SWEET ESCAPE

"Promise me one thing," she said. Her voice barely carried to his ears.

"What?"

"It's over in the morning. We go back. Shut it down. Family friends, photographer and subject. All the normal stuff is fine."

He couldn't help but touch the delicate line of her jaw again. She was like softness and determination all in one. "What's tonight, then?"

"An escape. That's all." Her fingers locked on his, their palms sliding together. "I get tired of thinking sometimes."

He took another kiss, this one fast and hard. His tongue swept into her mouth, stroked along the texture of her tongue. Mostly because he didn't want to acknowledge how true her words were.

Pulling her forward, into the foyer, he kicked the door shut with a nudge of his toes. "Well, then," he said. "We'll make sure you don't think, won't we?"

D0058926

Riding the Wave

A PACIFIC BLUE NOVEL

LORELIE BROWN

A SIGNET ECLIPSE BOOK

SIGNET ECLIPSE
Published by the Penguin Group
Penguin Group (USA) LLC, 375 Hudson Street,
New York, New York 10014

USA | Canada | UK | Ireland | Australia | New Zealand | India | South Africa | China
penguin.com
A Penguin Random House Company

First published by Signet Eclipse, an imprint of New American Library,
a division of Penguin Group (USA) LLC

First Printing, July 2014

ISBN 978-0-451-46842-0   5573 7877 08/14

Printed in the United States of America
10 9 8 7 6 5 4 3 2

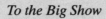

To the Big Show

Chapter 1

The past ten years of the waves down under hadn't been home to Tanner Wright, not like the gray-green swells of San Sebastian. He'd been raised on these Californian waves. His father taught him to surf on a long board, carve out what he could from the slush and be the man he was born to be. It hadn't been until they were halfway across the world, in a much brighter blue ocean, that he'd realized his dad wasn't half the man *he* was supposed to be.

Now Tanner was home again.

And Hank Wright was dead. Buried six months ago.

Tanner faced the waves of San Sebastian alone. The weight of the breeze pushed over his bare neck, scraping across his skin. His toes burrowed into the damp, cool sand. The sun rose behind him, over the expensive beach houses and stores that still hadn't turned to chains over the decade he'd been gone. The water was the same.

The surfers bobbing past the swells were the same too. Tanner ought to be with them but he carried a weight. San Sebastian had become an anchor.

In four weeks he'd have to not only surf here, but he'd

have to win. Or he'd lose his shot at this year's pro-surf World Championship. The points were too damn close. Jack Crews, pretty boy and part-time model, didn't fucking deserve the title. Tanner would be damned before he'd hand it over because he couldn't man up enough to surf.

A decent set surged, bringing a surfer cruising in with a deep layback before peeling off to the side again. Tanner hardly noticed. A woman popped up on the second wave, taking it all the way in. She didn't push any tricks, didn't grab for the rails or try to make air on a front that probably could have supported her.

She breathed pure grace. The easy acceptance of the moment she'd been handed and the tiny fraction of the giant ocean she rode. Her face turned up toward the still-rising sun, golden light kissing the rounded apples of her cheeks. A smile curved her generous mouth and she kept her eyes closed, apparently enjoying the feeling of floating into shore. The water soaking her ponytail made it look almost black, but he knew otherwise.

He couldn't help but smile as he eased down toward the edge of the water. Cool, foam-topped minisurf licked at his toes.

The woman glided in as far as she could standing on her board, but finally hopped off into knee-deep water when she wouldn't float anymore. She pushed back damp bangs with one hand as she scooped up her board.

Summer's deep grip meant that even a half hour after dawn it was warm enough for her to be wearing only a bikini top and black shorts. The red halter did good things to a figure entirely more curvy and filled out than he remembered.

"You never could spot a good trick, could you?" He

couldn't keep the laugh out of his voice. "All you had to do was shift and you'd have had a nice little cutback swish on the end."

Dark gray-green eyes went wide. The nose of her board dropped to the sand with a soft *thump* and a miniature splash. Her sharp words were in direct contradiction to her stunned look. "Swear to God, if you call me a lazy surfer one more time, I may toss you to the sharks."

Avalon Knox had always been a bit of a smart-ass. There was no denying the truth. "It's not my fault you passed up a pro career," Tanner teased.

She gave a wry smile and looked at him out of the corner of her eye. Lifting a hand to her hair, she skimmed loose strands back toward her ponytail. She hadn't had those pert breasts the last time he'd seen her. But then, she'd been at most fourteen years old and he'd been twenty. Looking at his sister's best friend would have gotten him strung up.

"Not everyone wants to go pro." She picked the board up and hitched it under her arm. "C'mon. I'll walk you back to the house."

"I'm not going to the house." The thought felt like scraping the inside of his skin with broken seashells. Tanner had never been able to separate the shitty memories of his father from his happy memories of his childhood home.

"You're not . . ." But her voice faded off. A light pink flush crept across her sternum. She put her board down again, this time setting the tail in the sand and standing it up. One arm curled around it. "You know, we didn't think you were going to be in town for another week or so. If you even made it at all."

The blow wasn't unexpected. He deserved no better.

It had been more than nine years since he'd been home. Seeing his sister and his mother in Hawaii every year or flying them out to Australia for his birthday wasn't the same thing. He'd invited Avalon too, but she'd passed every single time.

"I was injured last year. Pulled hamstring, remember?"

"Uh-huh." She scratched idle fingers across the plane of her stomach as she looked out over the water. Tanner looked too. It was safer out there. Out on the water, he knew who he was. A surfer.

On the shore, he remembered he was a surfer who hadn't won a world championship in nine years. Who got injured more often than not. Who wasn't one of the little kids still scrabbling his way up in the rankings.

She side-eyed him again. That was Avalon, poking at dark corners. Always had been. "And what about the five years before that?"

"That . . ." He looked back at her, away from the deep surf that had claimed his whole life and created his father's golden image. "That's none of your damn business, sweetheart."

She flinched visibly, the tendons at the base of her neck popping. Her tongue flicked out over her pink lips. "I see."

"No offense meant, of course."

"Most of the time when someone says 'no offense,' they mean they wanted to hit the max possible offense."

He shrugged. "Take it how you want. But if I'm not discussing it with my mother, I'm sure as hell not discussing it with you."

Avalon wasn't exactly a member of the family, but she was more than a friend too. She'd been twelve when Tanner's mom took Avalon under her wing for mentoring.

He'd been eighteen and striking out to hit the pro tour. Skinny little waifs hadn't held his interest compared to the beach bunnies who bounced their way down the sand. Plus he'd known Avalon a long time.

She wasn't the type to keep her mouth shut very well. He could practically see whitewater churning behind those almost gray eyes.

"The whole world wants to know, Tanner," she finally said. "Not just the family."

"You still work for *Surfer*?"

Her narrow shoulders lifted in a shrug. "I never really worked for them. I've sold them some photographs."

"You'd like to though, wouldn't you?" He tugged a pair of sunglasses that dangled by one arm from the pocket of his cargo shorts.

"Don't be an ass." She flicked her ponytail over her shoulder. "Of course I do. But I'm not going to sell out Sage or Eileen to get there."

That was Avalon too. Honest to a fault. "My mom and sister count, but me you'd sell out in a second, wouldn't you?"

The wide, bright grin she flashed him was everything appealing. He had the sudden, strange urge to taste it. Kiss that smile and see if it tasted as sweet as it looked. He could have shaken off the impulse if he wanted to. The years when he hadn't been in control of his own body were long gone, if you didn't count the times when it inconveniently gave out on him.

Avalon Knox . . . she wasn't off-limits. Not for any real reason beyond longtime ties to the family. From the way her gaze flicked over his shoulders now and then, maybe she wouldn't be averse to spending some time together while he was in California.

But then her smile turned out toward the water again. "You've been gone so long, you hardly count."

He laughed off the sudden sting of that blow. It was the hardest part of it all—that no one knew he'd been doing a good thing by staying away. Keeping his dad's secret meant keeping the family harmony. Who the hell was he to break his mother's heart?

And to be honest, there was a little envy there when it came to his sister. Sage still looked on Hank Wright as a god among men. Tanner remembered that feeling. He'd do anything to make sure Sage got to keep it.

Avalon's shoulder bumped into his arm in a friendly nudge. Her skin was still damp, and slightly chilled, but underneath was warm heat that was all her own. "Come back to the house. It'll be water under the bridge. Eileen'll make breakfast—you know it."

His mom put together an awesome spread when she got it into her head that her brood needed feeding. Regret pooled in his gut with something that felt strangely like fear. Even if his dad was gone, the house was still Hank's territory. "I don't think I can. I have a meeting with some WavePro reps."

"The big bucks," she teased.

He shrugged. He'd been lucky to be sponsored by WavePro when they were a tiny clothing line with only three styles of board shorts. The company had been the backbone of his support when he'd cut ties with Hank. Lately things had been strained because Tanner hadn't produced a major win. The San Sebastian Pro would have to be it. "Gotta keep 'em happy."

"Do you like working for them, though? I've got a meeting there this afternoon. Don't know what they want."

"They're businessmen at heart, but they know surfing too. Can't go too wrong."

Her mouth pulled into a firm line, but that quickly eased again into a kissable shape. "What are you doing out here, if you've got important places to be?"

"I got in so late last night, I didn't get a chance to look at the waves." He smiled down at her, testing. The way he'd like to lick the salt from her skin . . . He let it ease into his gaze. She didn't flinch. Her smile tucked deeper, the apples of her cheeks rounding. "I didn't expect to run into you."

The gentle curve of her chest, even before it swelled into her breasts, was something remarkable. He wanted to trace his tongue over it. "Life's full of weird little twists."

"It is." But he really did have to get going. "I'll be by the house this afternoon." Once he worked up the last bit of guts he'd need, but there was no reason to admit that. He'd have to hand over his balls. "Do me a favor?"

Her smile turned flat-out cheeky. The green in her eyes sparked brighter, washing away the gray. She cocked her hip. "Depends. I don't give away favors lightly."

The changes were definitely enjoyable. "Don't tell Mom you saw me."

"Want to surprise her?"

"Something like that." More like he still needed a little bit of time to gather himself before he could see her. The second his mom knew he'd landed in town, she'd be blowing up his phone. He wasn't a big enough asshole to be able to ignore that. After all, he always did everything he could to make up for the fact that he hadn't been home in years. It was hard enough keeping his dad's secret from miles away. He'd missed his family and the places he used to feel comfortable in his own skin. The pain of balancing everyone else's needs and wants and expectations had been the only thing sharp enough to balance the rest.

Eileen's kitchen had always been magic. As a teenager, sitting down at the counter while she set a glass of fresh-pressed juice and a sandwich in front of him . . . it was like having a switch flipped. Truths spilled out of him as easily as floating on the water on a flat day.

He'd only have to hope that being thirty-one and a full-grown man would provide immunity.

Spilling all the dirty details about Hank Wright's secret family on the other side of the world wouldn't help anyone. Hell, the man was dead. Let the truth die with him.

Chapter 2

By afternoon, Avalon had *almost* been able to forget the strange swirl of thoughts Tanner's reappearance had resurrected. Almost.

Walking into the WavePro offices blew that one out of the water.

Nestled in an anonymous complex barely redeemed by its beach-adjacent location, WavePro looked like any other set of stucco California offices.

The walls were covered with giant prints of surfing shots. Some of them front-lit, full-color, some of them artsy black-and-white portraits.

At least half of them were of Tanner.

His rugged, gorgeous face looked down at her from almost every angle.

Tugging at the cross-body strap of her camera bag, she sat on a cloth-covered couch. Her gaze drifted back to the shot of Tanner on the far wall. She couldn't help it. Another dead-on color composition. He stared directly into the camera, his bright blue eyes looking into hers. The scar cutting up from his mouth toward his left cheek was a faint line. Mostly it was the wicked tilt of his eyebrow that got to her.

Christ, she had to shake this. She wasn't a gawky fourteen-year-old drooling after her best friend's older brother anymore. Jumping Tanner's bones now could lead to major huge awkwardness come the next family Christmas.

There was no way she was repaying Sage and Eileen back like that. Along with Hank, they'd been her sole support when she'd been a teenager. *Gee, thanks for making sure I didn't end up knocked up at fifteen and working two part-time jobs to make ends meet. For repayment, mind if I bang the prodigal son?*

Besides, when he wasn't wearing that come-hitherish look he'd given her at the end of their chat, she remembered her annoyance all over again. Back to how much she owed the Wright family — when he'd cut tail and run. Never bothered to come home, not until his own dad was *dead*. The asshole. She didn't sleep with assholes.

Not even if they had six-packs worthy of national advertising. Not even if they could drop a rail so sick the front of the wave carved *itself*.

He was still the one who'd left. For years. He might set himself up as some sort of conquering hero, flying Sage and Eileen in for a month in Hawaii here and there. He wasn't the one who'd been here, who'd held their hands and given them hugs when Hank had died. Who'd taken care of all the stupid paperwork and told Eileen that no, it didn't really matter whether Hank's coffin had brass handles or silver.

Bitterness rose up in her chest like zaps from a jellyfish. She shoved it back down again just as quickly.

That solved that tingly girl bits problem, didn't it? If

she ever started thinking about his mouth too much, all she had to do was remind herself of his near-shithead status. Easy peasy.

"Miss Knox." The voice belonged to an older man standing in the open double doorway. Though silver streaked his hair, he still carried the deep tan of a long-time surfer. The founder of the company, Frank Wakowski.

At his side was a taller man with golden blond hair and an expression that said he'd rather lick paint than meet with Avalon. He sneered down his nose. A fresh-faced brunette wearing a pencil skirt and button-down shirt stood next to him. The man and the brunette seemed like intentional opposites in everything, down to attitude. Even their hair was on the opposite ends of the spectrum.

The hand Avalon held out was probably damp with sweat. "Mr. Wakowski, I'm honored to be here," she said as they shook. "WavePro is a huge name."

"We've worked hard to get where we are." His genial features spread in an open smile. "And I've heard you're quite the hard worker too."

Sudden nerves spiked her heartbeat up into her mouth with a heavy pulse. She'd racked her brain, but the only reason she could come up with for such a meeting was an opportunity. The fact that they'd asked for this meeting meant Mr. Crankyface could suck it.

She and Mr. Wakowski made small talk as they made their way into a standard-issue conference room. At least the version of Tanner in this room barely poked out of a heavy barrel, the entire right side of the image layered over with WavePro advertising.

Avalon knotted her hands beneath the pale oak conference table and did her best to modulate her voice so it didn't shake. She hated being nervous, but hated looking nervous even more.

The tall man had been introduced as Walt Palmer. He leaned forward with his elbows on the edge of the table. "Miss Knox, to be frank, you've never worked at the level we're asking for."

She lifted her brows. "To be frank, you're the ones who asked me here. Someone here must think I'm good enough."

Mr. Wakowski chuckled. "That'd be me. I've been seeing your shots frequently in smaller publications and online. There's an appealing element. I'm not entirely sure if the promise can be fulfilled, but we want something different."

"We wanted Scott, but it fell through."

The young woman, Ms. Harmon, seemed to be the in-house attorney. She lifted a single finger. "To be fair, it fell through because he bombed out in Tahiti and has since checked into rehab. We're lucky to have escaped that commitment, considering his lack of reliability."

Palmer's mouth pinched. "He might be unreliable, but he's good."

That certainly took care of the nerves. Avalon leaned back in her seat, hooking one thumb in the open end of her camera bag. She never went anywhere without the thing. The canvas and Velcro had become her friend and confidant in a lot of ways, along with the equipment within. She looked Mr. Wakowski straight in the eye. "If your assistant is done insulting me, perhaps you can get on to the offer."

"We want you to work with Tanner Wright for the entirety of his time in San Sebastian. His homecoming." Mr. Wakowski tapped his index fingers together as he stared intently at her. "Honestly, yes, we had another photographer planned. It fell through. So we've decided to offer you the opportunity."

Opportunity was definitely the word. "Commercial or feature?"

Ms. Harmon laid her hand flat on a folder that likely held the contracts and pushed it forward a few inches. "Both, hopefully."

"If Tanner wins this competition, he'll sew up the World Championship," said Mr. Wakowski. "Back in his hometown for the first time. The publicity is inherently positive."

Nervousness sank deeper into Avalon's bones, but this time a thrill of excitement ran alongside it. "Me. You want me to photograph Tanner Wright for the next four weeks."

"We do."

"He and I are friends, but not follow-around-constantly-level friends."

"We have a publicity clause in our contract with Tanner," Mr. Wakowski said calmly. "We'll invoke it if necessary."

The tall man's lips pressed into a thin smile. "Between the level of access WavePro gets and your personal connection, we expect plenty of good shots."

Oh crap, she wasn't sure if she could even do it. Their meeting this morning had been slightly volatile. Not to mention there were other worries. How she'd be perceived. She'd worked ridiculously hard trying to find her place in what was so very much a man's field. Was she willing to take a leg up because of her connections?

Hell yes, she was. She'd known plenty of men who'd gotten their break because they grew up surfing with the right people. She'd worry about the perception later.

This was big enough to make her career.

She stuck her hand across the table. "You've got yourselves a photographer."

Mr. Wakowski broke into a wide grin. He stood and took her hand, giving it a sturdy shake. "You're not going to regret this, Avalon."

Everything went rapidly after that, particularly the discussion of terms. Afterward, Palmer fled the room as if he were in danger of catching something nasty. Avalon held her hand out. "May I have the contracts, Ms. Harmon?"

"Please, call me Beth."

"Beth. I hope you don't mind me having the paperwork checked by my attorney."

Beth had sweet brown eyes that danced when she laughed. "Oh, I promise I'm not offended. I might think less of you if you didn't, for that matter. But everything's on the up-and-up. If you ask me, it's those surfer boys you need to watch out for."

The Wrights' place had been Avalon's second home for close to a decade even before she'd officially moved in. Most of the value in the tall, narrow beach house was in the location. For two kids and lots of random drop-ins all the time, the place was a little small.

But whenever Avalon kicked off her flip-flops at the front door and cool Spanish tiles hit the bottoms of her feet, she knew she could relax and let down her shields in a way she couldn't anywhere else. She put her camera bag on the couch, but not before pulling out her Canon. She loved the beat-up beast of a camera. "I'm home," she called. Her voice echoed through the narrow living room, then out the opened French doors on the far end of the kitchen.

Sage stuck her head out over the stairway railing above Avalon's head. "Get up here."

"Nice to see you too," she teased even as she skipped up the stairs. "Sure, my meeting went *awesome*. You're so nice to ask."

When she got up to the landing, where three rooms spidered out, there was no one there. Just the plain yellow walls adorned only by cobalt blue glasswork that Eileen had done herself during the "off hours" she had when she wasn't working at the family-owned surf shop, Wright Break.

As a role model, Eileen Wright was really something to live up to.

Sage's door squeaked open on the left, and the blonde reached out to grab Avalon. Next thing Avalon knew, Sage had dragged her over to the window.

"Look. Just look," Sage said in a near squeal, her delicate features jumping with excitement. It was hard sometimes to believe that Tanner and Sage came from the same stock. Where he was blunt-nosed and hard-jawed, his sister was all sweetness and beauty and looked like Eileen. The way Tanner took after Hank had made it all the more awful to watch their split.

Avalon obediently looked out the window. Though a canopy of green star jasmine half concealed them, she could see Eileen on the back patio in her favorite spot. She was curled into her padded papasan chair, a holdover from faded hippie days. The only difference was the person sprawled across a lounge chair next to her.

Tanner.

A crumpled mess of emotions turned over in Avalon's chest. Part wonder, to see him in the Wright family home again. Part excitement, to realize she'd been handed an a-freaking-mazing opportunity, all because she knew him.

And, yeah, part turn-on too, because Tanner was one fine specimen of man. He wore the same cargo shorts and slim, hugging T-shirt that he'd had on this morning at the beach. His legs were spread in a negligent sprawl and the way he had his arms crossed over his chest only made the T-shirt draw more snug over his shoulders. His hair looked spikier than this morning, as if he'd found some time to dip in the water before coming over.

Of course. Tanner always took the long way home, it seemed like.

Avalon flat-out didn't get it. If she'd ever been born part of a solid family like this one, there would be nothing in the world that would make her walk away. "How long's he been here?"

"About three hours. Rang the doorbell like he was a door-to-door salesman or some other kind of bullshit. I could choke him." Sage touched her fingertips to the glass in a move that looked way more sisterly than her words sounded.

"You didn't though."

"Nope. Of course not." She sighed, turned away from the window, and flopped across the bed—a little juvenile for a twenty-six-year-old woman. Sage scrubbed the heels of her hands across her eyes. "God forbid we scare him off. Mom's already planning a party though."

Sage used to have her own apartment, but that changed after her dad's death. Even though Avalon had already been living there, Sage moved back in to help her mom either shut down the surf store or sell it so she could retire—and to be near when Eileen needed her. As a result, the walls of Sage's room were still papered with magazine cutouts of fellow surfers and bands from her high school years—and hand-drawn sketches of the surfboards that she shaped for a living.

Avalon couldn't help but pick out the shots of Tanner. She couldn't get away from the man and she'd be even closer to him during the next four weeks. One way or the other she'd have to get over herself. "That's your mom, though. Any excuse for having people over."

"And cooking. God forbid anyone might go home hungry." Sage rolled her eyes but it was obvious she didn't mean it. Even being in Sage's presence was relaxing. Lots of calm and sunshine, all stemming from a happy, internal place.

Avalon envied that happy place so damn bad. Half the time she felt like she was scrambling to keep up, and the rest of the time she wanted to collapse. She straddled the desk chair and fiddled with her camera for a second.

She had to look up from under her lashes to ask. It didn't feel like her place, and yet she couldn't leave it be, either. "Are you gonna ask?"

"Ask what?"

God, that was Sage. Able to let any slight or problem go. "Are you going to ask Tanner what happened with your dad?"

Sage shook her head. A sheaf of hair slid over her shoulder as she rolled onto her tummy. "No. Not my business. It's past now."

Avalon snapped off a couple pictures. Sage barely blinked. The random picture taking was routine between the two of them. Part of Avalon's way of framing the world in more understandable ways.

Because she didn't get it. If her brother had been gone . . . She'd have to know why.

She wasn't sure at all if she'd be able to keep her mouth shut while spending the next month with Tanner.

Jesus. Suddenly, something made her sit up straight. It was possible he didn't even know yet. He hadn't said anything this morning. As if it weren't enough that she'd tagged around his family for close to a decade, now she'd be shadowing him personally.

She might have to tell him herself.

Chapter 3

Tanner had always liked his mom's back patio. The entire space was probably only twelve feet by twelve before the garage and alley cut it off, but his mom had a special touch for making it cozy. She'd squeezed in a couple chairs, eked out some plants and grass that didn't mind the high walls and getting only an hour of sunshine a day. Next to being out on the water, it was one of his favorite places in the world.

So the quiet burn of tears that had threatened when he'd stepped out onto the flagstones wasn't a surprise. He'd easily managed to choke them back.

His dad had been such a fucking dillhole. To put all this harmony at risk, and to put Tanner in the position of losing it. All the while, he got to look like a good guy, while Tanner was the ego-filled surf boy who wouldn't come home.

No one had ever known how much he missed the quiet moments spent with his mom in this space.

Eileen reached out and tapped his forearm. She kept doing that all the time, finding reasons to touch or pat him. Push his hair back out of his eyes. Once he'd thought she was two seconds from licking her thumb and rubbing his cheek.

He didn't mind, not really. It couldn't last long, but being with his mom again . . . It made him a little warm and fuzzy on the inside.

"Is there anyone in particular that you want me to invite for Friday?" she asked.

"Not really." Anyone he added to the guest list would be another set of eyes to stare and wonder where the hell he'd been. The weight ate at him. "If you've got a question, go ahead and ask, Mom."

"Do you have a girlfriend, sugar?" Amusement glowed from her still-smooth skin. His mom wasn't exactly over-the-hill, but a bit of silver paled out her honey-blond hair.

"No," he said, but he couldn't help the little chuckle that worked through him. Mothers were always the same, no matter what other drama swirled around them. "Now, if you don't mind, I'm out of here."

Her easy smile drooped a little. "So soon?"

"I've been visiting for hours now." He pushed out of his chair, but then leaned down to brush a kiss over her temple. "Besides, I'll be back tomorrow."

Her throat worked over a swallow. The corners of her mouth managed to push up again, but a certain wavering quality took over. He didn't like it. For a second, she looked almost old. Sickening guilt churned through him, that he could make her look like that.

But he shoved it down again as quickly. She'd look even worse if she knew the truth.

"Promise?" she asked, her voice light on the surface. Darkened blue eyes gave her away.

"Promise."

That easily, things were better. Maybe he'd actually be able to make it all work. To balance everything.

He couldn't afford to let all this family stuff take the fins out from under his board. Too much rode on the upcoming contest. He needed his head in the game.

On the front walk, he was slipping his sunglasses on when the door opened behind him. For half a second, he thought it would be Sage, wanting a word when their mom couldn't hear. But when he turned, Avalon stood on the front stoop.

She looked entirely different from the way she had at the beach, but in a way she was still the same. Her hair had been dried and maybe even styled somehow so that her bangs weren't just pushed out of the way. A thick fringe grazed above eyes that looked greener than they had this morning as well.

The biggest change was the fact that she was wearing way more clothes. The red bikini halter top was nowhere to be seen, replaced by a disappointingly respectable blouse. Not even a hint of cleavage. At least her skirt showed off a couple solid inches of smooth thigh above her knees.

Slender fingers hooked into her dark gray bag. "We should talk."

"I think we did that this morning."

Her soft-looking mouth quirked. "Something's come up."

It was weird as hell, looking at this version of Avalon and mentally layering it over the version he used to know: thin, wiry, and way too young. But that version was long gone, and he pushed the memory away. This was Avalon now. She was the one he had before him. Ignoring the past was what he was good at, after all.

"Do you mind if we don't go back inside?" Being in what had been his father's house had been bad enough. He'd had to employ intentional tunnel vision to make it past all the photographs and framed covers and his father's trophies. All the things that said what an awesome guy Hank was. No way could he do it again so soon.

She shrugged. "No worries. C'mon, we'll walk up the block to Manna's."

"Where?"

She struck out walking while she laughed at him. "I keep thinking of you as a local. But that's not quite right anymore, is it?"

He let her draw even before he started moving. She smelled like coconut and toasted sun and everything good he remembered about California girls. Plus, underneath it, something different. Something tastier that called right to the bottom of him, made him want to lick and suck. And bite. "No, I don't think it is. I . . . I don't think I'm a local anywhere right now."

She slanted a sideways look at him. The cross-strap of her messenger-style camera bag did delicious things to her tits, lifting them and pressing the cotton of her blouse against them. "That's got to be one of the saddest things I've heard in forever."

"Didn't mean it to be sad. Just is." He didn't have to measure his steps to walk alongside her. She moved with ferocity of purpose, intent and quick. Though her legs had to be shorter, she clipped along too fast for it to be a problem. "Don't feel bad for me."

"Oh, I don't." She grinned. A quick flick tossed her shoulder-length hair over her shoulder. Now that it wasn't soaking wet, the sun picked out red strands to caress. "Not in the least."

"Nice. You're real sweet—you know that?"

"You can't have it both ways, dude." She turned her face up toward the sun for a second. When he'd spotted her on her board, she'd been like that too. A true sun worshipper, probably. He couldn't blame her. He had the same instinct. Get to some water and sun and the rest of it would all shake out. "If you don't want me to pity you, you shouldn't get your panties in a twist when I don't."

"When you put it that way." He gently pushed his shoulder into hers. Not hard. Not enough to toss her off balance, but enough so that he felt that skin again. She was everything bright and soft. "So what makes it so sad, then?"

"This," she breathed. Her hands found the back pockets of her skirt, thrusting her shoulders back.

They'd come to the end of the road, where it dead-ended in sand and a footpath tracked through the reedy plants staking their claim at the very edge of the beach. Cars and trucks squeezed in where they could. The heat of the crystal-clear summer day meant the entire expanse of beach, all the way to the ocean, was a sea of people. Dark hair, brightly colored swimsuits, tan and-blue sun umbrellas. All of it covered the pale sand.

Some surfers bitched and moaned about San Sebastian. Said it was too crowded, too commercial. Tourists flocked in from miles around to fill out the small town. Tanner had always loved the contrast. In the morning, he could claim waves that ranked among the best in the world. In the afternoon, it'd all be handed over to inlanders so they could get a taste of wildness.

"You gave up all this. Apparently for nothing, if you don't have a home." Something sad darkened her eyes into a stormy color. "I could maybe get it if you'd chosen something else instead. But . . . nothing?"

Yeah, thanks. Like he needed any reminder of how bad the last few years had sucked. Of the kind of choices he'd been left with. Words burned his throat but he choked them down. She didn't deserve to take the lashings from all the tension he carried.

He'd have to do something soon to work off the buzz riding his skin. Maybe he'd grab a board and hit the water, if he could get through the crowds. And the freaking tide was out too, now that he thought about it.

He'd have to find another outlet. He couldn't help the track his gaze took toward Avalon. She'd be a spicy little armful—if she had any intention of giving him the time of day.

Though she had been the one who wanted to talk to him. Maybe she had more illicit purposes after all.

He couldn't help the little spike of amusement. Yeah, right. He was starting to believe his own hype. Too much more of that, and he'd be Jack Crews. And as useless a surfer too. He and Jack had made about the same amount of money through the years—lots of it. But Jack's attitude had suffered. "C'mon," he said, shaking free of his own head. That was a dangerous place to be too long. "Where are we headed?"

"This way." She turned south, then led the way down the beach about a hundred yards to a beach café slash bar. The door they pushed through was weathered to look like driftwood and the interior was cool and dark. The entire west wall was nothing but banks of open glass doors. Dark wood fans swirled air around in a lazy effort to add to the salt-tangy sea breeze.

There were tables outside, all of them crowded with

pasty white or lobster red tourists who clutched frothy drinks. The tables inside were half empty, as if it were a sin to come to the beach and not get all the sunstroke possible. At the far end, a nest of tables had been pushed together and seats dragged up. All of them were occupied by surfers.

Tanner recognized many of them, including James Montcrief, and so did Avalon from the way she smiled and waved. In fact, there was Jack Crews sitting at the head of the tables, as if Tanner's very thought of him had drawn the man. He forced his mouth into a smile and gave two tips of his fingers.

"Avalon, sweetheart, why're you keeping such shitty company?" Jack called. His eyes were narrow, but Tanner had heard plenty of chicks coo and giggle over him. He pushed his seat back and patted a knee. "You know I'll always make room for you."

"Like she wants to fight through your hordes," provided James. It was surprising to see him in town, since he'd left the World Championship circuit behind to become a free surfer. He must have been visiting Beth Harmon, his fiancée.

"Sorry, Jack," she answered. "We've got business to discuss. But maybe if you behave yourself I'll grace you with my presence later."

Business, did they? That certainly put an end to anything he'd been supposing. Probably had something to do with the way she'd been asking about WavePro earlier that morning.

"If anyone can keep me on my toes, it's you," Jack said with a grin. His teeth were so white, he'd probably had a recent bleach treatment.

Tanner didn't hate the guy, but he didn't understand

him, either. Jack seemed to go out of his way to court inlanders and kiss publicity ass. He drank too much, partied too hard, and he'd lost freaking heats in important competitions because he'd been hungover. Absolutely unprepared. But his sponsors never let him go because he drew attention.

Considering Tanner had spent the last nine years garnering the least possible attention he could get away with, all so no one would ask him about his dad, he couldn't comprehend.

"But please," said another voice out of the crowd, this one low and lilting with the slightest touch of a foreign tongue. "Do think about coming back. We could use your sort of pretty around."

A cold freeze trickled down Tanner's spine in direct opposition to the hot air on his skin. Even worse, Avalon's cheeks pinked with a blush. He didn't need to look for the speaker, but he did anyway. He couldn't help it.

Three seats down from Jack, separated by a dreadlocked, burned-out surfer stereotype and a bright-faced noob, sat Mako Wright.

His father's bastard.

Chapter 4

When Avalon had been thirteen, after the Wright family had practically adopted her but before she'd managed to break all the old ties of her life, she'd been at a beach bonfire that had gone very, very wrong. Too much alcohol and a too hefty sprinkling of skinheads had led to trouble once the hour got late. The air crackled with the very taste of violence, something sharp and bitter as everyone stared down enemies. Avalon had wrapped her hands around a red plastic cup and huddled into her hoodie, hoping no one would notice her before her ride was ready to go home. When an accidentally spilled drink led to a fistfight, which turned into a near riot, she'd run all the way home—a mile and a half in the dark.

In the shady bar, the air took on that same crackle. Bad sign.

Beside her, Tanner somehow bulked out without moving. She'd been standing and walking beside him for almost fifteen minutes, but until that moment she hadn't felt small. Suddenly, it was all she could think of. That he had probably twice the weight on her, all of it thick muscles. Not that any of that threat was pointed at her.

Instead, it was toward the man who'd spoken. He had high cheekbones and dark eyes with a slant that whispered of far-off waves. His mouth, too, was delicate in a way that most men couldn't pull off. Not him, though. He was all subtle intention and dark focus. On her.

She swallowed. She smiled.

"Okay, well . . ." Her voice trailed off. Tanner's arm had the consistency of concrete. His muscles were locked about as rigidly as possible. "Jack, everyone, thanks for the invite, but we'll be . . . See ya."

Hauling Tanner into a corner booth took all the subtle force she could muster. And she still could only move him because he eventually decided to *be* moved.

She ought to have been annoyed. Manly power shows had never been her style.

Instead something wicked and dark lit within her. It felt like cresting the top of a huge slab, waiting for the heavy weight of the wave to snatch her up.

She intentionally wedged him in so that his back was to the tables filled with surfers, then squeezed in next to him. If she'd sat across, she wouldn't have been able to resist looking. Wondering what the hell had set him off.

His dad had been a blusterer. Lots of complaining, a little bit of stomping around. But Tanner seemed to be the exact opposite. All quiet burn. Her fingers literally itched to have her camera. The sharp line of his jaw would photograph so freaking perfectly, even in the dim light. Her thumb rubbed across the latch of her messenger-style camera bag. But it'd probably be a bad idea.

"Do I get to know what your problem is?"

"No."

"Well, that's easy enough."

Rolling her eyes, she waved down the waitress. They

turned over as easily as prom dates, so Avalon didn't know this one's name. But she had quite the rack, wrapped up in a pink twist of fabric.

Avalon checked automatically to see if Tanner had noticed. Not that it made any sense—and hell, with what the waitress was sporting, she had looked too.

Tanner still stared straight ahead, as if willing himself to keep his gaze away from the table of surfers.

The bleached blond waitress smiled and it turned her otherwise vacant features pleasant. "What can I get you?"

"Just a Corona. Tanner?"

"Iced tea. Thanks."

The waitress bounced away with a nod.

Avalon fiddled with a cocktail napkin. "Tea?"

"I'm on my training regimen. Strictly limited alcohol."

The party behind them broke up, and Jack and James called a farewell to both of them. Avalon twisted in the booth to say good-bye, but Tanner only raised a hand over his head in an abrupt farewell. When the rest of the noisy group tumbled out the door, he deflated a few inches into the leather bench.

He blew out a noisy breath. "Sorry."

"I'm assuming you've got some problem with that dude?"

His mouth tweaked in something that approached a smile. The scar over his mouth leached white. "You could say that."

"But that's all you'll say, I'm guessing." She ought to have moved around the horseshoe-shaped bench to the other side of the table. There was no reason for her to be within touching distance of him. But she stayed.

He smelled like salt and man. Something that made her want to nuzzle.

When the waitress arrived with drinks, he smiled at her. Avalon spotted tension at his temples. The tiny fluting around his eyes that wasn't quite called wrinkles. When the blonde walked away, he kept looking in her direction, but Avalon didn't get the idea he was ogling her. More like avoiding looking directly at Avalon.

She wrapped her hands around the damp bottle. "You don't have to say anything, of course. You owe me no explanations. But I'm here to listen."

That got him to look at her. It went all the way down inside her, as if he were looking for a specific answer. "Tell me one thing, Avalon."

She swallowed past a mouth that felt as dry as if she'd swallowed a handful of sand. "Sure."

"Are you oh so eager and ready to listen because you want to . . . or because that's what you've always done with my family? Your role, let's say."

She flinched the tiniest bit, the tendons inside her elbows jumping. No matter how closely she searched his face, she couldn't see any meanness in it. A certain level of curiosity, she supposed. Maybe a bright flash of hope in the anticipating part of his lips.

There had only been a couple times in her life when she'd felt like she stood at such an easily delineated crossroad. One had been when she'd held two college acceptance letters and decided intentionally to stay near the Wrights so they didn't forget about her. The other had been when she'd looked at her college boyfriend and intentionally accepted the fact that he would always be too nervous to try surfing, even for her. At that moment, she'd accepted that he wasn't Tanner and never would be.

Her heart thrummed into overdrive. "Because I want to."

His lips lifted into a genuine smile. "Yeah? That's all right."

She ducked his gaze, looking at her beer, and she wasn't the gaze-ducking type. Easier to keep her fluttering girly bits in line if she wasn't looking at him. But crap, it wasn't even as easy as all that. "You should know something."

"That doesn't sound promising."

She couldn't help a little laugh at that. "Totally depends on your definition."

"My definition includes not being able to take you out for dinner tonight."

"You're kind of slick, aren't you?" She didn't want to admit what that line had done to her. Made her slippery and needy. "You know, I remember when you were nineteen and home after your first summer on the circuit. Didn't you have a crush on Amanda Hanterny? She shot you down."

"Ouch." He pinched his features into mock chagrin. "She said she wanted a boyfriend who'd be able to take her to prom. Thanks for bringing that one up."

"Yeah, your ego doesn't seem like it needs any stroking. Anyway. Issue. Us."

"There's an us already?" He took a lock of her hair between his thumb and forefinger. Though he wasn't touching any other part of her, a shiver slid over her collarbone. "I think I should be careful around you."

"Hush already." She was really going to have to spit this out before Mr. Slick got going too hard. "I've been hired by WavePro to do a spread on you. I thought you should hear it from me first."

He tugged lightly on the chunk of her hair. A tingle spread over her scalp and she had to swallow hard. Her legs pressed together against the sudden ache between her thighs, until her knees ground bone on bone.

"A photo shoot shouldn't be that big a deal. We'll take some pictures, and then you'll let me take you to dinner. As payment, I'll get to pick the restaurant."

Oh, this was not going to go over well. Tanner had never really been known to revel in the spotlight. "No, you don't understand. They want full access. I'm to be with you pretty much twenty-four-seven until the Pro."

"No way," he said automatically. He dropped the lock of her hair as quickly as if it had turned into a jellyfish stinger, and slipped so far away from her that he was practically on the other side of the booth.

"I wanted to be the one to tell you. I didn't want you to think I'd gone behind your back or anything. They came to me."

"You know what everyone's going to say about why, right?"

Bile burned through her chest. Everyone was going to say that—the boys' club of the surf world in action. But it didn't matter. She'd make sure it didn't, not when they saw the photos that resulted.

"I don't care." She pulled her Canon out of her bag like a medieval warrior pulling out a sword. Rather than beheading dragons, she laid it carefully on the highly polished table. Tanner was no Arthur anyhow. "If I wasn't friends with the family, everyone would say I got the gig because I was sleeping with you."

"But we both know that's not true." His voice was as silky as a spider web and as sticky. She wanted to be on him. With him. "If you and I were sleeping together, there'd be no forgetting that."

She rolled her eyes a tiny bit. "With that ego, you are entirely your father's son. How the hell could you stop talking to him when he was practically *you*?"

That was apparently the entirely wrong thing to say. He surged up from the booth, a muscle sharply carved in the side of his jaw. After peeling bills off a thick wad, he tossed down money to cover their drinks. "You'll do what you need to, and I'll do what my contract says I have to. But don't think you'll get any special consideration. I'm not talking about him."

"Tanner, I'm—" But before she could finish the sentence, he turned away like some sort of petulant teenager. Huffing an annoyed breath, she crossed her arms over her chest and sat back in the booth. The only person who got to treat her like she was nothing was her mother, and even that was a close call. She injected all the saccharine sweetness she could muster into her voice. "I'll drop by your place in the morning. Don't worry—Mr. Wakowski gave me the address."

He stopped short. Even the backs of his calves pulled into a sharp shelf of divided muscle. She could tuck a pencil under that rivet. The sunglasses he tugged from his cargo pocket were expensive, with a dragon emblem on the side and likely comped. All the top surfers got gear and clothing for free. He might not like his notoriety, but he sure benefited from it.

The slow pivot he did was all show. One more thing he was certainly good at, whether he wanted to admit it or not.

She snapped off a handful of pictures, the whir of the

lens like a subtle raspberry at him. He wanted to play at being as mercurial as the ocean before a storm, fine. She could be as much of an ass in return.

"There's one thing *you* ought to know," he said. His voice was a quiet purr, half threat, half promise that would forever go unexplored, at least with her. "Hank Wright was no god. There are things you don't know about him."

"And you do? You're the one who was gone. You don't want me to ask, fine." She stood as well. No way was she finishing this conversation from such a disadvantage, staring up at him. She'd never been much of one for doormatting. Her camera dangled, strap wound loosely around her wrist. She lifted it with a smile that felt only mean. Snapped off a couple more shots. "But I'm the one who was here. The whole time. So unless you're prepared to spill about the dark and dirty? You don't also get to rub it in my face."

Out of nowhere, the wrinkles across his forehead cleared. He grinned. She didn't want to admit how much she liked the shape of his eyes, the darker sweep of his brows above them. "It's a damned shame," he said.

She swallowed down her sudden confusion. It was so much easier to be annoyed. "What's that?"

He leaned down and brushed a kiss across her mouth, too short to be much more than a tease. She didn't even get a taste of him, and sure didn't get any more than the shock of a tingle. "That we won't get to follow up on this. Not anymore."

Chapter 5

It hadn't taken Tanner long to realize very little had changed in San Sebastian. The place was a funny mix of half organic-eating, biofuel-spouting, crunchy ex-hippies and half young, heavy-wave, cutting-edge surfers. The only difference from his last time in town was that both factions sported smartphones that they put to entirely different uses.

The surfer crowd filmed themselves doing wicked tricks and had it up on the web in less time than it took to dry their hair. The hippies flash-organized protests when the local grocery store was discovered to be passing off regular grapes as organic.

The downside meant Tanner had to weave and dodge through them all as they were nose-to-screen wandering down the main strip.

The good part was the eclectic offerings at the heart of the town, smack up against the beach, right where the street led inland from the pier. The rental house he'd taken was intentionally less than three blocks up the beach from the retail section. He'd pretty much planned on parking his SUV in the garage and walking all over town, the way he had when he'd been a kid.

So far, mission accomplished.

Late in the evening, he wandered his way toward some grub. His hands slipped deep in his pockets, it almost felt like he was slouching in an intentional reclamation of his teenage years.

He'd been such a shit. More attitude than one too-skinny body should have been able to handle. But no one had called him on it because he'd had the talent to back it all up.

His dad had told him plenty of times that nothing mattered but winning and making sure everyone knew you'd won—keeping up your image.

Hank had gotten that right, and lived up to it to the utmost. Even if it had left Tanner holding the bag when it came to guilt and secrets.

Tanner shoved those thoughts away and let everything else go. Nothing got through to him but the quiet shush of his sandals over the sandy sidewalks. The cool breeze coming in off the water, scented with the salt he'd always considered a vital part of anywhere resembling home. Now he had the real thing.

The front doors of his father's store—no, now it was his mother's—were propped wide open. A rack of cheap tourist T-shirts had been planted outside the threshold, but the quality goods were on the inside. All the last-minute essentials for a day of good surfing, plus Sage's surfboard-making studio in the back.

Tanner strolled on by. He might've even looked across the street as he passed the lit-up windows, in case his mom was manning the front counter. He'd come back, and he was dealing with the fallout of almost a decade of choices. Seeing his mom and Sage in Australia and Hawaii had always been bittersweet. He'd wanted so much to tell them the truth of what Hank was like, about the secrets Tanner was forced to keep. But he knew how painful it was to have their father's façade crushed. He didn't want to inflict that on them.

The slot next door had been a psychic's storefront when he'd been young. The place had always been draped in purple and gold, and Tanner had been fascinated with the dark-haired woman who'd run it. He'd never quite been able to figure out if she was a fraud preying on tourists or if she'd actually believed her spiel. Eventually he'd realized it didn't matter. She was there, she did her thing, and no one seemed to get hurt. Good enough.

But Madame Rozamund was apparently gone. A candy store now filled the narrow storefront. Pyrex bins and giant tubes filled with brightly colored munchies lined three and a half walls.

Oh, he was totally getting some of that, though after the Sebastian Pro. Training was training. He couldn't even say it sucked, not anymore. It just *was*. As much an ingrained part of him as the motions of surfing itself.

Though he passed a couple restaurants, he couldn't seem to pick one. Instead, he wandered to the foot of the pier. The real wood of his childhood had been replaced with recycled material that sprung under his steps. He turned back to face the town he'd willingly abandoned for the better part of a decade.

Tiny streaks of light burned through the growing twilight. Mostly it was the main street, running east, that was still bright and populated. The houses to the north and south of the pier were lighting up, most of them with towels drying on the back railings. Expensive-as-hell beachfront property had racks of surfboards and wetsuits pinned up on clotheslines.

The slow-burn contentedness that swept over Tanner wasn't as surprising as he'd have expected even two days ago.

He could practically taste the possibilities now. He was home. The town's memory was starting to untie from his father's. And Tanner dug that. They'd always been so intrinsically intertwined, the result of growing up in a small town where his father was a big shot. San Sebastian had always been Hank's world. Sometime during the years of following the world circuit, Tanner had forgotten that it was his world too. His home.

The only thing better would be making new memories in the place. Taking down a championship would be the best start. Another good one might be spending time with Avalon. Though she was his sister's best friend, they were all adults. Avalon could make her own choices. There was plenty of opportunity down that road for happy making. If it were up to him, it'd be her panties he'd be working on. If she was on board with the idea, naturally.

He smiled to himself as he leaned against the tar-stained railing of the pier. She wouldn't mind. He knew women and Avalon was definitely a special one. Both clever as hell and also into him. It had been there after he'd stolen that superfast kiss. She hadn't simpered, hadn't gasped. She'd only flashed him one of the cheekiest grins he'd ever seen.

But he wasn't allowed to continue his happy turn of thoughts. A dark, shadowy figure approached from the head of the pier. Tanner dismissed him at first, but then realized that that wasn't going to work.

An accented voice came out of the darkness. "So here we are. In our father's town and together."

The disks of Tanner's spine felt like they fused into one hard line of *what the fuck?* Small towns could bite it. Tanner's jaw thrust hard and he kept his gaze locked down the street the way he'd been. "My father. And, yeah, maybe the asshole was your father too. You're welcome to him. But there's no 'our father' because there's no us."

Mako's dark hair roostered up across the orange-streaked sunset behind him. It only got worse when he ran a hand through the mess. The narrow shape of his eyes bore very little resemblance to Hank Wright, but Tanner could still see the ghost of the man in the way Mako looked out sideways. All sly insistence that he could work things the way he wanted.

Hank had been insanely determined like that and willing to see only his own side, even if no one but Tanner seemed to realize it. Except he'd been more like a bulldozer than a snake. Slamming through resistance with smiles and jokes had been his specialty.

Tanner pushed away from the railing. He didn't need this; that's all there was to it. He had enough crap piling up in his life, and at some point he needed to make a choice as to what he was doing when he left the surf circuit. Mako simply didn't figure in the picture.

"Look," he said on a sigh. His bones felt weary, as if he were getting old before his time. He pinched the top of his forehead, where a sudden ache had set up. "I hope you have a very nice life, and I'm not being sarcastic. I don't wish anything against you. But . . . dealing with you means dealing with all the shit my dad left behind. I figure it's best to let the past stay buried."

He didn't want to be responsible for putting his mom through that pain, not if there was anything he could do about it. With Hank dead and buried, there was simply no reason to. As long as he could choke down the memories that being in Hank's house would bring, everything would be totally covered.

But Mako was shaking his head. "Thanks, but, no."

"What the hell do you want from me? Thanksgiving dinners?" The words flew sharp from Tanner, but he couldn't come close to stopping them. They swelled up from a dark and sickly place inside him that had been brewing for almost ten years. "I don't fucking think so."

Mako's eyes narrowed further and his chin tipped farther forward. "Oh look, it's like talking to Hank all over again."

"Fuck you."

"Thanks, brother, but I've got that much covered at least." The smile he spooled out was incredibly smug and had a sharp edge of cobra to it. As dangerous as he'd always thought the man. "These California girls really do know how to make a guy feel good. And they're so fucking gullible."

"You're pretty fucking smarmy, aren't you?" That Tanner had been right about Mako all these years was a strange, unpleasant mix of vindication and distaste.

Avalon was a local girl, but she wasn't gullible. Not by far. The idea of Mako taking advantage of her made Tanner's skin crawl. He wouldn't let it happen, not to her or to anyone like Sage, either. They were his important people, not this guy. Not Mako.

"Fuck you," Tanner said again, this time more slowly. He wanted the words to drive home. He wanted to hurt Mako like his very existence hurt Tanner.

"So creative. Good to know what I'm up against."

"Christ, why do we have to be up against anything?" Tanner shook his head. "Can't we go our separate ways? You know what? I'll start it." He waved briefly and turned away. "Have a good life. Peace out."

"I wanted to warn you that I did an interview with *SURFING*."

Tanner's feet stuttered to a stop. "Like hell."

"It should be out the week of the Pro." Mako's jaw hollowed, a sharp tic of muscle right in front of his ear. "I didn't pull any punches, either. It's all out there."

"You don't have the right to wreck my mom's and sister's lives."

Mako shook his head. The sun had dropped below the far line of the sea, swamping the town with dark. It seemed pretty appropriate for the discussion. Be damned if Tanner actually wanted to look at Mako.

"I think the world has the right to know what their precious surf idol was really like. Including the fact that he married your mom when she was only eighteen."

"And he was twenty. It's not that big a deal."

"It looks a hell of a lot less pretty when he's in his thirties and takes up with *my* mom when she's fifteen, doesn't it?"

Tanner's hands curled into determined fists. His dad might have made this fuckup but that didn't mean Tanner was going to let it get any worse. "You can't do this. Pull the article."

"That's not in my control." Except the way that Mako smirked said maybe he didn't give a shit anyway. He was wrecking things exactly the way he wanted to.

"I'll make your life a living hell." Tanner had money and he had position in the surf world. He wasn't exactly sure what Mako's weak point was, but if he threw all their dirty laundry out in the street, Tanner would dig until he made Mako pay.

Mako's mouth pressed flat. "You might want to ask who owns your mom's store."

"She does. Nice try." Tanner's half brother hopped right on over to extortion. Good to know.

"No, I mean the building itself. Wright Break is on a thirty-year lease. Did you know that? Buying the building was never a priority to *your dad*." Mako put an insidious emphasis on the last couple words, spitting them out with angry intent.

Tanner hadn't known. The business had never been his priority, either. As a teenager, his head had been more focused on making the world circuit than running a tiny surf shop. As an adult, he'd known that his dad had cut him out of the will, so it really didn't matter. But the place was still his mother's lifeblood, the thing that kept her days filled.

Not to mention Sage's surfboard shaping was done out of the back half of the building.

"You can't evict them."

"You sure, bro?" Mako was still spitting words around. The anger in the air was an almost palpable thing. "But as their landlord I can certainly inspect the premises. Introduce myself."

"Stay the fuck away from them."

Mako's lips curled into a smile but Tanner didn't feel particularly reassured. Pretty much the opposite. Bile rose at the back of his throat. The guy flat-out sucked. "No. I'm not withdrawing my interview. Plus, I'm meeting Eileen and Sage. I'm tired of being the dirty secret who has to hide in the corner. It'll be up to you whether you . . . soften them up first."

Tanner wanted to vomit. Right on Mako's bare toes if at all possible. "I'm not sure who I want to punch more. You or Hank." Tanner couldn't take any more. He turned to walk away, but the twenty-year-old part of him that still fucking resented what he'd learned about his father couldn't resist. He flipped a bird back over his shoulder.

"Nice. Classy," Mako said. "I feel almost like a real brother."

"One thing I can promise you," Tanner said as he walked away. "You'll never be my brother."

Chapter 6

The north side of San Sebastian was lined by a state park. The south side abutted the very pricey homes of Damian Cove. To the east were the outer edges of less nice suburban sprawl that covered vast stretches of Southern California—of course, that was the area where Avalon's mother lived.

The dingy condo complex was made up of a half dozen buildings, each with eight units. The unit Candy lived in was at the far back of the setup, but at least it overlooked the pool. It was a green-tinged pool where the local teenagers smoked pot. What a bonus.

On second thought, Candy probably did count it as a bonus when she was running low from her own suppliers. Easy access to score.

Avalon hitched the bag of groceries she carried a little higher and rang the bell. Quiet chimes echoed on the other side, followed by the clattering of high heels.

"Coming. Hold your horses," Candy called. She always sounded like she was about to laugh, if that made any sort of sense. Like she was always poised on the verge of looking for fun, anticipating finding a good time.

The door popped opened. At least Candy's smile didn't falter when she saw Avalon, not this time. "Darling," she cooed, "what a surprise."

Avalon lifted her eyebrows on a tiny flush of annoyance. "Funny thing. When my mom calls and asks me to come by, I usually do."

"You're so responsible like that." Candy managed to make it sound like an indictment.

She fluttered a hand, then pushed back a heavy fall of bright blond hair. For an afternoon with no company expected, she was certainly dressed well. Her capris clung to a carefully maintained figure and the low-cut silk blouse showed off plenty of assets. The boyfriend she'd had during Avalon's junior year of high school had paid for those.

Avalon had spent three weeks straight at the Wright house while her mom "recovered" from the surgery. Sure, the last week of recovery had been in Vegas, but, as Candy explained, sometimes a girl needed a little mental recovery after the physical stuff.

Avalon gave the brown bag in her arms a little wiggle. "Mind if I come in, Mother?"

"Oh! Of course not," Candy said on a wide smile. She opened the door with an extra flourish and stepped back. Her four-inch heels clattered over linoleum as she led the way toward the kitchen.

Avalon set the bag on the island. Sometimes Avalon swore Candy dated blue-collar men so she could bring them home and have them do chores. Hopefully she'd date a tile worker soon. She could do with some new counters. The white tile had lost its glaze over the years and the grout needed replacing, but her mom would spend thousands on clothing before she sank a penny on home repair, if she could help it.

In the fridge, Avalon found nothing but a box of wine and stacked take-out boxes. She shook her head. "You live like a frat boy, Mom."

Candy slipped onto a barstool. She already had a glass of white wine between her fingers. "That sounds a little like envy, darling."

Avalon managed to hold back the snort as she filled her mom's vegetable drawers with an assortment of fruit. She'd gotten the prewashed, precut versions along with a couple expensive tubs of ready-to-eat berries. If she hadn't, the stuff would be wilting and molding the next time she came by.

Her mom liked stuff the easy way. She'd lived her whole life by the model, and in a way it was working out for her.

"I have good news," Avalon said, but she kept her face carefully turned toward the fridge. There were certain concessions she had to make in order to keep at least a semblance of a mother-daughter relationship going. One of those meant not looking her mother in the eyes at certain times, in order to not see the disappointment.

"Oh?" Even without looking, Avalon could picture Candy's carefully manicured, filled-in brows lifting and her highly lipsticked lips parting. "Did you finally snag yourself a man?"

The sting didn't go away, not even when compared to the hot rush of thoughts of Tanner. The two feelings wove together under her skin in an uncomfortable mix.

That mixed slush of feeling was one of the hardest parts of her relationship with her mother. Avalon had never been able to come to terms with the fact that she still desperately loved the same woman she resented.

She shook her head, carefully keeping her hands from

shaking as she loaded a package of pineapple slices in the bottom drawer. "No. I got an awesome commission."

"Oh." The disappointment was audible in one tiny syllable. "You've put so much stock in that career of yours. It's about time it started to take off. What's the commission?"

There, that was almost the validation she needed. If she didn't see her mother's face, she could pretend that there wouldn't be a tiny sneer of disgust knotted on her forehead. "I'm following Tanner Wright for the month leading up to the Sebastian Pro. Documentary-style. He's got a good chance at winning the WCT, exactly ten years after his first championship. It's a huge opportunity for me. Guaranteed spread in *SURFING* magazine. This could be my big break."

She had to explain these little details because her mother made absolutely no pretense of following either Avalon's surrogate family or the world in which Avalon had built her life. Surfing was nothing to her mother except that thing Avalon did.

"Tanner Wright?" Candy laughed and then the wineglass clinked against the tile counter. "I knew I made the right call all those years ago."

"What call?" Avalon said, almost against her will. She winced as soon as it came out of her mouth.

"Why, letting you spend all that time with the Wrights. I knew they'd set you up well, and just look."

Avalon ran out of things to put away. She shut the fridge and carefully laid the brown bag out on the counter. Her hands worked at folding the sack as she looked up from under her lashes.

The expression on her mother's delicate features was a little difficult to interpret. Or maybe, difficult to understand. Her collagen-plumped mouth seemed set in a self-satisfied smile and Avalon couldn't understand what she thought she'd done that was so great.

She'd *let* Avalon spend time with Sage under Eileen's guidance because it was easier. It had taken less time out of her dating schedule. Explaining the sullen thirteen-year-old girl sitting on the couch was a little bit difficult when she'd led her boyfriend to believe she was only twenty-nine.

Though lately she'd given up twenty-nine for thirty-nine. She couldn't keep that gig up forever, much to her chagrin.

"Mom, repeat after me: Congratulations, Avalon."

She lifted the glass of wine and took a healthy swallow. "What? I already said congratulations."

That was her mom, exactly. Not abusive or intentionally cruel. Just . . . absent. Even when she was there. Avalon held down the soft wash of familiar pain.

Candy did her best. That was what counted.

And for those times when Candy hadn't done what was best for Avalon, Eileen had always been there to pick up the slack. Hence, why Avalon would slice a vein open for Eileen if she ever asked. The fact that Eileen wouldn't ask for that level of sacrifice was one more reason for her devotion.

Candy twiddled her fingers. "Anyway, that's done with. Why don't you get a drink? Sit down and chat awhile."

Done with. How neatly and tidily Candy glossed over the most important development in Avalon's career since she'd left school.

Of course, if she were to tell Candy about flirting with Tanner, that'd be a different story. Candy would be all over that and provide intricately detailed advice.

Putting a finger on what, exactly, Candy was became difficult. Though she liked drugs now and then, she wasn't exactly an addict. When a man came along who didn't like her pot habit, she easily put it aside. And though she adored her afternoon wine, she wasn't an alcoholic. She was . . . a wanderer. Someone without purpose beyond what a steady string of boyfriends and husbands gave her.

Avalon thanked her lucky stars constantly for the gift of photography. For having a goal and a life. She was going to be a professional surf photographer. Eventually being a stringer for a major magazine wasn't unfeasible. Everything else could follow along eventually, if it worked out.

She declined the offer of a drink. White wine wasn't her favorite, as she'd told her mom time and time again, and Candy didn't seem to have anything else in the house.

Avalon folded her arms across the counter and leaned on them. "So, Mom. How much do you need?"

Candy widened her eyes. "What makes you think I need money?"

Avalon rolled her lips in, the better to hold back the smile. It was either laugh at the situation or cry way too often. Her mom played the same games over and over. That Avalon played along was her cross to bear. "Hmm, dunno. Maybe because you only invite me over 'to hang out' when you need cash?"

Candy's mane of blond hair tossed back over her shoulder. "That's not true!"

It was absolutely and totally true. Candy was nothing if not predictable. Hanging out meant a request for money. An invitation to the spa meant maternal guilt over her failings. A dinner meant a new boyfriend that she wanted to introduce. Strata and deposits, everyone had their place. Avalon knew hers by now. "How much?"

Candy huffed, looking out toward the tiny living room. But she slanted a glance back at Avalon out the corner of her eyes. "If you're going to insist on money, I wouldn't turn away five hundred."

"Five?" Avalon asked on a fast jolt of surprise. Her hands spread flat over the cool tile. She did a couple fast calculations in her head, most of them revolving around the time of the month. "Your mortgage is due in three days. Are you going to be short?"

Candy's manicured fingernails drummed along the edge of the counter. She wiggled a tiny bit. "It's not my fault, Avalon. Really."

She sighed. "What was it this time?"

"I wish you wouldn't look at me like that. Teddy wanted to take me on a cruise, and my boss approved the days. It's not my fault that bitch in human resources didn't tell me that I'd be in the hole on vacation days."

A sharp pain lanced down Avalon's neck. All tension— she knew that—but even the careful application of breathing techniques Eileen had taught her couldn't put a dent in the mom-headache. Avalon dropped her head against the sudden pressure inside her skull. "Most people keep track of their own vacation days."

Candy huffed. "I'm sure it must be easy for you, since your job is running around the world to beaches. But some of us are working stiffs. My paycheck was three-fifty light!"

"Where's the other one-fifty, Mom?"

"What?"

Avalon shook her head. Another helpless laugh built. "Your mortgage is five hundred short. But your paycheck was only missing three fifty. Where'd the other one-fifty go?"

A hot pink blush scored Candy's cheeks, even under the layer of bronzer. At least she had the grace to be embarrassed. "This really beautiful pair of shoes. They were on sale and I figured . . ."

She'd figured she might as well since she was already going to have to call Avalon. That was an easy one.

Avalon nodded anyway. She had the money, no hardship out of her budget. Especially since she'd had to slink back to the Wrights' house after she and Matthew, her postcollege boyfriend, had split, so she wasn't paying rent. "I'll call the bank and pay it direct."

And honestly, it was worth it when Candy bounced up and darted around the island to toss her arms around Avalon. She shut her eyes and breathed in the sweet scent of perfume.

No matter her faults, no matter how much Avalon dreaded becoming rudderless like Candy . . . she still loved her mom. She was still going to help.

Considering the lengths she'd go to for the Wrights, it'd be criminal not to pay her mom's mortgage once in a while.

Chapter 7

Two days later, Tanner had already had enough of Avalon. For being such a cutie, she could be hella annoying when she got something between her teeth. For now she seemed to be following him like Little Bo Peep's lost sheep.

It might be okay if she talked now and then. But she'd gotten that stuck in her craw too. "Pretend I'm not here," was the most she said as a periodic reminder.

So he'd snuck out. It was nothing more than he'd done to any other photographer a time or two.

Besides, it was practically a requirement. He needed a chance to get hold of the surf. To make it behave under his board in a way he'd be able to channel come competition time. Not like it was working, though. Not yet.

Board under his arm, he trudged up the beach, sand sticking to his bare feet and flicking up onto the back of his calves.

All he'd needed was one good set on his own. In peace. How the hell was he supposed to nail the World Championship if he wasn't given enough time to fucking surf?

The points were too damn close to let this one go.

Jack Crews was five hundred behind him. If Crews won, he and Tanner could go neck and neck for the last two events of the season. If Tanner won, he'd be so much ahead of the rest of the pack that no number of Crews's wins could take the title away from him. He'd have it completely sewn up.

"Nice to see you too." The unspoken "asshole" didn't go by unheard.

Avalon perched on the back railing of his deck, the ubiquitous camera bag slung across her chest.

Christ, her shorts were tiny. Or, more important, her legs looked amazingly long beneath them, her toes tucked into the vertical slats of the railing. The slim, hugging T-shirt she wore had some sort of bear monster on it and her hair had been scooped up into a messy ponytail again. Tendrils skimmed along her slender neck.

"I woke up earlier than I meant to," he lied. "Headed out before dawn."

"'I'm going to sleep in, probably hit the gym later in the morning.'" She even mocked his facial expression, putting on a pseudoserious mien.

He shrugged as he propped his board up next to the door. He dug a key out of the pocket on the inside of his shorts, then unlocked the door. "Changed my plans."

The house he'd rented was pretty awesome. Definitely a step up from the WavePro flophouse he'd shared with seven other surfers his first years after breaking with his dad. The beachside house was cool and dim after a morning of hard work. He fished a Powerade out of the fridge, then chugged it down while he leaned against the marble counter. He was shedding sand everywhere probably, but it didn't matter. The floors through the lower level were all made of reclaimed wood in small, highly polished rectangles that looked and acted like tile. It could take a beating and only look better for it.

Avalon followed him inside a moment later. "Thanks for the invite."

"WavePro made sure you didn't need one."

Her bag went down on the counter next to him. He'd seen that dark gray canvas bag so often the past couple days, it felt almost as familiar as his own skin. But this time, there was something different. The corner of a black portfolio case poked out the flap this time. He tugged it free another couple inches. "What's this?"

"My work."

"Let me see."

She grabbed a glass from an overhead cabinet while giving him a slant-eyed look. "I don't take orders well."

He hadn't even known he had the stubby, flat-sided glasses she grabbed. The rental had come fully furnished, and it wasn't a tiny place. There weren't a lot of rooms but they were all spacious, airy, and perfectly decorated. Easier that way when he only needed it for a month. But at the same time, it was more comfortable than a hotel room.

When his kitchen wasn't occupied with a faintly hostile female, that was.

Though he fully admitted part of that was his fault. He should have taken her surfing with him. It was bound to happen eventually. But between seeing both Jack and Mako, and then the shit Mako had sprung on him . . . He needed to take the edge off, pretty much.

He could go for a lot more time on the waves alone too.

She poured orange juice into her glass, then leaned

against the far counter. In a kitchen as big as this one, that put plenty of distance between them. The smile that curved her mouth was all sharp angles and a tiny bit of contempt.

"Please, let me see your pictures," he gritted out.

"Sure." She grinned, but hid it behind the glass of juice. Seemed she liked making him twist. "Go ahead."

He tugged the case free, then flipped it open. The shots were beautiful . . . but cold, in a way. Bright blue ocean, surfers doing their thing. Some of them were black-and-white and gritty in a style he'd seen a million times before. All very competent. "Nice," he eventually said.

She put her juice down with a clink. The tendons climbing up the back of her neck popped into stark relief as white lines carved under her cheeks. She silently walked across the kitchen, flipped her portfolio closed, gathered up her camera bag, and then walked out of the kitchen without saying another word.

Shit, there was only one way to interpret that one. He'd hurt her feelings in a way he hadn't meant to at all. In the heavy silence of the room, he sighed.

He couldn't let it go. There was a vast difference between her being annoyed with him because he'd snuck out to surf or stolen an inappropriate kiss and her being actually hurt.

He found her in the living room.

She'd laid out two cameras, including their waterproof housings, and was quietly wiping away sand. Her mouth had acquired an upward turn, but it didn't look real. Almost as if it had been scribbled over her real expression.

He leaned a shoulder against the stucco wall. The paint was cool and rough. "Look, I'm sorry."

The look she angled up at him from under her brows seemed intentionally blank. She was sharper than that. He much preferred her being a smart-ass.

"I'm not sure what you're talking about." She snapped a lens from a camera body, then pulled out a soft brush. "Do you think you'll be surfing a set again this afternoon? One I can actually photograph, I mean."

"About your pictures. They're nice, really. As good as anything I've seen in *Surfer*."

"You said that." She flashed another smile. "It's fine. I get it."

Something didn't add up. "What do you get?"

Her mouth twisted into a bitter knot, but her gaze dropped to her hands. "Same shit I've been hearing from everywhere around me. I'm missing the spark. Fine for commercial. Maybe I should stick to magazine ads. But, you know, fuck that noise. I'm not giving up."

"No one said you should." Shit, the last thing he needed to do was give her more ammo, but he couldn't help himself. "I'm not giving up on my goals, either."

She lifted her eyebrows. "Says the man who's one competition away from winning the World Championship, pretty much. Good to know you'll stick to it." Her voice practically dripped sarcasm.

He wondered if she'd be quite that snarky if she knew her thin shirt revealed quite the view. Her breasts were small enough that she'd gone without a bra. There was nothing beneath her worn-soft T-shirt but her bare skin and the gentle swells of her breasts.

"Yeah. Make fun. That's fine," he managed to say.

He was probably one injury shy of over-the-hill. Didn't it figure that the first time he managed to admit it to someone, she'd blown him off?

The hamstring injury that had kept him away from San Sebastian last year had been no joke, no exaggeration. Maybe previous years he'd made excuses to stay away, but not a year ago. No one but his physical therapist knew how hard it had been to come back from that injury, either.

He wasn't some green kid fresh from the juniors anymore. Not made of rubber. If he didn't nail the championship this year, he was pretty sure he'd never get another chance and he wouldn't forget that.

One World Championship might be enough for most people. But he'd been twenty-one when he'd won his, barely conscious of a world beyond the nose of his board. Now he wanted to go out on top.

Retire in his thirties. The idea was a joke. But that was what he wanted. Take life all sorts of easy. Coronas on the back deck of a beach house, no more physical therapy or training or watching every move.

He scrubbed a hand over his head, breaking loose some of the sand. "Whatever. Not so easy for us old guys on the circuit, either."

She snorted. "Old? Kelly Slater is forty-one."

But he'd already walked out of the room, headed up the stairs to the master suite. There was a walk-in shower with his name all over it. He flicked the spigots on, then yanked his board shorts down and tossed them over the hamper in the corner. Then remembered he'd left his towels on the bench at the foot of his bed.

A surprise waited at the door to his bedroom. Avalon had followed. Bright red flashed over her cheeks. She slapped a hand over her mouth.

But she didn't look away, either. Her eyes sparkled.

Tanner picked up one of the fluffy, dark gray towels

from the bench. Deliberately, he took his time flicking it out, then wrapping it around his hips. Avalon bounced on her toes, excitement buzzing through her very pores.

"Can I help you?" he purred. The last thing he should do was sleep with her, not while she was officially covering him for WavePro but he didn't mind setting the groundwork for later, either. Avalon was too luscious to pass up.

She lowered her hand but had to tap her sternum once or twice as she coughed. The red finally faded from her cheeks. "The door was open. I didn't think . . ."

He lifted an eyebrow. "Don't let me stop you."

She coughed again, glancing off to the side. "I wanted to say I'm sorry. I know you've had a few injuries. They must be getting harder and harder to bounce back from."

Christ, that was true. He didn't want to think about them any more than he had to, but that was why he had to win this year's championship, why he couldn't give up even a handful of points. He wasn't likely to have another shot.

That didn't mean he needed to listen to Avalon tell him how he was over-the-hill, either. He turned his smile sharp. "Don't tell me you've been following my career."

Another hot wash of pink rolled over her cheeks, even as she puffed an annoyed breath and flicked a glance up at the ceiling. "Don't be ridiculous."

Except he'd seen it. The quick flash that gave her away. "Holy crap, you have."

Then she genuinely laughed. "God, not like that. Don't make it any more than it is. You're Sage's brother and I already have to keep up-to-date for market research. That's it."

He tucked the towel a little more snugly around his

hips and looked out at her from under his brow. Was she really so relaxed, or was that her pulse fluttering wildly at the base of her throat? "You sure about that?"

In half a second, her eyes went wide and her lips parted on a quiet gasp. "Oh gee, Tanner. Don't make me say it. How I've always felt."

He couldn't help but step forward, close enough to smell her sweet fragrance. "How's that?"

"I've felt—" She rose up on her toes. The wash of her breath sent goose bumps down his neck. "I've felt like you were a huge jackass with an ego too big for your own good."

With a giggle, she patted his cheek, then swished her way out of the room. Her ass twitched with each step she took, laughter echoing along behind her.

Tanner couldn't help but chuckle as she walked away. Yeah, he'd deserved that one.

He tossed the towel onto the rack by the shower and stepped into the glassed enclosure. Water struck him from both sides, steaming away the stiffness of a morning of surfing. More proof he wasn't as young as he used to be.

Hell, maybe he even needed to think about settling down. Damned if he'd hook up with a chick as smart-mouthed as Avalon, though. He knew what was good for him, and it wasn't listening to crap like that for the rest of his days.

Chapter 8

Not once since she was fourteen had Avalon been nervous walking up the front path of the Wright residence. They'd been her second home, her saviors. The very first time she'd spent more than two nights in a row had been when she'd been sixteen and her mom took off for Bakersfield. No one in her right mind willingly went to shitty, landlocked Bakersfield, never mind to follow a boyfriend who had to be back in time to make a parole check-in. But Candy took off with barely more than four hours' warning. The fact that Avalon had midterms the next week hadn't meant anything to her.

So she'd crashed on Sage's floor.

Eventually the "guest" bedroom had morphed into hers. First a spare toothbrush in the upstairs bathroom, then extra clothes for after surfing.

The whole time she kept expecting her mom to raise a fuss. Claim the life she'd made and was supposed to raise. But Candy hadn't.

Avalon had become part of the Wrights in everything but name. When things had gone wrong with Matthew, her postcollege boyfriend, and Avalon had found herself without a place to live after she'd been dumped, she'd been welcomed back without even a question. She'd luckily been close enough to help when Hank died. Hell, she'd been there last night, left this morning. It was only that she was arriving in time for Tanner's party that made anything odd.

Which meant that standing on the front stoop smoothing down her skirt with damp palms was ridiculous. Asinine.

Unavoidable.

Her heart seemed ready and willing to thump its way out of her damn chest, never mind her need for it. She really had to get her mind off Tanner's body. The man had no shame at all.

God, she was fucked up, but she was beginning to like him for it.

He was completely and totally assured of his place in the world. She could do with a little of that. Though most of the time she was sure she hid it well, it felt like she was scrambling. Trying to grab at what she *could* get, not what she deserved. Like she'd snag scraps while no one else was looking.

Even she knew it was what was wrong with her photography. That missing spark had to do with her. She couldn't get too mad at Tanner earlier today because—while she'd hoped he'd adore her photos—she hadn't been surprised at all when he hadn't.

That train of thought killed the frothing waves in her stomach easily enough. Walking into the house became nothing. So what if she saw Tanner? It was his welcome-home party; he was bound to be there eventually. Instead she found Eileen and Sage bustling around the kitchen, putting together trays of vegetables and pitchers of drinks.

Eileen dropped baby carrots and opened her arms to Avalon. "Baby! I heard, I'm so proud of you."

Stepping into Eileen's hug was one of the easiest things in Avalon's world. She smelled faintly of patchouli from a holistic antiarthritis cream that she swore by but it wasn't enough to be overpowering. A tiny reminder that Eileen wasn't always the businesswoman she'd had to be to run a surf store for twenty years.

She closed her eyes and sucked up the comfort. Let her bones unclench for a moment. When she'd hugged Candy the other day, it hadn't felt like this. They'd been all inflexible angles and stiff shoulders. That almost made her more sad.

Chasing Tanner all over Southern California meant she hadn't had a chance to talk to Eileen about the assignment. "You don't mind?"

"Mind you following my handsome son around for over three weeks? Not at all." She leaned back, her smile lit with easy relaxation. Tiny wrinkles fanned out from the pale eyes both her children had inherited. "Slip me a few that I can put up on my walls and I'll make that chocolate turtle pie you like so much."

"Pinkie swear?"

"Of course."

Sage poured blush wine into glasses, then pushed two across the counter. "Celebration time."

She smiled past the prickle at the back of her eyes. This was home. These were the people she'd do anything for. Even if it meant coping with Tanner or, more specifically, not letting him get under her skin. Tanner would eventually leave for the circuit. She needed this family.

"I probably shouldn't," she protested but a glass of

wine might relax the knot of nerves between her shoulder blades.

Eileen kept trying to teach her how to relax and let go. She wasn't exactly the type. Three hours later, when the house was crowded with people and her cheeks were tired from holding a smile, she'd had enough.

She'd been following Tanner around—of course—and he'd been completely working the room. Chatting, laughing, talking surf conditions with old buddies. Some of the guests had been on the pro circuit with him for years, and some he hadn't seen in almost a decade. He treated them all with the same strangely empty surface cheer.

Framing him between the targets of her lens, it was almost like she saw him differently from everyone else. She wondered if anyone could see the odd buzzing within him, the way the corners of his eyes tightened every time he looked away from whomever he was talking to.

When he walked by a cabinet filled with his father's old surf trophies, it was like a low-level bomb went off under his skin. His shoulders went sharp and hard, the back of his neck flushed faintly red.

She snapped off a few shots.

Tanner was back to ignoring her again, but that was fine too. She liked it better that way. At least then she wasn't picturing the heavy sweep of his muscles, the sleek tendons that dove down his ribs to his waist. A vein to the left of his hipbone. God, that had been a yummy view, one that had made her mouth water. Inappropriately. Her mouth watered *inappropriately* over a photography subject.

She had to keep that line up. Somehow.

People were used to her buzzing around parties with a camera in hand. Hardly anyone even asked about the fact that Tanner was her target. She didn't mind that. There'd be enough fallout and behind-the-back whispering once her spread hit *SURFING*.

A satisfied smile tucked up the corners of her mouth. She flicked her bangs out of her eyes as she traded out cameras up in her room. This? Was going to be so damn sweet. Best job of her life.

The level of payoff was worth ten times the hassle from Tanner.

For example, by the time she made it back downstairs, the frustrating man was gone. Disappeared. Bodies of all shapes and sizes—though almost everyone dressed in shorts and slim T-shirts—filled the space almost wall to wall.

But nowhere among them was tousled blond hair over a harshly hewn smile. Nowhere was the scar she found so intriguing. A taste of rough danger in an otherwise beautiful man.

Muttering under her breath, she dashed back upstairs and searched the bedrooms. Nothing. Even the room that had once been his was empty. It didn't even hold a trace of him anymore, all blue-walled guest room with white furniture. Eileen had kept most of Tanner's high school and junior surf trophies, but Hank had insisted they be packed away. Said if the boy couldn't be bothered to step foot in the family home, he shouldn't be a part of it.

They were both about as bullheaded as possible.

It hadn't been a surprise to anyone when they'd butted heads—you can't have two alphas in the same household—and the shock hadn't set in until they'd both failed to get over it.

Avalon had almost given up searching for Tanner and was in the process of pulling the door closed behind her, when a flash of white caught her gaze.

Except it was outside the window.

She stepped back into the room. "Tanner?"

There was no answer, but the white shifted again. The corner of a sleeve, she figured. The window was open to the evening's breeze coming in off the ocean a block away, and it smelled of salt. More home.

As she got closer, she realized the screen had been popped out of the window and rested against the wall in the dim shadow of the bed. Tanner sat outside the window on the low, gently sloping roof of the garage. His knees were pulled into his chest, his wrists draped over them so his fingers dangled between. His shoulders made a thick curve of muscle under his gleaming white shirt.

He glanced at her out the corner of his eye. "Hello, Avalon." The way he said her voice was half purr, half caress. All tease. In it she heard a reminder of this morning and the view she'd been privy to.

She wasn't one to back down from challenges. Never had been. Especially not when they were so damn delicious looking. She ducked her shoulders under the window and hitched one hip on the roof so she was pretty much sitting next to him. "Mind if I join you?"

The camera was an almost unnoticeable weight in her hand. Practically an extension of the way she blinked. She ran off a couple shots, barely even pointing the lens. That angle of his jaw, the way his skin glowed with health and happiness wasn't something she could pass up. Her camera whirred in quick succession with the *snap-snap-snap* of the button.

His chest lifted on a sigh. "First rule. If you're coming out here, you've got to put the camera down. Or go down to the party. I'll be back in ten, and you can get all the shots you want."

She bit her bottom lip, then wiggled the tip of her tongue over the tender flesh. Putting the camera down was harder than she'd expected but she'd always been there for her friends. Even if he was difficult—even if she had dirty thoughts about what she'd like to do to his body if he were any other man—she wanted to consider him a friend.

She needed to, on some level. Friends were safer than the strange animosity and lust they bounced between.

Ducking back inside the room, she set the Fuji down on the nightstand, next to a brass lamp. When he'd been living in this room, there had been a Hawaiian hula girl there. The first season he'd gone off to surf in Tahiti, Avalon snuck in nightly and swished the girl's skirt. Not anymore.

She wondered what he thought about having been wiped out of what used to be his home.

It wouldn't have happened if he'd stuck around. Sage's room had stayed the same until she'd needed to come home. After Avalon couldn't put up with Matthew's whining anymore and came home, her room had been waiting. She'd thought her relationship with Matthew was headed toward an engagement at any moment, but they'd had a blowup instead. At least she'd had her own bed and the room she'd decorated to keep her company while she dealt with admitting her blindness. It had only been Tanner's room that had been completely redecorated.

She slipped back out onto the tiered roof of the garage. The slope wasn't too extreme, but it was certainly noticeable as she settled onto her ass. Tanner had the wall of the house to lean against, but she had to plant her hands flat at her hips to feel more secure. She settled into the feeling like she settled into a heavy slab of a wave.

"I knew you weren't much of a party boy, but this seems extreme."

"This actually isn't about them. Not much, at least."

He stared off past the roof of the house across the street. She followed his gaze. For a minute, all she saw was suburbia, neatly tiled and slated roofs all lined up in a row, and past that the dark glimmer of the water under a half moon. The water frothed white in the surge she loved so much.

Avalon didn't poke. There was a special element to a summer night where the warmth never left the air, but the dark could fix problems. Or at least soothe them for a little while. Minutes stacked up in quiet companionship.

Tanner sighed contentedly. "Now I'm home."

"What?"

"I used to come out here and sit when I still lived here. Watch the water. Think about that day's waves. Feel exhausted or upset or whatever drama my teenage self was rolling around in. Just . . . process. Almost every night. Mom gave up on keeping a screen on the window."

Carefully, slowly, she lifted her feet and folded her knees to her chest. She still felt fairly steady. In body, at least, since her mind was rolling. "Not surfing, not your mom, not the house itself. This rooftop. This is home?"

"Yeah. I guess in a way it is."

"You, Tanner Wright, are an idiot."

Chapter 9

Tanner's immediate reaction was to bristle. He hadn't exactly invited her. Under no circumstances had he asked her opinion. Then he smiled. Leaned his shoulders back against the wall as prickly stucco caught at his shirt. "Jealous much?"

"Of you?" She gave a neatly dismissive huff. Two fingers flicked her bangs to the side. "No chance."

He was struck with the sudden wish to see her hair damp and plastered to her temples again. No seawater needed; he'd make her work up a sweat. She had gorgeous legs that he could wrap around his hips.

He pushed all that down. No time, no place. He had a championship on the line. If that wasn't enough, he had seen firsthand what happened to relationships broken by his hellacious travel schedule. Splitsville, pronto. The longest relationship he'd managed was six months. Nothing to brag about, but she'd gotten hella bored, hella fast being without him. "No, not of me. Of my family."

Her smile looked a little smug. "Well, yeah. That's a given. Have you met my mom?"

The hand he rubbed over the back of his head was

pushed by chagrin. "Um. Maybe? I'm the first one to admit that I was fairly self-centered in high school."

"I think you might have. At Sage's sixteenth birthday." She winced a little, curling her hands around her thighs. "That was a mess."

God, he did remember that. It had been one of the last times he'd been home. At that point, he'd known about Mako, but he'd bought his dad's story about it being a onetime mistake. He'd learned soon after how much Hank lied. The truth had been so much more painful, an ongoing betrayal of everything their family stood for.

As a matter of fact, that hot mess of a birthday party had somewhat propelled the situation along. If he remembered right, the bleached blonde had been Avalon's mom. The distraction over the inappropriately dressed woman who'd brought along a boyfriend ten years younger than her enabled Tanner to hit the keg more often than he otherwise would have. He'd barely been able to keep his mouth shut around his mom. After his further discoveries in Tahiti a few months later, he'd known he couldn't go home.

Her chin rose. "Yeah, I see it. You remember."

"See what?"

"That look." She turned her gaze back out toward the far line of roofs. "Anyone who remembers my mom gets it eventually. A little distaste, heavy on the disgust. And often some doubt. Am I like her? Will I turn out like her?"

"You asking me, sweetheart? 'Cause I don't know you near well enough to answer that." He waggled his eyebrows. The moment had gotten way too deep for his liking. "Though you give me half a chance and I'll find out."

Her laugh was pretty. Light, surprisingly musical. He'd

have thought, based on her voice, that she'd have had more of a husky chuckle. "You keep trying, Tanner. You've got only your pride to hurt. Come on. There's a party downstairs. Everyone's waiting on you."

She slipped back in the window with an easy twist of her hips. Inside, she dusted off the curve of her ass. Quite the pert curve, no less.

Drawn by that firm swell, he was in without thinking about it. But standing in what had once been his room, memories hit him all over again.

The weight of the secret threatened to drown him every time his mom smiled at him. And she was waiting downstairs to do a lot of that. Time was running out, in more than one way. It wasn't enough that he was here again, dealing with the pictures of Hank everywhere he turned. Mako had given that damn interview. Everything was ticking down.

He wasn't sure he could take it.

Somewhere along the years, he'd lost his way. Now that his dad was dead, it became harder every day to understand why he kept a shitty man's secret. Except Avalon was pretty much proof of why, wasn't she?

With no family of her own, she'd latched onto his sister and his mother. They'd welcomed her because they had that purity of spirit he'd been lacking all his life. They chilled and relaxed when he was driven to tear and shred his way through life. That was his father's influence, pushing him to bigger and better. It wasn't enough to have one championship; nail two. It wasn't enough to have three sponsorships; you should find another. Drive. Ambition.

The strange thing was, he wondered if Avalon, under the surfer-chick front, had the same sort of buzz under her skin.

His hand darted out, almost without any conscious thought behind it. Her skin was smoother than liquid silk. Slicker than salt water between his fingers. He'd caught her by the waist, two fingers snaking under the bottom hem of her shirt.

Her lips parted silently. In the shadowy darkness of the room, moonlight picked out her eyes to make them gleam. Her head tilted slightly to the side. "What are you doing, Tanner?"

"I wasn't kidding, you know." He tugged her a little closer. A little nearer. Silence swirled around them, locking their breath together. Salt, sweet, the tiniest edge of a gasp. "Everything else aside . . . I want to know you."

The smile she was biting back became something suspiciously like a snort of laughter. Lines cut under the apples of her cheeks as she tensed her mouth. "Has that line ever worked for you? Maybe when you snuck girls in here?"

"I didn't," he said, but it felt kind of like bluster, even to him. The back of his neck flushed hot. At least it was too dark for her to see the blush.

Her chin lifted even higher, but she didn't step away. If anything, she leaned nearer. The cotton shirt brushed over his chest. Her eyes looked darker than normal, the pupils large pools. "Wanna try again? Liars don't get in my panties."

"Didn't realize that was a possibility."

"Possibility, yes. Guarantee, no. But lying to me's the safest way to not get a shot."

He followed the long, sleek line of her arms from her wrists all the way up to her shoulders. Then traced over the straight blade of collarbone hiding beneath her shirt. Most girls who showed up at circuit parties wore a hell of a lot less. Bikinis, most of the time. While Avalon could have totally gotten away with that, she'd worn a V-neck shirt that gave only a hint of her cleavage. He'd seen her body before at the beach, but he was still hit with a sense of wonder. Curiosity. What she'd taste like once he'd unwrapped her.

He swallowed, dragging his gaze back up to her face. "What am I not supposed to be lying about, again?"

"Girls. In this room."

"Yes. A bunch of them. I got them to come up after dark or when no one was home."

"Inez Montoya." Her head tilted to give him better access as he traced over the satin work that made up her skin. She still hadn't touched him in any way.

She rested within his arms, but not a part of him. Not yet. He'd fix that soon enough.

It was becoming rapidly apparent that getting through the San Sebastian Pro without tasting Avalon was a ridiculous goal. "Yeah, Inez was one of them." He hadn't thought of that dark-haired beauty in years. It had been about six weeks after he'd graduated high school, when he'd gone to his first official ASP event.

Something about Avalon drove every woman out of his head. Her energy, maybe. Her smile sent a liquid rush through him. "I peeked."

"Like hell."

"I was thirteen. You didn't close the door all the way. Man, did she have a nice rack."

His jaw dropped open. "No, you didn't."

"Did too. I didn't stick around for long, but . . ." She lifted up on her toes, close enough to whisper in his ear. The sweet scent of her wrapped around him. "I always wondered what it'd be like to kiss you."

That was an invitation if he'd ever heard one. He kissed her.

At first he'd meant to stay soft. A tease. Something to get his mind off the swelling voices downstairs. The party he wouldn't be able to avoid forever. The weight of the stares might be easier to bear if he had Avalon's mouth.

But it got away from him. *She* got away from him.

Probably when she licked her tongue over his bottom lip, then took it between her teeth. Tugged. The sharp bite went straight to his cock. He filled, hardened, and the flashover want had him walking her backward. His arms wrapped low around her ass, grabbing that curve.

His fingertips found bare, silky skin at the hem of her skirt as he pushed her back into the wall.

Sinewy arms wound over his shoulders. Her wrists latched behind his neck, pulling their torsos together as if one. Her soft breasts cushioned his chest.

The way she kissed went straight to his head. She took and took, as if every motion was worship. Every taste a gift she gave him. He knew without saying a word that she'd ask for exactly what she needed from him. No guessing. No secrets.

God, that sounded good.

He hitched her higher against the wall, one arm between her and the cool wallpaper. They could fuck like this and it would be epic. Amazing. But it wasn't time for that. Not yet.

Maybe not until he'd put the San Sebastian Pro behind him. He had to keep his head about him. Once in a decade was too much to risk on a woman. But he'd have to make sure that she understood it'd be a temporary thing, nothing long-term.

Drawing his mouth away from Avalon's was even

more difficult than he expected, though. She kissed him back with enthusiasm that went all the way to his cock. The soft protest that dwelled in her throat stroked his ego. He pressed kisses over the line of her jaw, easing her back. She leaned her head against the wall with a sigh and looked at him from under her thick lashes, but said nothing.

He licked the last taste of her off his mouth. Something sweet, like oranges. "God, I needed that," he breathed.

Her wrists tugged at the back of his neck. She laughed quietly. "That. Not me. Way to make a girl feel special."

"You know what I meant." Letting her down proved harder than he'd expected. He liked having a reason to grab her ass. It was a damn good one.

That ass twitched as she walked across the room. "What I do know is that you're the last person in the world I should be fooling around with."

"Funny, that felt like your tongue in my mouth, all right." He wasn't even sure why he was arguing his case. If anything, he ought to walk away and keep his energy for the next couple weeks of surfing.

But he'd rucked up her shirt somewhere in that kiss. It twisted higher on one side of her waist, revealing a silk-soft stretch of skin that ended to the left of her belly button. He wanted to drop to his knees and lick that skin. See if it tasted half as sweet as her mouth, or if she'd be all ocean salt.

"Oh, it was." She picked up the camera. Her fingers curled around it with a particular level of affection. She flicked away a microscopic fleck of dirt. "People will say I got the gig because I was already in your pants."

"No, they'll be too busy saying you got the gig because you grew up with my sister. Won't bother to look past their noses." He shoved his fists into the pockets of his cargo shorts. His body was taking its sweet time calming down. Probably because every time he started to reel himself in, he looked at the tiny patch of skin above her waistband. "No one would have to know."

"I'd be your dirty little secret?"

"Nah," he said, drawing the word out. "I'd be yours. Totally different."

She laughed. Throwing her head back turned her neck into a pale column. Scooping up her camera bag, she slung it over her shoulder, then adjusted the strap across her chest like armor. "I have no idea how you got the reputation of a ladies' man."

He shrugged. "Me neither."

"Lucky for you, I'm an odd girl." She stepped close, rising up on her toes. Her soft cheek skated over his jaw as her mouth lifted toward his ear. "I'll think about it. If you quit ditching me to surf on your own."

The smile rose from somewhere way down deep inside him, like a sunken ship rising again. Up through the depths this party had tried to drown him with. "You don't mean that."

"Nope. Not really." She patted the center of his chest with one hand, but then snapped off a few pictures with the left. The damned camera was like an extension of her. She didn't even bother with the viewfinder half the time. "But if you go surf on your own, I'll toss every pair of your board shorts on a bonfire and you can swim naked. I don't think I'd mind that much, but the tourist crowds might have something to say about it."

Chapter 10

Playing with fire was too damned much fun. That was the only problem with Tanner. She wasn't going to be able to stay away from him. Avalon's knees shook as she made her way down the stairs to the main level of the house. Her fingers left a faint trail of sweat over the wrought-iron banister while her heart was a wickedly thumping beast.

Holy sweet baby Jesus, could the man kiss. He'd turned her upside down and given her insides a good shake, like she was some kind of snow globe. A little play toy to amuse him and distract him from unpleasantness.

She'd be damned if she was going down that easily. As soon as he won, he'd be gone. Her penchant for emotionally unavailable men was bad enough. She'd realized her relationship limitations after Matthew. No need to add physically unavailable.

But going down at all . . . Yeah, that looked likely. She wanted more of those kisses. More of his rough, raw grip on her hips. The way he'd picked her up and held her against the wall had been amazing. She stuffed down a shiver as her foot landed on the bottom step. She needed more of that. More of him.

The years hadn't seen her celibate exactly, not by a long shot. But Matthew had left her kind of raw. The problem hadn't even been that he'd dumped her. It had been that he'd dumped her when she'd been so obliviously confident they'd made a great couple. Only after the fact had she realized where they'd failed. The signs she should have caught to make him happier.

There hadn't been anyone lately. Tasty opportunities didn't often present themselves while she did her best to scramble to the top of the photography world. This one was too good to pass up, really.

But she'd have to step carefully.

Weaving her way through the throng of bodies that pressed around her, she kept her camera up. Snapped a shot of the surf manager canoodling in the corner with an up-and-coming women's champion. Another picture of three supposed rivals who were listening to a fourth telling a story by waving his hands above his head. Probably describing some epic air he'd caught off a wave.

This world was her home. The strange mix of the surfers' laid-back personas swirled in with the cutthroat business of promotions and a healthy helping of athletic devotion and determination. But she needed her own entry. She'd spent four years collecting a bachelor's in photography but she'd spent enough years in the surfing world. She'd earned her place.

The photos of Tanner would prove it. She'd have the same incisive eye as the rest of her peers, the same editing to get the right frame on the shot. Maybe, if she played her cards right, she'd have some brilliant orgasms to go along with.

The kitchen was relatively empty, the quiet bouncing off the tiled counters. Sage had staked out a place near the fridge, sitting at the right angle of two countertops and holding a beer.

Avalon snagged herself a drink out of an ice-filled tub set to the side of the room, then levered to sit next to her friend. "You making it?"

Sage nodded. Her mouth curved into a beautiful but wistful-looking smile. "I miss Dad."

At a party like this, Hank Wright would have owned the room Avalon walked through. He'd have held court from the living room, but not in any bad way. People wanted to listen to Hank, wanted to impress him. He'd have corralled them into less smashing pandemonium, more of a chill vibe.

The soda flowed sweetly over her tongue, but it still couldn't wash the taste of Tanner out of her mouth. "This wouldn't even be happening if your dad were around. Not the same way."

Not with Tanner here, being the unspoken portion.

"I know." Sage pushed a sheaf of hair off her bare shoulder. "Which I think only makes missing him worse. He'd have loved it. Loved having everyone under one roof."

"And it never happened." She didn't get it, didn't get Tanner. It was for the best that she didn't have time for anything in-depth with the man. A long-term relationship was off the table not only because he'd be leaving in a month, but also because Avalon hoped that she'd be able to understand any man she got involved with. At least a little bit. More than she'd managed before. She flicked at the tab to her soda with the corner of her thumb, over and over, making a tinny noise.

Until Sage put her hand over Avalon's. "Please stop, darling."

She smiled weakly. "Sorry." Too much churned in her head. Most of the time, she wished for Sage's easy calm. Even when Sage was missing her father so badly, she seemed relaxed.

Avalon ought to give up and go take some photographs. It was her job, after all, which gave her a yummy little thrill. She was making it. Finally. But after the interlude upstairs, after Tanner's mouth and the thrilling way he'd held her, she needed some calm. Some relaxation.

She'd never learned how to get there on her own. She always soaked it up from Sage.

Two men stepped through the open archway, their shoes ringing on the tile. One was vaguely familiar and the other was Jack Crews. Pretty boy of the world champions— in a way. He wore a perfectly pressed, pin-striped button-down shirt over slim dark trousers. Five levels fancier than anyone else at the party, but he pulled it off with ease. At his side walked a tall, slender Asian man with black hair, the same man who'd gotten Tanner riled at the bar.

Jack gave a wide, bright smile that creased the corners of his blue eyes. The smile almost outshadowed the faint bruise at the corner of his jaw. He'd been fighting again. "I heard I could find the sweet stuff in here."

She grinned. There'd always been a soft spot in her heart for Jack. Hank had taken him under his wing after Tanner had flown the coop.

"You heard right." She pushed off the counter and flew into his open arms. "You're late enough."

"Had to pick up a guest." Keeping his arm hooked around her shoulders, he waved a hand toward the man at his side. "Avalon and Sage, this is Mako Wright."

"How funny," Sage said on a light laugh. "That's my last name too."

He gave a slight bow of his head, but the way he held his mouth was sharp. His eyes were dark shadows that gave little emotion away. "It's a common enough name."

Sage shrugged. "Sure is. Means you're extra welcome around here."

His mouth curled in a slightly devious-looking smile but his reply was polite enough as he and Sage drifted to the far side of the kitchen island. Sage was rambling on about the history of the name, all stuff her father had told her a hundred times. Avalon didn't really like the way Mako kept watching her. In a way, he seemed as shark-like as his name. Nearly reptilian in his level of intensity.

Avalon held back a shiver under Jack's linen-clad arm. He sent her a curious look out of the corner of his eyes. This close, the carefully scruff-covered jawline looked pettably sharp. Jack had to be one of the prettiest men she'd ever seen but still, she couldn't think of anything but Tanner's blunt features.

She looped her arm around Jack's waist anyway and nestled closer. "Why didn't we ever hook up?"

"Because you were clever enough to realize what a bad influence I'd be on you." He tossed the words about lightly enough, but his eyes told on him. Jack's childhood had been even more messed up than hers, though she didn't know all the details. He hadn't been lucky enough to meet the Wrights until he was in his twenties.

He played hard and fought harder. Somehow he was always rising to the defense of some poor—and usually female—bartender getting the sharp side of an asshole's tongue. Or there was the time he'd taken on three men because they'd pinched a cocktail waitress's ass. He had radar for damsel-oriented distress, and almost all of it ended up with him brawling in a back alley.

The upside-down look of his mouth, with its lower lip held slightly tighter than the top, had sent plenty of surfer groupies fluttering and squealing. There wasn't a single heat where he didn't have girls in bikinis waiting on the sand.

Avalon had never found herself pinned up against a wall being kissed by him. Or kissing back. Never wanted to, for that matter. "I don't think that's it."

"Let's ditch this pop stand and I'll show you a good time, then." His hair was so short-cropped that it was a bristly cap.

Nothing to brush back, no golden mess to tousle. "You're lying again."

He looked forward, catching Sage in his sights. His mouth pulled, the line of his cheekbones becoming a sharp blade. The corners of his eyes tucked deeper. "I am."

"Why?"

"Why not?" He flashed another smile, but she shook her head. Tugged on the back of his shirt.

"Tell."

"Because some people in this world are broken, and some are not." The expression he turned on her made her want to pet him, tell him everything would be all right in the end. "Some of us have broken pieces and we need to find somewhere to fit them into. You and me? Our pieces don't fit."

Too much, too heavy. She had enough crap to deal with and maybe it made her a shitty friend, but she couldn't take on his stuff at the moment. She grinned and rested her head on his shoulder in a coy gesture. "Boys and girls. Things fit. I promise."

He laughed. "Wanna prove it?"

"With you? Not on your life." Definitely not when she still had Tanner's taste in her mouth. Or when her girl bits were still tingly and wanting Tanner's bits. "You know what, though? Once I'm done with this WavePro contract, I'd like to do a shoot with you."

He tugged lightly on her ponytail. "I was wondering when you were gonna ask. I was worried I wasn't handsome enough for your lens."

She laughed. Couldn't help it. A rising level of confidence left her buoyant. "You *so* don't think that's the problem."

"I'll tell my manager you're going to call. Work out the schedule."

"Thanks, Jack."

Sage laughed at something Mako said, then reached out to pat his shoulder. The gesture was entirely friendly, but under Avalon's fingertips, Jack's side went rock hard. His freaking *side*, over his ribs, as if Avalon needed any more proof of how fit he was. But there was something else about it. She tilted her head up, looking at the angular lines of his face.

Maybe there was another reason she and Jack had never hooked up.

Maybe they both had a propensity for Wrights. Wouldn't that be a sad, sad idea?

From the other rooms, the general level of noise swelled. She sighed. "I need to get back out there."

"Gotta find Tanner?" Sage grinned at her.

Jack squeezed her shoulder. "I can't remember if I mentioned that I'm ridiculously proud of you."

"What's this?" Mako asked. Intonation gave his voice a foreign vibe, but Avalon couldn't place it.

"Our Avalon has been chosen for the next WavePro photo layout. They're known for making a surf photog's career," Sage said. The genuine pleasure in Sage's voice was what marked her as good and pure all the way down to her toes. "She's following my brother around."

"Tanner, yes?" Mako asked. But something about the way he asked . . . Avalon was confident he already knew. "The one you mentioned, Jack?"

"Yes." Jack took his arm from around Avalon's shoulders, then smoothed down the front of his shirt. "And now come on. We need to hunt down the prodigal son. Gotta remind him how I'll be taking the points right out of his hand once we're in the water."

"Tanner'll mop the floor with you," Sage said. Even when she was smack talking, she could only smile.

Jack shook his head with mock seriousness. "Hate to be the one to tell you, but your brother's getting old." He turned toward the entryway. "Isn't that right, Tanner?"

Tanner stood there, but his gaze wasn't fixed on Jack. Instead, he was all about Mako. Tanner's hands had fisted at his sides, and his shoulders bulked into a deep, heavy line of muscle. He'd gone white, as if he'd never seen a day of sun in his entire life.

"Get out of my house." She'd never heard his voice that low or growling. "Or I'll throw you the fuck out."

Chapter 11

Tanner had always assumed the expression *seeing red* was something of an exaggeration. But the second he stepped foot in his mother's kitchen and saw Mako's smirking face behind the counter, his sight had literally washed red. The blood rushed in his skull with a sudden *whoosh*, like he was being held under by a hard-core slab, his board long gone and nothing but dark in his senses.

Every speck of air in the world had frozen and he'd choke on the shards.

Mako rocked forward on his toes, hands spreading wide at his hips in that universal sign. Begging for an ass beating. He had the audacity to fucking smile.

Sage set her beer down slowly and stepped forward, her eyes cloudy with confusion. But she still had her lips plastered into a smile. She lifted one hand toward Tanner and put the other in the center of Mako's chest. "Come on, boys. Don't let rivalries get out of hand."

Jack eased between them, as if he were being subtle. He managed to smile too, but it didn't go anywhere near his eyes. "There's no trouble here, right?"

A fist-sized knot lodged between Tanner's shoulder blades. His chest bowed out in counterpressure. Kill, hurt, fight. All he wanted. Everything he'd boiled down to for the moment. A claim on his space. "Don't talk about shit you don't know, Jack. And, Sage, this isn't your place."

Avalon's mouth dropped open. Her hands fell to her hips, her elbows angled out. "Not her place? You're insane. If you've forgotten, this is her house, not yours."

The soothing noise Sage made went nowhere. "It's okay, Avalon. That's not exactly our biggest worry right now."

"No, our biggest worry is this shitbag," Tanner snapped. All he could think about was the magazine article that was probably already being printed. "And how he needs to get the hell out before I wipe the floor with him."

Mako turned his palms upward, as if trying to seem like less of a threat. But he knew exactly what it would mean walking into this home. Exactly what he'd put at risk.

The first time the two had met, Mako had made it perfectly clear that he resented the family Hank Wright had in America. He'd flat-out said he'd do what he could to make them hurt if he ever had a chance. The *SURFING* exposé was probably the culmination of his every fantasy. To meet Sage under false pretenses only confirmed his sliminess.

There was no way Tanner could allow that. "Didn't I tell you to go home, Mako? Your kind needs to be kept far away at the other end of the globe."

Avalon's eyes went wide. On second thought, Tanner realized how that sounded, but she didn't know the whole story. Didn't know the history.

"Just saying hello, friend. That's all." He showed gleaming

white teeth but no real amusement. "I heard there was a party and I tagged along."

"With you?" Tanner spat the words at Jack. "You brought him?"

Jack lifted a single eyebrow. "You wanna reconsider how you're talking to me?"

The growl grew in Tanner's throat, swelling up from his chest. His biceps snapped hard, and his fists curled in on themselves. He lunged forward before he could think about it, but it wasn't Jack's body he came up against. It was Avalon and her slim curves.

She set both her hands in the center of his chest and pushed. "Down, man. Chill."

"They can fuck off."

"I know, I know." Her eyes were wide, but calm. So strange—the smile tucking in the corners of her lips seemed real. She wasn't the least bit afraid of him, even though he felt like ripping Mako limb from limb. "Jack, get your boy out of here."

"Right." He grabbed Mako by the upper arm, but for a second the other man didn't move.

Other man. Tanner could almost spit. Would if it wasn't his mother's kitchen floor involved. That was his half brother. Almost as big a shithead as their father.

Eventually, Mako shifted, letting Jack drag him away. They made for the back door, hopefully so Jack could take him straight to the alley and as far away as possible. At this hour, LAX and an airplane was probably too much to hope for.

"Don't come back," Tanner yelled over Avalon's head.

"Not tonight, I won't." Mako waggled his fingers in a mocking wave. "But the company was so fine, who knows about next time?"

Tanner surged up on the balls of his feet again, but before he could get around Avalon they were gone.

A strange silence washed over the room. The only noise was the still-roaring beat of his blood in his ears, plus a harsh panting that he eventually realized was his own breathing. He unlocked his fists finger by finger.

Avalon's hands still rested on his chest. Her mouth had opened on a silent gasp. "When did you become an asshole, Tanner?"

He shook his head in protest. "You don't know. There's things that . . ."

He wasn't the bad guy in this situation. He'd even tried to be Mako's friend when he'd first found out, thinking maybe a mutual disgust for Hank would draw them together. Or failing that, the bonds of brothers. But the guy had made his position perfectly clear.

A shark could have eaten Tanner for all Mako cared. Fuck, he'd have probably chopped Tanner up into chum and spooned him into the ocean if given half a chance.

Sage clasped her hands before her stomach. "Tanner, it's not right to maintain that level of aggression carried over from competition. It'll eat you alive."

"For the last fucking time, there's shit neither of you know. He's not just a competitor." The words exploded from him like shrapnel, hurt coming up his throat much as if it really had been tiny shreds of metal.

He straight-armed through the back door, into his mother's patio garden. But the tiny walled-in place didn't give him the relaxation it usually did.

The wrapped-up power jittering down his arms had to go somewhere. Punching the wall hadn't been in his repertoire since he'd been a seventeen-year-old kid pissed because his dad wouldn't let him take off for the Worlds until he was another year older and done with school. He still had the scar on his third knuckle to prove that one.

But he was considering it tonight.

The back door opened, spilling a triangle of golden light and noise across the patio blocks. "I don't need to be soothed, Sage."

But the voice that answered was decidedly huskier than his sister's. "I was more worried you intended to follow them and kill that guy. I'm not so great at soothing."

He pressed his hands over his temples and squeezed. Tight. With the ebb of his killing impulse, his head was starting to hurt. "Yeah? And how'd you stop me?"

She ranged around the dark edges of the tiny patio. Out of reach. That was probably better. If he was on the verge of hitting walls, he certainly shouldn't have someone as delicate as Avalon in his hands. At least she didn't have a camera in hand. He didn't think he could have handled it.

She slid her hands in her back pockets, then shrugged. "Probably call the cops if necessary."

"Look, I'm sorry you saw that."

The look she slid over her shoulder was altogether knowing. A siren to call him to the rocks. "But I did. And Sage did. Your mother could have walked in at any moment. A whole party of friends and family waited one room away. People you work with. I didn't think you were that much of a hothead, Tanner."

"There are things you don't know." His fists strained until he thought his knuckles would pop.

"So you keep saying." She leaned her shoulders against the wall. In the dark, he couldn't see any more of her eyes beyond a soft gleam. Her mouth was a gray shadow. "But you're not explaining."

"I can't." But that was his automatic response.

The one he'd honed over years and years of protecting his father—and, more specifically, his mother. Keeping her feelings safe, even if she never knew it.

The time for keeping quiet was long over. Tanner had a deadline now.

Mako had made it perfectly clear that he was in town. He had no problems stepping foot in what Tanner considered his territory. He couldn't keep his mother safe if Mako wasn't content to stay in Tahiti and Australia anymore.

Tanner dropped into a deck chair, his knees spread wide. "Fuck," he muttered.

Avalon eased off the wall. She'd seemed laid-back during the whole confrontation, and when he'd been popping and ready to go, but now that his anger eased, she bounced up subtly. As if shedding a skin, like the relaxed part hadn't really been her. Really she was eager and curious in a way that burned outward.

"Spit it out, Tanner." She eased a hip onto the glass table. Her feet landed between his outstretched legs, but she wasn't quite touching him. "You'll feel better if you do."

"I doubt that."

The weight of the secret might disappear, sure. He wouldn't have everyone staring at him, wondering why he'd been such a shitty son for all those years. But it would only be a trade.

He'd break his mother's heart. But Mako intended to do it anyway. . . .

It would be better coming from him. Not less painful, no. There was no way he could spin anything that hard.

Hell, if there was, he'd have told her a long time ago. But it might be less of a betrayal.

He scrubbed his palms over his eye sockets, then pushed hard. Anything to hold back the pressure in his skull. "I don't want to do this."

"Then don't."

"Easier said than done."

"You could always run it by me first. If you wanted to." Her cheeks looked leaner when she wasn't smiling, less rounded. But her mouth still seemed lush.

He'd much rather return to the portion of the night where he'd been kissing her. Holding her. Thinking so easily about fucking her.

He couldn't help but touch her. Two fingers trailed along her thigh beneath the skirt. Every time he touched her skin, it seemed softer. But that had to be all in his head.

This was neither the time nor the place. He pulled his hand back, laced both together over his stomach. His muscles had latched hard, as if he were bracing to be swallowed up by a huge barrel wave. Blowing out his tension with a breath that lasted only a second.

The time had come. Mako wasn't going away, which meant he'd have to tell. Sit his mom down and tell the nasty secret he'd held and watch her heart break.

This was going to be a fucking blast.

He shoved up out of his seat with abrupt and barely leashed fury. The move brought him even closer to Avalon. But she didn't flinch. Only looked up at him with those big mossy-colored eyes, her forehead wrinkled in expectation.

"You about to hulk out or something? Because I think those guys are long gone."

He shook his head. There was no way he'd ever admit

the way his stomach churned. "I have to have a talk with my mom."

Her eyebrows lifted even farther and her lips parted. "*The* talk? Like, the where the hell you've been talk?"

The laughter caught him out of nowhere, zipping through him. Avalon was good for him, it seemed. "Yes, that one."

"It's about damn time."

"I know."

"This is a good thing. No family can survive with secrets."

The irony of that one chewed away at his nerves. "Trust me on this. She's not going to like it. Not in the least."

But as he turned to walk away, her hand flew out and caught him by the wrist. Against his arm, her fingers looked reed slender. Graceful. "Wait. If you're sure it's going to be that bad, wait an hour. Give her this night. She's wanted this party for the longest time."

It had been years. An hour wouldn't matter. In fact, it felt almost like a relief. He nodded, probably bobbing his head as fast as an eager puppy. But it faded so fast. This was a reprieve, not a release.

He'd still be facing the music at the end of the night.

Chapter 12

The next hour passed in a strange haze for Avalon. She was so damn curious. At one point, she wanted to stand on the birchwood coffee table, wave her hands over her head, and tell everyone else to get the hell out.

But she'd been right to make Tanner wait. Eileen was on top of the world, floating through the crowds of people like a brightly colored butterfly in her multicolored silk blouse. The dark green skirt had once been her favorite, hauled out for multiple dates with Hank. She'd put it away for more than six months.

Until now.

Even her expression looked lighter. She'd always been serene, but that wasn't the same thing as being *happy*. Nothing Avalon did had been able to put that glow back in her smile but having Tanner home did it. Having this party to welcome him had apparently given her a sense of purpose and joy. Because she was sucking it up.

Avalon stood at the far side of the room, fiddling with her primary Canon, switching out the lens. Mostly for fun at this point. She'd gotten all the industry-at-work shots she'd likely need.

Even Tanner was worn out, though she wasn't sure how she knew that. The way his eyelids tensed, probably. Maybe a faint whitening of the scar over his mouth. No one else would likely think so. Three feet away, he was still talking and joking with the towheaded teenager who'd dominated the junior surf circuit this year. The kid hadn't come out and asked Tanner if he should go pro — the kid probably already had a manager, not to mention his parents — but it was obvious he was interested in Tanner's opinion.

Weirder than that was the fact that Tanner was avidly and competently talking to the kid, weighing the pros and cons. Tanner even mentioned college once or twice, though he'd walked away from the opportunity himself.

Avalon lifted her camera and snapped off a shot, in case. The exhaustion riding Tanner seemed clearer to her through her viewfinder. But it was the way he kept sneaking looks at his mom that was most obvious.

That most tugged at her heart, if Avalon were to be honest.

Though she was pretty sure it was the general attachment she had to the Wright family. Nothing special to Tanner.

She wanted to be able to walk up behind him and dig fingertips into that deep slab of muscle across his shoulders. The stiffness there said he had to be tense as hell.

But she resisted the impulse.

It turned out to be easy to do when a pale-skinned redhead inveigled her way into the conversation. Avalon turned away in disgust. If that girl was actually a surfer, Avalon would eat the bikini covering her fake tits. Strings and all.

But as she packed up her camera, she might have

smirked. Tanner had pinned Avalon against the upstairs wall. Not some implanted bimbo.

Eventually the crowds thinned. Eileen walked the last couple to the door, then waved from the front step. Tanner sat in an overstuffed chair, his legs sprawled wide in his usual manner. Sage perched on the half-wall between the living room and the den.

Eileen shut the door and leaned against it. She tucked her shawl more closely around her shoulders. "I do love a good party."

Avalon smiled, but it was a bit difficult. Her heart had taken up residence in her throat as soon as the door snapped closed. The worry on Tanner's face when he'd insisted that his mom would be hurt by the truth of his split from his father ... He'd believed it completely. No matter her doubts about him, he wasn't a stupid man.

He both knew his mother and loved her wholly. That had never been in doubt.

Tanner smiled at Eileen, but it was obviously forced. "You've always thrown good ones."

A happy smile fluttering around her mouth, she started gathering up wineglasses, most of them still stained red. "A party is an excuse for people to get together and be happy. It's pretty difficult to throw a bad one."

"Mom, put those down," Sage said through a yawn. "We've got the cleaners coming tomorrow for the express purpose of picking up."

"Remind me to make sure they get under the curio cabinet in the den. I think I saw Phillip drop a whole handful of munchies." She sighed, flipping a hank of blond hair from her eyes. "That man's been such a mess since his wife died. He needs a keeper."

Sage leaned her head against the wall at her side. "No

more strays, Mom. You're not playing matchmaker again. How many times did Christine call you in the middle of the night last time? When it didn't work?"

"Pish." Eileen waved a hand at her daughter, no matter the wineglasses dangling from her fingers. "I'm doing no such thing. It's a human being's duty to sow joy in the world, that's all."

A pang struck Avalon in the chest, underneath her sternum. She loved these two like they were her own. More, probably. Sometimes she wondered if it was possible to love someone she didn't admire.

And she didn't admire the tangled mess her mother had made of her life.

Eileen set her first load of glasses on the sideboard, then started gathering a second. "Though, Tanner, I heard you were fighting. In my kitchen too." She shook her head in a chiding waggle. "I thought I raised you better than that. No matter the provocation, fighting is not the answer. I know Jack is bad about that, but—"

"It wasn't Jack's fault," Sage insisted, cutting off her mother. "Tanner, what was your problem with Mako? He seemed perfectly normal to me. Maybe a little full of himself. He said something about wanting to come by the store." She flashed her patented smile, the one that never failed to make Avalon smile back.

But apparently her brother was immune to it.

Tanner's gaze caught Avalon's. Dark worry lodged behind his eyes. She nodded at him, though he'd never exactly asked for permission.

Coming out of the chair, he caught his mom by the hands. Blunt-tipped fingers took the wineglasses away from her and set them down side by side on the low coffee table. "I need to talk to you."

"So talk," she answered, still smiling. "No reason I can't keep picking up. I don't sleep well if I know there's clutter. My surroundings are out of alignment."

"No." His voice was low, as if he were trying to speak only to her. Avalon slung her camera bag across her chest in preparation to go upstairs. "It's about why I stayed away. About my fight with Dad."

Eileen's arms relaxed, no longer reaching for the glasses, but the smile stayed in place. "Then talk. It's fine."

"Alone."

She crossed her arms over her chest. At the other side of the room, Sage sat up straighter. She shot a look at Avalon, obviously asking what the hell was going on, but Avalon could only shrug. She didn't have any more idea than anyone else.

Though she was mostly all earth mother, Eileen had a stubborn side. Her mouth set into a flat line. "No. There's nothing you can't say in front of them. They deserve to know where you've been too. Your sister's missed you as much as I have."

"That's probably not a good idea." The back of Tanner's neck reddened. His shoulders lifted.

"It is if I say it is."

Eileen's hair was still the gold-touched blond it had been when Avalon had first met her. Sage had brought Avalon home from the beach for lunch and Eileen had whipped up a salmon and green bean salad. Avalon hadn't wanted to eat it, but Eileen had presented the same implacable calm she cloaked herself in now. So Avalon had chowed down on salmon and veggies, which she'd been sure she'd hate.

If she wanted Tanner to speak in front of Sage and Avalon, then that's what would happen. There was no defeating Eileen when she got that look. His chest lifted on a deep sigh.

"At least sit down then." He still had her by the wrists, until he let them go to hold her shoulders.

"That I can do," she said with her nose lifting toward the air. She tucked her flowing skirt under her as she sat.

Tanner sighed again as he sank down to sit on the coffee table directly in front of his mother. "This isn't very easy for me to say."

"Spit it out, then." Eileen reached out to smooth Tanner's tousled hair. "Get it over with. Your father loved you, I hope you know. Always did. If anything, I've wondered if you two fought over being too much alike."

Tanner's big shoulders shuddered. Actually shuddered. Avalon would do anything to be able to see his face, but his head was bowed and turned away from her. His voice rumbled, but she couldn't hear him. Neither had Sage from the confused hold of her expression. She mouthed a "What?" at Avalon, but she had to shrug her shoulders.

But apparently Eileen hadn't heard, either. Or hadn't liked what she heard. "What did you say?" Her voice shook.

"Dad cheated on you."

Eileen shook her head slowly. "No, you're wrong."

"I'm not." He tried to take his mother's hands again, but she snatched them away. She pulled back into herself, shoulders curling in. "I only know because of Mako."

"Mako? I met that boy tonight." Her face blanched white but for two hectic dots of color high on her cheeks. "What's he got to do with anything?"

"He's Dad's son." His voice was wrecked. Shaky and grumbling at the same time. The difference between his

shoulders and narrow waist became even more pro-
nounced as his tension ratcheted up.

A soft gasp came from Sage. Shaking fingers rose to
her mouth. She slipped down from her counter-height
perch, but she didn't go far. She only leaned back against
the wall, as if her legs wouldn't hold her.

Avalon knew the feeling. Her blood had slugged to a
chillish hold and her stomach churned. And Hank Wright
hadn't even been her actual father.

She'd always thought him a good man. Fathering a
second son, not by his wife . . .

She could almost understand where Tanner had been
all this time. Almost.

"I fought with Dad because he refused to tell you.
And I didn't think it was my place."

"You stayed away all those years because of *this*?"
Eileen tugged at the brightly colored scarf over her
shoulders. "That's no reason. No reason at all."

Tanner sighed again. "I couldn't look at him. Not here,
in this home that you poured so much work into. I
couldn't look at him without losing my mind. And I
couldn't bear hurting you like that."

Avalon crossed her arms over her chest, holding in
the hurt. She couldn't fall apart, not when Sage and Eileen were so shaken up. And they weren't the crying,
sobbing mess she wanted to be. She drew a deep, shaky
breath. Not her place, really. She had to get herself under
control.

Even if it felt like Tanner was picking apart her very
dreams. She'd always wanted her marriage, whenever
she had one, to be like Eileen and Hank's. Respectful
and loving—and apparently fake as hell.

Eileen kept shaking her head as if she could deny

what Tanner was saying. "There's no way you could possibly know that. It's not like he would have told you."

"He didn't. I met the woman. In Tahiti, the second time I went for the ASP." He flicked a glance over his shoulder at Avalon. He was almost as much of a mess as Eileen. Definitely more than Sage, who stood so quietly. Pulling into herself without ever moving an inch. "I tried talking to Mako back then, but he wasn't having any of it. I think he resents me. Resents all of us. It's made him an asshole."

"That's enough of that." Eileen held up a hand before she stood on shaky legs. Tanner reached for her again, but she stepped back, out of his hands. "No reason for talk like that."

"Mom, there's something else you should know." Tanner stood up as well. Behind his mother, he reached for her, only for his hands to drop again. "Mako has apparently given an interview. He told everything."

Eileen's hand shook when she reached up to pull her shawl closer around her shoulders. Her knuckles stood out in stark relief. "I suppose that's his right," she said, but her voice broke on the words. Her fingertips rose to her temple. "I have to go lie down."

Sage tried to stop her as she walked out of the room, but she wasn't having any of it. She held up her hand again, her neck curved down in a way Avalon had never seen before.

Tears prickled at the back of Avalon's eyes. This was awful. So horrible that she didn't even have words for it. Her stomach flipped over and over as the pretty little world she'd been permitted into fell apart. But she had to hold it together. If it was this painful for her, she couldn't imagine what it felt like to Sage. God, to Eileen.

She had to be falling apart inside. Avalon scratched her nails into the tender skin inside her elbows. The pain made her hiss, drawing her back down to earth. She didn't exactly have the right to fall apart when Sage and Eileen needed her.

Eileen stopped at the foot of the stairs. "How long?" she asked, her back to them all.

"I don't know what you mean." Deep lines carved around Tanner's mouth.

"How long was it going on? From start to finish."

He rocked back on his heels, shoving his hands in his pockets. His chin lowered to his chest. "I don't know."

"I didn't think you would." Her sigh was as soft as the summer breeze coming in off the waves. "That right there . . . That's why you didn't have any right to keep this secret, Tanner. Because you waited until your father was dead, I don't have anyone to ask."

Chapter 13

That had gone about as well as Tanner had expected it to. Something along the lines of dropping a nuclear explosion in his mother's living room. Or like feeding her to sharks. His stomach churned so hard that he thought he might throw up. He hadn't had this awful a feeling since that disastrous night in Tahiti when he'd first seen Mako's mother.

His mom walked upstairs with slow, careful steps. She seemed a shadow of what she'd been a few moments ago. And he'd done that to her.

He'd have never told her at all if it wasn't for Mako giving that goddamned interview, all to make trouble. Tanner's guilt was a live, slithering thing. It turned his insides upside down. He'd carried these secrets for so long. He shouldn't have had to be the one to see Eileen's face fall apart when she heard.

If anyone should have had to deal with that, it was Hank.

The picture to the right of the stairwell was of Tanner and his dad, posing on the beach after Tanner's first junior win. He'd managed to avoid looking at it all night.

Hank Wright had been a big man, even two inches taller than Tanner was when grown. At twelve, Tanner had barely come up to his ribs. But he'd been so ridiculously happy that he'd have a trophy that could go alongside his dad's.

And it had. In the trophy case, right next to Hank's early-eighties World Championship, because winning mattered in their family. It wasn't there anymore, though. No telling where the shiny trophy had gone now.

His mom's feet disappeared past the line of the landing, heading up to her top-floor bedroom. That didn't mean he was off the hook.

Avalon stared at him. Her eyes were flat gray with something incredibly painful. How did she think he felt, huh? He hadn't wanted to hold on to all this horrible stuff for a decade.

That left Sage. Except, by the time he turned around, she'd disappeared.

"Goddamn it," he muttered.

"She probably went down to the beach." He'd never heard Avalon speak so quietly before. She ducked her head, effectively hiding her eyes behind her thick fringe of bangs. The line of her plump mouth was a decided frown.

"Don't blame her." He'd be at the beach as soon as he could get away from this disaster. And Sage had always been a private person, prone to nursing her hurts in silence.

"Oh, I don't blame *her*," Avalon said, her eyes slitting until they were barely more than dark glimmers, even in the bright lights of the living room. "I don't blame her at all. I blame *you*."

He'd been expecting the blow, but that didn't mean it

HAAS, ROBERTA LEC
Unclaim : 04/09/2015

Held date   :
Pickup location :

Title   :
Call number   :

Item barcode   :
Assigned ITdate :

Notes:

was any easier to take. His guts felt like they'd been stirred up, then smashed back in upside down.

"Of course you would." He made himself shrug, since he'd expected it all along. But his mom's condemnation had hurt more than he'd expected. More than he wanted it to. Adding a thick layer of scorn from Avalon tipped him over the line. He had to get the hell out of here.

He wasn't going to stick around and listen to her crap all over him. No point in that. The fact that he managed to not slam the back door behind him had to be a win on some level, but he didn't much care.

The night had gone quiet. Even the college kids had seemingly quit for the night. Only a soft breeze swished palm fronds. Tanner was halfway down the block, toward his rental house, when he heard another sound.

Footsteps shushing over sand-dusted sidewalk. He drew his shoulders back. He wanted to get home. It was kind of sad that a rental house would feel more home-like than the place he'd left, but at this moment he needed quiet. Somewhere that wasn't totally saturated with thoughts and memories of his dad.

He didn't need Avalon chasing him and rubbing his nose in the shit storm he'd unleashed.

But her hand wrapped around his forearm, no matter how he'd wished she wouldn't. She was noticeably smaller than him, delicate-looking with her narrow shoulders and slim hips, but her grip said otherwise. She dug in with surprising strength, trying to drag him to a stop.

Plus, she had nails.

He finally stopped, but Christ, he didn't want to look at her. He stayed where he was, fists deep in his pockets and his gaze locked on the bare inch of beach he could see at the end of the street. "What do you want, Avalon?"

"You think you can dump shit like that and bail?"

"What the hell was I supposed to do?" He spun on a heel. Since the moon was the only glow, her skin looked paler than normal. Almost ghostlike. It looked like it had when they'd been sitting on the roof together.

Going back to that moment would be nice, but it wouldn't happen. Not after everything. The shock of seeing Mako in his mom's kitchen had been nothing compared to the devastation he'd seen on his mom's face. Just like he always feared.

"Was I supposed to sit around the living room and wait? Twiddle my fucking thumbs in case my mother decided to speak to me again?"

"Yes, as a matter of fact." Her chin was tilted forward like a bulldog's, filled with determined intent. Her mouth pulled into a small knot. "It's called *being there*. For your family. Not that you'd have any experience with it."

"I don't need your crap, Avalon." He turned again, stalking away. The reverberation up his calves said he might be stomping, but he didn't particularly care. The shits given might be mighty, but not by him. "I've got enough to deal with."

Her footsteps clattered along behind him until she drew up even at his side. The arms she swung had fists at the end. Who exactly did she plan to beat up? Tanner?

It wasn't fucking fair. He'd been the one doing his best to keep the family safe in ignorance for years. But he'd known on some level that this day would come. His staying away had only drawn out the inevitable.

"What do you have to deal with?" Avalon said with a snarky kind of insinuation. "Oh no, you might not win the World Championship. Again. Whatever will you do? At least you've made it once."

He slammed to a stop, neighbors and sidewalks be damned. "So fucking what? I've made it once. My name's gone down in Wikipedia. That's supposed to be good enough? I'm supposed to quit for the rest of my life?"

Her mouth gaped. "No. But I'd think sticking around for a night to discuss something important would be a little higher on your priorities."

"I didn't even want to tell them to begin with." They were at the front door of the rental house. A tiny bit of sand-resistant grass clung to the ten-foot square between the sidewalk and the house. He always felt bad for grass planted in San Sebastian. Kind of a lost cause.

He fished keys out and unlocked the door. Inside was even darker. He'd forgotten to leave a light on. Again. Stepping in, he tossed his key ring into a bowl on the front table. A mirror showed he looked like shit.

He wasn't nearly as young as he used to be. Just this side of washed up at thirty-one. It was a joke.

"Well?" He dumped the contents of his pockets into the bowl with the keys. He'd never much liked being weighed down. Best-case scenario meant he had only a pair of shorts and a single key. And his board. He was always on the move, which was exactly why he couldn't have a girlfriend. Avalon deserved better, but he didn't seem to be stopping himself. "You coming in?"

Her head tilted. She still stood outside on the front stoop, arms crossed over her chest. "Seriously?"

"Why not?"

"Maybe because you 'don't need any more of my shit'?"

"I don't." He curled a hand around the edge of the door, leaned his shoulder into it. "But I've got a plan."

"You do?" Her very voice dripped doubtfulness.

"I'm going to take you out on the water. We'll talk a

little bit, bitch a lot more. When we've both calmed down, we'll come back in and take a shower. Together."

She laughed, a short, sharp chuff of doubt. And shock, if he read it right. But she didn't draw away. If anything, she leaned closer. Stepped one foot nearer, lifting onto the next step. "You think that'll work on me?"

"Maybe." He shrugged and smiled. "I know for damn sure it'd work on me."

He needed the ocean. The clean feel of being in cool water after the sun was gone. During the day, golden rays made it easy to ignore or forget how cold the Pacific could get. At night, it went right down to a man's bones and cleared him out.

Showering with Avalon—hopefully with more to follow—would only be the perfect capper.

He needed that kind of distraction, that pure feeling to blow out the noise in his head. Surfing gave him the same sort of rush, that oneness with his body. The kiss he'd stolen off Avalon earlier convinced him that she'd provide the same rush.

And he could make her feel good in return.

"What the hell does it say about me that I'm so tempted?" She stepped a little closer. Hovering in the doorway, she looked part wraith, part fairy. Something ethereal. Which made sense with the way she sort of floated over the waves every time he'd seen her surf.

"It says you're human. That you know we'd be good." Reaching out, he uncurled her hand from her bent elbow. Drew her closer.

Her fingers shook the tiniest bit in his grasp. He smoothed them straight, laced his fingers with hers. Once they'd locked, a weight slipped from him. Yeah, this was what he'd needed. Some sense of connection. Avalon tied him to the earth, and made him feel a little more solid. He tugged lightly, and she came. Close enough that he could smell her again, the warm spice rising off her hair.

He kissed her. Softly. Lightly, his lips sliding over hers. She gave a quiet gasp and he only took it into his mouth.

Here, between them, there was no other shit. No other drama once he closed the gap. Everyone else could slide away and he could ignore them a little longer.

He needed this. Needed Avalon. If she didn't agree, he'd be left alone with his thoughts. With the memory of the night's strange ups and downs.

He tugged her hand, until they were snugly palm-to-palm, their hands one unit at their sides. Still he kissed her, flicking his tongue over her bottom lip.

When he drew back, her eyes were shut, her mouth still slightly open. Her chin tilted up as if begging him to kiss her again. With his free hand, he smoothed the backs of his fingers over her jaw. "Come in."

Her eyes opened. In the white glow of the moon, they looked strangely dark. He didn't like it. The one thing he was noticing about Avalon was how readable she was. Those eyes of hers gave everything away, always had. Even the first time he'd met her, when she'd been a too-young-to-notice girl, he'd seen desperation in her eyes. Thank God that emotion was gone at least. He didn't want to feel like too much of a shithead. At least no more than he already was.

"Promise me one thing," she said. Her voice barely carried to his ears.

"What?"

"It's over in the morning. We go back. Shut it down. Family friends, photographer and subject. All the normal stuff is fine."

He couldn't help but touch the delicate line of her jaw again. She was like softness and determination all in one. "What's tonight, then?"

"An escape. That's all." Her fingers locked on his, their palms sliding together. "I get tired of thinking sometimes."

He took another kiss, this one fast and hard. His tongue swept into her mouth, stroked along the texture of her tongue. Mostly because he didn't want to acknowledge how true her words were.

Pulling her forward, into the foyer, he kicked the door shut with a nudge of his toes. "Well, then," he said. "We'll make sure you don't think, won't we?"

Chapter 14

The way Tanner looked at her was intoxicating. He made her completely dizzy, even before he kissed her with such sweetness. But she couldn't make herself answer, not in words. She only let him pull her across the threshold. Maybe she'd leech sanity from him, a quiet moment outside the world.

Even as he pulled her toward the back of the house, she had nothing to say for herself.

He'd lined what was supposed to be the dining room with all sorts of boards. She didn't even want to do the math on how much money it took to have that many surfboards lined up for use on a whim. For her, he tugged a Lost brand board out of a rack, then stacked it beside his at the back door.

When he pulled her into his arms, she went willingly, tired of feeling like she was letting him drag her through the night. If she was making this choice, she'd make it wholeheartedly and reach for it all with grabby hands.

The touches over her waist snuck under her T-shirt. Lowering his head, he nuzzled her neck. She stretched up, back, letting him have all he wanted. At the same time, she curved her hands around his strong back. Sturdy. He seemed so solid. She could grab on for a ride and he'd never falter.

"Do you have a swimsuit?"

A helpless giggle slipped from her throat. Such a prosaic, ordinary question when she thought she might explode. The night had been too much. Too long, too many highs, and way too many lows that she couldn't even think about. And here it was, past midnight, and she was about to go out in the water.

Insanity.

That she'd gladly embrace.

"I have one in my bag." She always did. Being a surf photographer meant she had to be ready to jump in the water at any moment.

He spoke against the tender skin of her throat, his lips moving softly. "Put it on."

"Yeah, let me hit the bathroom, and I'll be right back." Her hand was already digging in her side-slung bag, in the back pocket.

But just as her fingers touched the slick material, he shook his head. "No. Here."

He looked at her. The dim light made his features blunter. His nose a little more crudely carved, the line of his brow deeper and heavier. A tiny splash of caveman in a handsome guy. "Change right here."

The protest that rose to her lips was automatic—but it didn't go anywhere. She couldn't manage to say it. Her mouth went sand-dry and her throat clicked as she tried to swallow. "Here?"

He smirked at her. A tiny curl of his lips. The pads of his fingers scraped over her waist, above her hipbones. A shiver worked its way down to her pussy, from that touch. He challenged her just by breathing, it seemed. "Yeah. Here. And I'm not going to turn around."

She squirmed inside her skin. She'd always liked her body, for the most part. Maybe the inside of her thighs could use a little extra toning, but she didn't do too poorly. Never in her life had she ever had a guy complain about her body. Not that she'd have put up with that for more than a nanosecond.

But all that had been in the moment. Mutual clothes-tearing and lustful groping. Tanner seemed to be asking for something else entirely. Something a little more demonstrative.

More open.

She nibbled on her bottom lip, but her hand went to the strap of her bag anyway. Drew it over her head.

Through it all, Tanner kept his gaze locked on her. On her face, not the motions of her body. The intensity combined with his wicked idea made her nipples bead up, tingling.

He backed up until he leaned against the dining table still planted in the center of the room. He wrapped his hands around the edge of the table, his ass barely seated. But for the casual position, he still looked focused. On her.

Heady stuff. Powerful. More of him going straight to her head and wiping out the rest of the mess strewn through the night.

Stripping out of her T-shirt and skirt became almost automatic. She moved fast, whipping her hair around her head as she yanked the shirt off. Standing there in her matching panties and bra was as hard as she'd expected. At least they were some of her cute ones: heather gray, but with bright blue lace trimming at the edges.

Tanner's response was everything she could have hoped for. His breath hissed on an inward pull, his chest lifting. The parting of his lips made her think of where else they could go.

When she unhooked her bra, he stood up straight. She couldn't help a teasing, mean cup of her breasts. Even her thumbs passing over her nipples sent a soft wash of pleasure through her center.

The panties she drew down her thighs were already damp. She had to swallow down her fear again. It was like getting inspected, in a way. Slightly cold, but in a way she couldn't explain. Not a coldness of excitement, because the moment was incredibly hotter than any other experience she'd ever had. But being so bold took her out of her own head, so she hardly knew her own thoughts.

God, she'd been locked inside her own head for so long.

She might have been smirking a little as she tugged her bikini from the bag at her feet. And her ass wiggled a little, definitely.

How could she be blamed for it, when Tanner gave her such lovely feedback? The groan he let go went straight to her pussy. A new flood of dampness soaked her tiny red bikini bottom as she pulled it snugly over herself. She took her sweet time with the top. For the first time, she wished the slightly sport-bra-like top were smaller. She'd take the wish back the next time she was surfing, but for now, she wanted less material. Something a little sexier, so that when she cupped her breasts into position, more would show.

But Tanner didn't seem to mind. His gaze darted back up to her face. "Now, that was mean."

She smiled as she smoothed the bottoms over her ass. "You got what you asked for."

"Fuck yeah, I did." He grinned. Tucking his board under his arm, he led the way out the door and down the beach. The sand almost seemed to glow, shining white under the moonlight. It flicked up behind them in soft clouds.

There was something peaceful about the very act of walking across a beach. Soothing, like dropping down into a certain layer of her mind. One she liked a lot better than her normal frenetic pace.

They stood at the edge of the water, miniature white froth licking at their toes. Cold, despite the cloying warmth still in the air. Even the hard-packed sand held the chill of the water. The rhythmic roar of the surf was the only sound.

"The waves suck." She let the fins of her board droop toward the sand. "One to two feet at most."

"We're not here to surf. Not this time." He strode out into the water as if it wasn't going to freeze his bits off. "C'mon. Don't chicken out now."

She'd never been out in the surf at night. There was a different cast to the waves. They were barely a surge topped with white froth, despite their relative lack of height. The light sparkled off the water in a straight line from where the moon hovered to their point on the beach. It felt different and yet similar at the same time.

Her heart gave a small tumble that wasn't just in fear, but in anticipation as she watched Tanner's back. The tiny muscles and ligaments there did shaky stuff to her insides.

She followed.

The water was damn cold. Once she was up to her waist, she flopped on her board and paddled the rest of the way. Tanner kept going, diving in past the small swells of waves and letting them crash over his body. But he didn't stop in the normal lineup spots for surfing, so neither did Avalon.

Eventually, he stopped. He sat up on his board, straddling it and planting his hands flat between his outstretched thighs. The water swelled and dipped, but it felt mostly flat. Because of the dark, the horizon was practically invisible. They were both alone together and adrift in a vast wideness.

The disconcerting feeling made her look down at her board. White, bright. Cleanly focused. She looked up again and that was quickly lost. But she breathed through the agitation, letting herself go free. And suddenly felt as relaxed as she'd ever been in her life.

Her feet dangled in the cold water, but she hardly noticed. She felt little. Small and overwhelmed by the world, but in the best possible way.

"This is nice." The words felt pretty damn insufficient, but she'd never been very expressive. Not without a camera, at least. She'd need a very wide-angle lens to capture this moment. Or maybe she'd do the opposite and focus very closely on the dark, glassy water to demonstrate the blissful emptiness of that sort of darkness.

"It is." Tanner looked up toward the sky, his neck a thick column that made her think about biting and licking. His arms stood out in stark relief, heavy curves.

"Do you ever surf in the dark?"

"Once or twice." His gaze fixed on her. "Mostly I come out here when I want to be alone. Have some quiet."

"But you brought me out here."

"I've got dirty plans for you afterward, remember," he said. The words were light, but she heard something else underneath them. A depth and caress.

Or she wanted to, at any rate. She had a stupid habit of that, though. Her mom had counted on it to break her heart more times than she could count. Being a twelve-year-old left alone for two weeks while Mom went on vacation with her boyfriend meant she was extra susceptible to hearing sincerity in voices that didn't actually carry it. But with the Wrights, she'd learned to actually trust.

And now the Wrights couldn't even trust one another. The way Eileen had withdrawn upstairs . . . Avalon had never seen her quite that hurt before. Nor had she ever blamed Tanner like that for anything.

Avalon couldn't let the family collapse. They'd always had problems, but she wasn't going to let it go too far. Not this time.

She spread her fingers on the board, across the tacky surf wax and roughed-up grip. She didn't want to ask, not really. But she had to. The words burbled up of their own will. "How long have you known?"

Tanner's sigh was one of the saddest things she'd ever heard. "I'm guessing there's no chance of convincing you to let it go."

"You've lost your mind if you think so."

"You keep saying that to me."

She flicked water from her fingertips in his general direction. "I'm not convinced yet that I shouldn't be researching the best lockup facilities."

"You can be pretty damn mean sometimes." But he didn't actually seem to mind. He'd planted his hands flat on his board, bowing his shoulders into the move even as he looked up at the stars. "I'd think you'd be nicer to anyone with the last name Wright. Earn your place."

A surprising flash of pain went through her at that,

even though he was obviously teasing. He was probably trying to distract her from asking about tonight's revelations.

But that didn't keep it from ringing true on some level.

The cold water swirling around her calves loosed a chill through her. She pushed a smile up to her mouth, though not a big one. Just that tiny bend that said she didn't care. "How long? Spit it out."

"What if I said flat-out that I didn't want to talk about it?"

"Then you wouldn't have brought me out here." She kicked gently until her toes touched the back of his calf, behind his knee. The ocean made his skin slick, but she could still feel the light hairs. "You'd have taken me up to your room and we'd have stayed there until neither of us could see straight. But you wanted to talk first."

"You're sure of that."

Of course she was. It was what she did for all the Wrights. She listened, let them vent. Took their problems on herself. It was part of being a family, as near as she could tell. She paddled her board, twisting until she was right next to Tanner.

He carried a particular warmth that emanated from his skin, despite the dark and the cold water and the licking breeze. Something solidly comforting. She wanted to tuck along his side and bury her face against his ribs.

Instead she touched his knee, cupped her fingers over him. "Tell me, Tanner. You'll feel better for it."

Chapter 15

Tanner was not at all convinced of that. Catharsis was not exactly his deal. His mom had always been on about that, talking about closure and all sorts of other crunchy granola stuff. But he'd had his eyes on the prize, on taking the championship.

And sure as shit, telling her had not been any big letting go. Watching her face crumple had been everything he feared.

Goddamn that Mako. The asshole didn't have any right to come tromping through and fuck it all to hell and gone. San Sebastian was Tanner's mother's world.

Avalon's fingers tightened on his knee. "You're kind of wound up, aren't you? You're practically twitching."

"Whoever said I wasn't?"

She shrugged. "I don't know. Your mom's so laid-back, it's amazing. I try to be like her."

He couldn't help a little snort. "You'll never be like my mom." Half of Avalon's appeal was her vibrant energy. Making her like Eileen would dampen her spark.

"And *you* won't dodge the question forever, no matter how hard you try." Slim fingers tapped the top of his knee in insistent rhythm. Two inches up and they could be under the hem of his board shorts.

"I've known since my second year on the ASP." There, that sounded simple enough. Didn't quite convey the heart-stopping terror he'd felt when he'd first found out.

Which had never exactly made sense to him. Terror? It wasn't like he'd been in a two-wave hold-down, feeling his lungs burn for air as the ocean tried to keep him smacked to the sea floor. But it had felt oddly similar. Like having his world shaken upside down.

Like he'd never known the man who'd raised him.

"How did you find out? What happened?" Her voice had softened. Eased. She was being kind to him.

He didn't like Avalon kind. He liked her sharp and dueling with him. Or naked. That had been damned fine. He could willingly go back to that. The shadows had made her a ghostly goddess, all curves and dips and her nipples in bright relief.

Maybe if he kept that image in his head, this shit would all be easier to deal with.

"Mako happened. I was in Tahiti for the Billabong Pro. He was a little fuck, only fourteen. But he hitch-hiked to the staging area for the heats. Waited for me. I came off a damn good run to find him there."

He trailed off. That easily, he was back there again. Riding high, the sand soft and silky beneath his feet. He'd already dropped his board on the rack, stretching out the worst of the kinks in his back. It had also been the year of his first World Championship and he'd always associated the two together. Made Tanner wonder if that had been part of his problem in never nailing the championship again. He needed the win this time. Needed it with something that verged on craving.

"Tahiti? Your second year?" She looked back toward land. Moonlight glided over the pure line of her shoulders. "I remember that event."

Who didn't? He'd fucked up the final heat royally. Despite having gone in on top, he'd barely managed to stand up on a wave. Kind of hard to do when it felt like there'd been no world under his feet anymore. He'd been lucky to take second. But admitting that would be entirely too raw. "Been following my career, have you, Avalon?"

He liked that image. She'd have still been way too young then, probably only fourteen. But he could picture *this* version of Avalon with *Surfer* spread out in front of her. After she finished analyzing all the photos as competition, maybe she'd flip through a second time looking for him.

She shot that down quick enough with a soft laugh. "No. I remember because Kelly Slater kicked your ass in that last heat. I had a crush on Kelly my whole freshman year."

"Fuck Kelly Slater."

Her soft chuckle spiraled up into a full-on, head-thrown-back laugh. "Dude, there's press who'd pay big money to hear you say that."

"And you're technically press."

Her eyes went wide and fixed on him. "Not tonight. I want to make sure you know that. I'm not press tonight."

Under the water he hooked his foot around her ankle and tugged her closer. The kiss he took leaning out over the water tasted like salt of course, but beneath it was more. Her. Sweetness and earnestness.

"I know." The words breathed over her lips, and they were so close, his exhalation washed back at him.

She smiled, a soft curve that he wanted to taste again. "What did your dad say?"

"Seriously?" He pulled back until he was sitting firmly over his own board. "I'm kissing you in the middle of the water and you're thinking about my dad? I think I'm losing my touch."

"Oh, shut it. You do damned well for yourself and you know it. We need to get this out of the way." Her fingertips trailed over the inside of his thigh. A deliberate provocation? He couldn't tell. He liked that about Avalon. There was something about her that kept him on his toes. "So we can move on to other things."

Her bikini was sexy-small. Barely covered the dip of her pussy, more tease than anything else. "By all means. Let's move on."

She snapped her fingers under his nose. "Up here, please? For now?" But she was grinning at him. "Your dad. Did you talk to him?"

Christ, answering her questions was easier when he concentrated on her fuckable little body. "Yeah. I did. He convinced me it was once, an accident practically. Oops, he fell in a local girl. Didn't ever happen again."

"You don't sound convinced."

"Now, I'm not." His heart rate was going up again, like he was that twenty-year-old kid confronting the dad he'd once adored. He swallowed down the memory. "Then, I bought it hook, line and sinker."

"Until?"

He blinked his gaze back into focus. The tiny red bikini cupped her breasts lovingly. A single drop of water gleamed under a ray of moonlight, then dipped and ran down her cleavage in a slow plunge. He liked watching that drop far more than he liked remembering how things had gone from crappy to miserable. "Until the next year, when the tour went back to Tahiti. And I couldn't find Dad in his hotel room one night. I asked around until I finally found his buddy Bondo, who told me where the asshole was."

"Oh, Tanner, you didn't." Her eyes were wide, her mouth a soft O shape in the dark.

"Yup. I went. Tiny little house, with surfboards in the front yard. I banged the door until Dad came out."

She scrubbed her hand across the back of her neck. The pinch of her mouth and wrinkle over her nose chagrined him. It was bad enough to have to make this trip down memory lane. He didn't need her pitying him. "Jesus, Tanner."

"I know." He made himself shrug. "It was all screaming and this short little woman clinging to Dad's arm. How much more drama can you get?"

"No, not that." She pinned him with a look that had way too much sympathy in it for his tastes. "It had to hurt. Finding out like that. I know how much it sucks to have a parent lie to you."

Her mom had been flighty to the utmost power. It was why his mom had taken Avalon under her wing. If anyone was going to understand that pain, it'd definitely be Avalon.

But that didn't mean he liked rolling around in it. "I moved on."

"You're so full of it. Please do tell me how not talking to your dad for nine years is any sort of moving on."

"It was better for everyone. Telling something like that . . . Not my damn place. It should have been Dad, if it had to come from anyone." He spread his hands wide over the board. Latched his muscles into place. "And I didn't think I could keep my mouth shut if I looked at him in that house. My house. Every bit of my childhood became a lie."

Something dark pinched her features. "You don't think that's a little melodramatic?"

"Maybe. But that's what it felt like."

He didn't want to think about this, not anymore. After almost a decade spent ignoring it, he was going to get more than he wanted over the next few days. His mom would likely want to go a few rounds, get to the "emotional core" of what he'd told her. Because that was the type of woman she was.

Tanner rubbed the back of his hand over his mouth. There'd be enough time for that sort of flaying-open tomorrow. Now he wanted something easier to understand.

And beyond everything, the connection that he and Avalon had on the physical level made sense to him. He'd never had a more responsive woman in his arms. Their moment in his old bedroom, in the middle of the party, hadn't been long but it had been perfect. Exactly what he needed to know how good it would be between them.

"Is that enough for tonight?" He looked back at her.

The dark pools of her eyes glimmered in the moonlight. He had the feeling that, despite the numerous times he'd looked off to the horizon, she'd watched him the whole time. The small rush he got off that was exhilarating.

His sister would have his head if she knew what he was thinking about doing to Avalon.

Good thing she wasn't anywhere around.

"Enough?"

"Questions. Laying me open. I'm going to get plenty tomorrow from everyone else."

"One more." She trailed her fingertips through the water, leaving a shimmering wake in her path. "Did you try to talk to him? Mako? Before he went to the press?"

The smile that lifted Tanner's mouth didn't feel that comfortable. Mostly hard anger. "Yeah. I've tried talking to him. Obviously it didn't work."

"It's got to be hard to look at you. Know you were the one who Hank raised."

"Avalon?"

"Hmm?"

He moved close enough that he could wrap his hand around her elbow. Tugged her even closer. Their knees bumped, then their thighs as their boards came into alignment. He stroked the very tips of his fingers over her jaw.

Her shoulders worked over a shudder and her eyes drifted shut.

Leaning close meant feeling the heat coming off her in waves. He let his mouth hover over the shell of her ear. "He's dug himself a big enough hole that I'm done with him. For good. I don't give a flying shit how he feels."

Her eyes snapped open. The melting near-curve of her spine jerked upright. "Tanner Wright. That's mean."

"It's the truth." The fingertips he grazed over her jaw became a stronger stroke. More take than touch. The back of her neck was delicate as he gripped it. "Want to know what else is the truth?"

Her slender neck thickened infinitesimally with a swallow. But she didn't pull away. If anything, she leaned nearer, into his grip. "What's that?"

"I want to kiss you."

The vision of her body had been floating at the back

of his mind. How she'd looked, the way the moonlight had skimmed over her curves. The slightly nervous, but mostly defiant way her chin had risen so that she looked at him through the screen of her lashes. Together, incredibly tempting.

Her mouth tasted as good as he remembered. All cool hesitation and a splash of salt. His own heady margarita.

For the first seconds, her mouth was slack under his. He thought for a moment he'd pushed too hard, tried to take too much. She'd pull back and realize any sort of involvement with him was a mistake.

But then she flashed to life with a gasp. Her lips sipped at his. Her tongue moved first, slicking along his bottom lip.

Tanner let his eyes close. She felt like safe harbor. He could come to shore with her and they'd stay away from the world.

He'd have enough fresh hell over the next few days. He'd already put enough behind him too. For now, all he needed was something good to sink into.

And the tastes of her mouth he'd stolen convinced him exactly how good she'd be.

One hand wound around the back of his neck, diving into his hair. But that wasn't enough for Avalon. Her fingers wound through the strands and tugged. Hard. That fast, he was rock hard, despite the cold water that occasionally sloshed over his ass.

There was nothing but Avalon.

For now, Avalon was more than enough. She was the whole ocean wrapped up into one rushing, sweeping feeling. He'd let it take him, even as he took Avalon.

Chapter 16

Avalon couldn't remember the last time she'd been kissed like this. Even their kiss earlier, in his old bedroom, didn't compete with this . . . this . . . dude. Avalon could hardly even put words to it. Full-on melding? Absolute connection?

For all that she'd thought she'd build a life with Matthew, his kisses had felt perfunctory, like he'd been doing what needed to be done. Tanner kissed her as if he couldn't get enough. As if he didn't have anywhere else in the world to be. As if even getting her into bed was a much lower priority than simply kissing the hell out of her.

It almost seemed like he wanted to use her as an escape hatch. A way out of his own head.

She probably should be offended.

But holy damn, when the result was being kissed hard enough to make her toes curl, why the hell would she care?

His hair verged on short around his neck and ears, but that didn't prevent her from getting a good grip at his crown. She didn't want him going anywhere, not when he was making such lovely silent promises.

Their knees bumped and she had to pull harder to keep him from floating away. The grip his fingers burned into her waist was no less hard. Almost desperate.

Their mouths came apart with a quiet gasp.

Avalon licked her lips. She felt like she could still taste him, but that didn't make much sense. That salt was every bit as much the sea; not him.

She felt marked anyhow. Like her lips were slightly swollen. The tingle under her skin burned higher.

"We should head in." Her voice sounded slightly unsteady, which only made sense.

"You make that sound so normal."

He had beautiful eyes. She'd never tell him, never use that word, because he'd likely blow her off in that guy kind of way. But even with their blue color obscured in the dark, the shape of them left her breathless. The way his gaze bore into her. She thought she might be able to live off that connection.

He cocked his head, casting his voice into a light parody of cheeriness. "No big. We're done on the water, so it's time to head in."

"How should I have said it?"

His mouth opened but only for a moment. His heavy-lidded eyes flashed a bit of sly humor at her. "No. I think we'll leave that one be. C'mon."

With that, he led the way back to shore. Since the waves were so tiny, they didn't bother surfing in. Once their feet touched the hard-packed sand below the tide line, they linked hands. Their fingers twined together even though neither of them breathed a word.

Avalon drank in Tanner's proximity, his heavy strength and solid warmth. Anyone caught within his shadow would be protected, even if things went too far. The difference between protecting and sheltering seemed to be escaping Tanner.

Her fingers cinched his. They walked along in silence as if breathing the same existence. It was almost too easy, and Avalon couldn't trust it, at least not for long. She could already feel the sand rushing between her fingers, the hourglass running out.

That was fine. The feeling of impermanence had become a blessing in her life. She'd learned that it heralded the beginning of a wonderful time, excitement. There was no point in not grabbing on with both hands if the moment wasn't going to last. She might as well take what she could.

At the back door of Tanner's rental house, she waited patiently as he unlocked the door, letting the tail of her board droop toward the wooden deck. If they had been closer, she would have nestled up behind him and licked that spot at the tip of his spine that drew her attention so well. He'd left a light burning over the blue-painted door. The twitch and play of his shoulder muscles was a thing of beauty.

Soon she'd get a chance to touch and play as she liked. But that wasn't the same thing as cuddling. Or laying her cheek against the divot of his spine.

Her fingers curled into her palm, folding safely in on herself. She should do it anyway. The risk was so little, and the reward of his flesh would be so great.

But before she'd managed to overcome the trembling knot in her stomach, it was too late. Tanner tossed open the door, set his board inside, and then leaned hers against the wall next to his.

Then he shut the door again. Leaning against it, he gave her a wicked grin. In the pale light of the energy-efficient bulb, his teeth looked as white as a shark's.

"Tell me what we're doing here."

She let her head tilt and let a sultry smile curve her mouth. The practice she'd put into this look as a teenager was worth it when his eyelids went heavy and his chest thickened on a deep breath. "I had been under the impression that was obvious."

The touch he trailed down the inside of her arm sent a wicked shiver through her. The weight landed in her pussy, making her swell with heat that battled against her damp swimsuit.

"No." His grip looped around her wrist. She'd never been tiny, but he made her feel delicate. Breakable, but only in the best possible way. "I mean, how bold do you want to be?"

"Bold enough to make it worth it."

When this all ended, she would need something big and bold enough to take away with her. A fully absorbing memory for when she was once again alone in her bed, playing with her battery-operated friend.

Tanner liked that answer. He pulled her closer, then stole a kiss, which was instantly reciprocated. The way he swanned through life, so fully assured of his right to what he wanted, made her head spin. She needed a little of that, even if it was only a taste by proxy.

When he lifted his head again, it was all she could do not to sway into his arms. "What are you hinting at?"

"I've always wanted to do something. It's late enough, I think." He wound his fingers up through the back of her hair. Tiny tugs and pulls told her he was removing her hair tie. "And you, Avalon, seem brave enough to try it with me."

The idea gave her a little rush. That she'd be able to

give him something no other woman had, sent a hot coil of *yes* down her spine and through her pussy.

She rose up on her toes, letting her kiss be enough of an answer. The way he grabbed her hips sent more power running through her, until her head almost buzzed with it. Until even her toes tingled.

He hitched her higher in his grip, yanking her up. Their torsos came together. The pressure against her breasts was enough to send another rush of wet to her core.

Almost involuntarily, she gave a little hop. Almost a test—would he catch her? He did.

Big hands curled around her ass, warm under the edge of her wet bikini bottom. His fingers were callused and his grip was hard and unrelenting. As if now that he had her in his hold, he wasn't letting go.

She crossed her forearms behind his neck, not wanting to admit how much she liked that. She wanted more too. All the way through. It was more than want—it was need. His touch, his existence. She needed to give him what he desired.

Everything she had, she poured into their kiss. More of her energy through and through, until his tongue in her mouth sent tiny wiggles of pleasure through her. The depths of her head went haywire, taking enjoyment further and further.

The world almost seemed to sway under their touch.

But then she realized it really did sway—because Tanner had walked her toward the side of the deck. There, tucked underneath the balcony of the upper floor, was a half-walled outdoor shower for washing off sand. All the nice houses along the beach had them, and this one was one of the nicer Avalon had seen, with tiled walls and both hot and cold water.

Tanner set her down on her feet in the corner. He flattened his hands at the wall beside her head. The dark became deeper in their close slice of the world, the porch light half concealed by the artfully worn boards.

She could only make out shadows and planes of Tanner's face. It gave him a slightly sinister edge, until she reached up to touch. Her fingers slid along his jaw. A slight hint of scruff, the golden hairs invisible in this light, roughed up her skin. "Here?" she breathed.

The idea was dirty. Filthy. Wonderfully so. She'd etch herself in a corner of his mind, something that would belong to her. During the day, she'd never consider such a thing. The tourist-packed sand and the neighbors would guarantee they'd be busted. Seen. Caught.

Christ, even that thought sent a dirty shiver through her. She let her fingers dive back into Tanner's hair. The strands weren't exactly soft, but they had a wiry texture she found fascinating.

Or maybe she liked touching him.

She smiled. Yeah. She did like that. Any chance to touch him and she would take it.

"Here." He kissed her again, a fast sweep. She'd give him anything for more of those drugging kisses that made her head spin. "Not everything. I don't have any condoms on me. But there's something I've been thinking about."

He flattened his hand wide over her bare stomach. The wiggling inside her fluttered to a stop, then surged higher in a heavy thud in her chest. She'd give anything to wipe the shadows away from their hiding spot. She wanted to see the way he looked at her. But she'd have to give up the moment to do that. Give up the chance.

RIDING THE WAVE 131

"How long?" She'd like to be able to give him something he'd been thinking about for years. A special little boost.

But what he said next was even better.

"Since I saw you come in off the waves my first morning home I've wanted to drop to my knees and lick you." He spoke between kisses, little quiet whispers that streaked down her limbs in promise.

How in the name of God could she even consider passing that up? She nodded her agreement.

The nerves almost came back when he reached past her to turn on the water. It splashed down on them, at first cold but a couple quick moments turned it warm. The whole time, Tanner's gaze was fixed on her face as he moved by rote.

When the water poured warm, he kissed her again. Hard enough that her eyes drifted shut and she thought she might melt backward into the cool tile that lined the walls. The shower drove off the salt-sharp smell of the ocean. Her world narrowed.

Tanner. Only Tanner. Everything else could scurry away. She didn't need it.

His touch. His kiss. The sweep of his hands over her hips. The confident way he tugged her bikini bottoms down her legs. He followed them down, onto his knees.

Thick weight lodged in her chest. She could barely breathe at having a man like that on his knees before her. She stroked back his coarse hair, watching a tiny bit of moonlight work its way through a slat in the wall to gleam off the strands. They weren't particularly concealed.

She wasn't sure she cared. She'd nothing left but this chance, this moment. The heady responsibility of having him on his knees before her.

He ducked his head, licked over the ridge of her hip-bone. She hissed in a breath at the enticing pleasure. There wasn't a moment of this she'd give up. It felt as if she was finally getting repaid, but for what, she had no idea. Lusting after him from afar? That was ridiculous.

The trace of his tongue over her seam sent her chin dropping loosely to her chest. Her fingers clenched in his hair. More. She needed more of that teasing. But she needed it harder, deeper.

More altogether.

"Tanner," she said, and the tone of her voice was almost a warning. But of what, she still didn't know.

"Hmm?" He hummed the response against her lips. The trembling sent a pulse of feeling up through her. So goddamn close.

She shifted her feet apart a few inches. She had to plant her hands flat on opposite sides of the shower, wedging herself in, because her knees were trembling so freaking hard. If this went on much longer, she might lose her mind. Come right out of her skin in a ratcheting-high sense of anticipation.

Outside the open door of the cubicle, the moon must have risen above the neighbor's roof. Light poured over Tanner's face. The blunt beauty of his features struck a chord within her. His hands stroked up the insides of her thighs.

"Did you want something?" He purred it right up against her pussy. The vibrations made her hips twitch in an involuntary way. The devious smile at his mouth made her even more impatient.

One hand dove deep in his hair and tugged. "Now, Tanner. Don't make me wait any longer."

Chapter 17

Tanner spread his fingers wide over Avalon's trim waist. Her skin felt like spun silk. He'd never felt a softer woman.

But there was nothing soft about the grip she had on his hair.

Part of him dug it, liked the little bite of pain along his scalp. But most of him got a strangely smirky feeling. He'd soon show her who was really in charge.

The tiny pets and strokes he made over her flat stomach gave away who was the real boss. She twitched under every touch, wiggling in a very appealing way. Her hips surged toward him, silently begging.

The water pattered down around them, combining with the cubicle and the relative dark to provide an impression of privacy. It wasn't real privacy, nothing that would protect them from the prying eyes of neighbors. Avalon's feet and his knees between them would be easily spotted in the daytime.

Only the cover of night gave them the slightest screen of respectability. And still Avalon wanted him badly enough to risk it. That rocked him all the way down to his gut. For his part, he loved the rush. It felt kind of like riding high on a wave three times his height.

But he finally had her under his mouth. Where he'd wanted her. The first moment he'd seen her riding in, he'd wanted to shake her up. And, yeah, maybe he'd realized that she wasn't near as self-assured as she wanted everyone to believe. But that didn't take care of this need he had to see her all mussed and wrecked.

He huffed an intentionally humid breath over the lips of her pussy. She was trimmed close, a little patch of dark hair pointing right toward bare lips. The soft gasp she gave went straight to his cock.

The caw of seagulls broke his fascination. They didn't have all the time in the world.

The first lick made him wish for an eternity. She tasted damn good. A little salt from the ocean, but mostly crisp woman taste. He loved the quiet sounds that broke from her.

He rolled his tongue over her full length at first, then went hunting for her clit. When her hands locked across the back of his head, nails digging in, he knew he'd found the right spot.

His entire body thrummed in response to what he worked out of Avalon. She turned him inside out with only her responsiveness. The choked gasps she gave, the way her hips twitched under his attentions.

The world narrowed to his task, the licking and sucking and nibbling that seemed to be driving her nuts. Mission accomplished.

"Tanner," she said on a breath. Her voice squeaked upward at the end. "Please, God, Tanner." The words all poured together, turning into one big smash of pleading.

She tossed her head back, seemingly without even noticing the water that sluiced over her face. The shower sprayed and gleamed on her curves. A rivulet ran down between her breasts, over the thin line of her swimsuit, then past the plane of her stomach. When it got to the edge of her pussy, he licked it up in one long, slow move, tasting both the clean purity of the shower water and the salty sheen left on her skin by the ocean.

She jerked her feet farther apart, nudging him with her pelvis. "Please. Don't stop. Whatever you do."

Fuck, he liked that. Liked having Avalon at his mercy, liked unlocking every bit of her. Liked knowing she was getting everything she needed—from him.

He pulled his mouth off her. The snug channel of her pussy enveloped two of his fingers. He curled them, watching up the length of her body for what made her ribs jump on a huge exhale. There. That was what he needed.

But in response, he had to give Avalon what she needed too. Because he'd be damned if he was done with her. Next stop would be his bedroom. He couldn't help another lick of her clit.

He wrapped his free hand around her thigh. He pushed up, until she rested half her weight on him. She leaned her shoulders back against the tile of the shower stall, trusting him. Tucking her knee over his shoulder was easy; then he had a free hand that he could pet over her sleek body.

The smooth marble tiles of the shower walls extended to the floor, but the sandy coating was beginning to work sensation through his knees. He'd need to get off them soon, but not until he was ready. Not until Avalon had come all over him.

He reached up to palm her breast, slipping under the barely damp material. Her nipples tightened under his attention.

"Tell me what you want." He punctuated his order with another lick of her, around the two fingers he still worked in and out of her.

"Come," she managed to squeak. Barely a word. He'd snatched those away from her. Taken her whole into himself.

"What's that?" He buried his smile against her flesh. Goddamn, she was soaking him. He loved it. The elation that ran through him had little comparison. He couldn't help but tease her a little. Not to be mean, but because he felt so damn good. "Use your words, love."

"Don't be an asshole." The tug she took out of his hair didn't do much to kill his high. "You know what I want."

"I sure as hell do." He stroked fingers in and out of her, adding one more.

She gasped, the sound sliding deeper until it was nearly a groan. She slammed her forearm across her mouth. He couldn't see the lush curve of her lips, but he understood. If she wanted to scream, she'd have to cover it.

And he was going to try like hell to make her scream.

"Yes," he said. "Keep that right there. Better quiet those noises. Don't be too loud." He rocked his teeth against the inside tendon of her slim thigh. "You'll get us caught."

She jerked up on her toes, slamming her wet pussy toward him with a moan. But she didn't say a word.

"Like that idea?" He wanted to push her, to pressure her. Wanted some sort of admission. "Want to be caught? Want everyone to see me on my knees, licking you? Driving you crazy?"

"Please, make me come," she finally said. Half whisper and half gasp and all pleading. She'd own him with sentences like that, if only she knew. He'd do anything to get more of them. "Please, Tanner. Make it worth it."

Fuck, how could he pass up on that? He fucked her with his fingers, adding his mouth back to the mix. Long, hard flicks and the barest nibble. Until finally he locked his teeth around her clit and sucked it deep.

And felt her break apart all over him. Her pussy clenched over his intruding fingers. The soft keen she gave wound upward into a flat-out scream muffled only by her arm. Her legs shook and her stomach jumped.

Tanner felt like the goddamn king of the mountain. He'd done that. Worked her over until she'd come so hard she'd probably seen stars.

He kept up the attention, letting her draw her knee down off his shoulder. He soothed her with deep, sure touches, petting her stomach as he rocked back into a squat.

His knees protested the move. More proof he wasn't the kid he used to be, with salt water running through his veins instead of blood. By morning, he'd probably be regretting this.

But he couldn't make himself care right now. And he'd be damned if he was done.

Avalon's eyes had gone cloudy, unfocused but pinned on him at the same time. Her tongue slid over her lips and she gasped one last time.

Deliberately, he lifted his fingers to his mouth to lick them clean. He loved the way she tasted, and the gobsmacked look on her face was worth it. Her lips parted. The pulse at the dip of her clavicles pounded.

He rose to his feet. Now that he didn't have his face buried in Avalon's pussy, the water pattering over them became an annoyance. He snapped it off, then pushed Avalon's wet hair out of her face.

"You still with me?" He liked the delicate lines of her

cheeks, the soft curve of her jaw. And he really freaking liked the way she nestled into his palm.

"Where else would I be?"

He brushed his lips over hers, needing to taste that relaxation. Needing a way out of his own head. And nothing had worked as well as when he'd been driving Avalon out of hers.

Even holding her bikini bottoms out for her took on a fun edge. She stepped into them and the move brought her even closer, so he could smell her skin.

He laced their fingers together, then led her back to the quiet house. The white rush of waves blended into the background, the only noise beyond the slam of Tanner's blood in his ears.

Avalon's hand was unbelievably warm in his. Small enough too, to make him feel like a big ol' manly man. It was a feeling he didn't get that much, but there was something about this whole night that already had him standing taller.

An overwhelming sense of protectiveness mixed with guilt dogged his heels. He knew he was using her on a certain level, to avoid the messiness and unpleasantness of the next few days. He was staring down a bit of a shit storm.

But as he led Avalon through the silent house, up the stairs to his bedroom, he pushed it all away. She had told him she was using him too. They both needed to forget.

As they stepped inside the bedroom, his bare feet dragged to a stop on the plush carpet. The place looked like an expensive hotel room, even though it wasn't. The walls were covered with watercolors of some stretch of beach that was certainly not San Sebastian. The headboard of the bed was an anonymous white-cane deal, but it was king-sized and spread with a dark gold blanket.

Because he'd had less than a week in the place, he still fumbled for the light switch. But a second later the room was flooded with light.

Tanner blinked against the sudden glare, glancing at Avalon. This was definitely going to be different from dropping to his knees in the shower.

There were only the two of them and whatever they could make.

So he wanted to make sure he gave her everything, gave her enough of an experience to make up for the fact that they had no future. He couldn't permanently take up banging his sister's best friend, and that wasn't even taking into account how often he was gone. He spent such a large portion of time on the circuit, maintaining a girlfriend was an impossibility. Kristin had made that more than clear when she called him five times a day and cried every time he left.

Not that he'd cared before.

Did he care now?

He didn't have the fucking *time*, to be perfectly honest. Avalon was an awesome chick, and she'd be able to give some lucky man everything he wanted. Everything he needed.

His hand folded tighter around hers at that thought.

Any bastard who got a chance with Avalon would have to appreciate how amazing she was. Tanner would have to make sure of it.

She tugged on her hand. "Getting a little intense there, Tanner?"

He pushed a smile up to his lips. This was the time they

had. In a little more than two weeks he'd either put the cap on a decent career or be halfway to burying it. Either way, he was obligated to finish out the rest of the year's World Championship circuit. He'd be moving on whether he had a San Sebastian trophy or not.

"Do you blame me?" He spun them around until he could sit at the end of the bed. When he tugged on her hands, she stepped between his knees without even hesitating. "This whole night has been one level of intensity after the other. I like what we've got going now much better."

He skimmed his thumbs over the ridge of her hips. When she shivered, her body shimmied along with it. The apples of her cheeks weren't so high now, not when she stared at him with dark depths of her eyes.

"I like it too." She nodded. Her hands fluttered a moment before coming to rest on his shoulders. But once she landed, her grip became firm. More intensity. Her fingertips gouged into the muscles behind his neck.

He wanted to groan, it felt so good. Hard spikes of goodness arrowed down to his shoulder blades.

"But the question remains." She scratched over his shoulders with her thumbnails this time. An entirely different sensation. This woman was going to flip his world as much as he wanted to flip hers. "What's the *next* level?"

Chapter 18

Avalon's knees were still weak. Wobbly. Her pussy throbbed with the aftereffects of the orgasm Tanner had wrung from her.

And she was still greedy for more.

The question had slipped out of her mouth almost unchecked. What's next, indeed. Most girls would have been thrilled with what she'd already gotten.

In the fall of her junior year of high school, she'd started dating her first boyfriend, Jeff Deveraux. They'd been together most of the year, until two weeks before prom when she'd had her first lesson in being used. As in, he dumped her once he didn't need a ride to swim practice anymore.

But she figured she'd actually come out pretty lucky in that relationship. There'd been plenty of her friends who'd told her they didn't come when they'd lost their virginity. She had.

It had made her kind of greedy. She had a high bar and men didn't always make it.

Tanner had made her come so hard she'd thought she'd stop breathing.

And she still wanted to climb him like a monkey.

She scratched her nails over his thick muscles. The way he arched up into it was a little bit of a rush. He was a beast; all power and strength. She'd seen some surfers who were nothing but ligaments and bones. They tended to flick over the waves in tiny, liquid moves.

Not Tanner. He'd always owned the wave. Owned the moment.

Now it felt like he could own her if she wasn't careful. She'd have to give so much of herself to be worthy of that sort of attention.

She simply didn't know if she had that kind of effort to give at the moment.

When he buried his face against her stomach, it sent a hard shudder up through her spine. His hair tickled her bare cleavage until she pushed her fingers through it, shoved it back.

"The next level," he said against her skin, "is anything you want it to be."

She couldn't help the little laugh that burbled up from her chest. "Here I am, again. Telling you that you're freaking insane. Is this going to be a trend with us?"

"In the first place, no, it won't be a trend." He grabbed her by the hips, then flipped her and gently lowered her to the bed in a move so slick her head spun. The man was certainly practiced.

But she liked being on her back, looking up at him. His blunt features had a kind of hard-edged sincerity she liked. She traced his top lip with a single finger, feeling the barely noticeable ridge of his scar.

Her mouth went dry. She managed not to ask if he meant because there was no "us." She already knew the answer to that one. Of course there wasn't. Tanner needed the type of girl who could wait at home for him. There was too much Avalon still needed to conquer. Not to mention she couldn't afford to have her name permanently linked with Tanner's in a romantic way. It'd be bad enough if even one word of this one night got out.

People would say she was trying to ride Tanner's coattails into the ranks of surfer photogs. The whispers about family connections would be nothing compared to the outright mocking she'd catch if anyone knew they'd slept together.

So she only smiled. Her toes trailed up the back of his calf. She liked the rough texture of his hair. "And the second?"

"I'm not freaking crazy. You name it, I've got it, it's yours." He settled onto his elbows, one big arch of muscle over her. The plank of his body was solid enough to make her feel protected.

"You're so full of shit."

"Am not." The childish words took on a sensuous lilt based only on his wickedly quirked smile.

"You'd go down on me again?"

"Why not?" He brushed a kiss over her mouth, trailing his tongue over her bottom lip. Then he sucked it into his mouth to nibble. "You tasted so goddamn good, I think I could lick you for hours."

The dirty words sent a rough shiver through her. But she didn't buy it, either. The hand she flattened over his chest found rock-hard muscles, pulled firm with tension—tension she was causing. She could get behind that program.

But when she swept her hand down his stomach, skimming her fingers over his barely damp board shorts, she smiled. The cock she'd felt pressed against her earlier had definitely perked up to play. "And this? Won't bother you any?"

He surged into her grip, but that was it. The ends of her hair tangled around his hand. "Blue balls are a myth. I figured you'd have known that one."

She grinned. Weird, to have this sort of happy buzz when she'd otherwise be oh so drama. She flat-out liked spending time with Tanner, no matter what was going on. "Of course I know that, numb nuts."

"Actually, no. Not numb. That's what we're discussing at this very moment."

The fingertips she drilled into his ribs had only one purpose—to tickle. But he didn't budge. "Nonticklish people are no fun."

"Then you'll be relieved to know there's exactly one spot on me that's ticklish."

She narrowed her eyes. "Where?"

"If you think I'm telling you, you're the freaking insane one."

"Nice. Real nice, Wright."

His touches ran over her skin and through her bones like she could float away on them. The heady rush threatened to drown her even while they teased. He could easily take everything she had to give and still want more. Still need more.

She'd run out of pieces to give him. Better they had only this time, then move on.

Lifting her mouth to his for more kisses was easier. Bodies she knew. The rest of it . . . She'd rather not even think about the rest of it.

Thank God he sent her spinning in a way she understood. Her body arched into his, her breasts rubbing over his skin. The thin material of her bikini top was too much and not enough at the same time.

The fast, methodical way he stripped it off her was a relief. The artificial air-conditioning breeze had only a second to send goose bumps over her arms before Tanner's nearness was back to warm her. His breath tingled her nipples; then he sucked one tip into his mouth.

He was good. Almost too good if she stopped to think about it, but she wouldn't let herself. There was only the way his hands glided and stroked over her skin, the easy way he slipped off her swimsuit bottoms.

The way he cupped her pussy had ownership written all over it. A full hand, fingertips barely cresting the curve of her ass. Until his thumb delved surely between her lips, slicked her moisture all over her skin.

She gasped, grabbing hard to his shoulders. Her eyes flashed open to stare at the plain ceiling. With the things he did to her, she ought to have seen stars, moons, something entirely more exciting than white plaster. The man was a fucking genius; that was for sure.

"Now, please." The words flew out on their own. How the hell did he make her beg so easily? This could be a problem.

He pressed openmouthed kisses along her shoulders, trailing up her neck. A spinning excitement made her curve her spine toward him, but she couldn't get much closer. Not with the heavy thigh he pinned across her legs.

"Nope," he said into the sensitive skin of her neck. His words were like rasping strokes along her flesh. "I've decided you need to come again first. Let me do what I need to."

"Lie back and think of England?"

"I didn't think Prince William was your type." He grinned against the top curve of her breast. The glance he flicked up at her sparked pure laughter up from her center. "But don't let me stop you."

She tucked her laugh against the inside of her arm, but that didn't help. The cough she forced didn't help her failing-to-be-serious face. He was going to get tired of her soon. Matthew had hated how she couldn't keep her "mind on the prize," as he said. "Keep calm and carry on. I can do that."

He flat-out laughed, mouth open against her sternum. The rumble sent dark pleasure through her.

"Can you?" He punctuated the words with a hard thrust in her core. The pleasure slammed up through her in one hard rush. "I think I might be doing this all wrong, then."

"Oh God, you're not. You're right. Do that. Do that more."

Her arms went over her head, fingers twining in the expensive duvet. The next breath she let go eased trembles she hadn't even realized she'd been holding back.

"Right here." He spread his free hand low over her stomach. The weight of his hand pushed through to her center. "Let go right here."

Her gaze locked on his. All their humor leeched out at the last second. She gasped on a sudden rush. There was no way she'd gotten that close that quickly. But she was there. Her head spun. Through it all, there was only him. Tanner filling her mind as she came.

That was all it took. Her hands got greedy and she filled her mouth with the taste of him. They crawled over each other, and Tanner produced a condom from God only knew where before he kicked off his board shorts. But then the protection was on, and, fucking Christ, then he was *in* her. Either he was ridiculously big or she was ridiculously turned on, but either way, it worked.

So freaking well.

He surged over her, his arms locked straight and his palms planted by her head. She was overwhelmed by him. She was overwhelmed by who she was with him. Everything else dropped away, until there was only their minuscule corner of the world.

The way he moved in her, made her feel. Her eyes drifted shut, the better to run from the crackling-fire rush. She wanted to close her arms around it, hold the smoldering blitz close. Hide away.

But she felt his grip across the back of her neck. A thumb stroked hard over her jaw. "Here. Look at me."

She slicked her tongue over her bottom lip. The muscles of his back played under her wide-spread hands. Blinking took way too much effort, but she tried it. Bit her lip when a hard fuck stole her breath. "Yeah. I'm looking."

His hand slid up her neck, to the base of her skull. Wound through her hair. Tugged. Hard.

The sudden snap of pain didn't distract from the pleasure building deep in her body. If anything, it added.

"No. Look at *me*." His eyes were so bloody bright. A neon kind of blue she'd never seen in them before, all of it focused on her.

She wasn't sure she could handle that kind of responsibility. Wasn't sure she could give him enough in return. And the higher he lifted her, the farther she'd have to fall when he didn't need her anymore.

But she couldn't look away from him, either. Together they might explode.

It felt almost like she came in self-defense. The whip-cord passion that released her muscles freed her. She let the power draw her head back, let her eyes drift shut on a long moan.

She locked her wrists behind his neck, hitched her leg higher over his hip. Let the last few strokes as he came draw out her own orgasm, but only from behind the dark safety of her closed eyes.

It was better that way. Safer.

Chapter 19

Waking with his face buried in a pillow and his arm around a slender waist, Tanner had approximately five point two seconds of peace. At least it lasted longer after he'd come last night. That had been all Avalon, though. The way she'd twined around him, brushing his hair back from his face, had been enough to keep his high going. To stay out of his head a while longer.

But now she was asleep. The light in the room was slightly gray due to the west-facing windows but Avalon's hair still managed to shine with dark red gleams, spread in a dark cloud over her shoulders. She slept on her stomach, like him, but she'd hitched one knee up toward her side.

Admitting what an attractive curve the position made of her ass would probably be a little pervy, considering how knocked-out she seemed to be.

For a minute, he considered waking her up. It wouldn't take much. Some strategic kisses and then he could fold up to her from behind. A few kisses to her neck and he could likely be inside her again in the time it'd take to get the condom on.

He slid out of bed instead.

In the morning's hazy light, everything seemed entirely more complicated. Sleeping with Avalon hadn't been quite as *easy* as he'd thought. To be truthful, he'd expected a quickie variation. More protracted, sure, but with the same sort of pump-and-go type of vibe.

Instead he'd locked his hand around the back of her neck and forced her to focus on him.

Not at all his usual mutual-orgasm routine.

But he'd hated the way she'd avoiding looking at him.

In the bathroom mirror, his face was rough looking. His eyes unfocused. Splashing water on his skin helped, and so did the rest of his routine, but by the time he stumbled downstairs to the kitchen, he still didn't feel right.

How much of that he could lay at Avalon's feet was debatable. There were also his other, way more massive problems. Like winning the San Sebastian Pro. Or, hey, how about the way he'd decimated his family last night? That'd make for some emo hours if he were so inclined.

The buzz of his phone against the granite kitchen countertop was a relief from the suck-hole his head had become. Until he saw Sage's face smiling at him from the caller ID.

Coffeepot in one hand, he thought about not answering. For way longer than a good brother would admit. The shit storm of the next few days was already coming for him. No reason to grab it up any faster than he needed to.

He snatched up the phone, thumbed the answer. "Hey, you."

"I'd decided that you were already out surfing."

Tanner had come to believe he knew Sage's voice better than he knew her face. He might've spent the past

decade away from his hometown, but there had been no
way to give up his little sister. She hadn't let him. At first
the phone calls had come mostly from her, but he'd absolutely grown used to them. Now they talked at least
twice a week, no matter what finagling they had to do in
order to work around the time zones.

"Excuse me?" Water gurgled into the pot. Coffee was
his one regular indulgence lately. He might have to eat
pretty healthy to stay competitive with the younger groms
on the circuit, but he couldn't seem to give up his caf-
feine.

"Either you were out surfing, or you actually screened
my calls. Mine. Your precious baby sister who you love
more than anyone else in the world." She was so obviously straining for her normal level of cheer and laid-
back attitude. And failing. A thick quality told him she'd
either been crying or was going to soon.

Tanner had done that to her. His hands kept working
through the motions of making coffee, but his gaze
turned to stare out the windows. This was what he'd worried about all along.

God*damn* their dad for putting him in this position.

"Screening is a sin against the universe," he finally
said. The coffee machine burbled away.

"So you hit the waves, then?" The music Sage always
blasted in her shop crashed in the background before
abruptly being cut off again. She'd probably swiped off
the iPod. At this hour, she'd be alone in her dusty shop,
probably hand-shaping her favorite pieces. "Because
I've got this prime sub-six-footer with three fins that'd be
sweet out there today."

"No, didn't surf. Not this morning." The truth flew out
of his mouth before he had a chance to think twice about

it. He'd never lied to his little sister before, not even when she'd been seven. Her hair in wispy blond pigtails, she'd asked him if the Easter Bunny was real and he'd managed to duck that one.

But he'd never banged her best friend, either.

The gaze he darted up revealed only a white plaster ceiling. As if he'd gone all Clark Kent–ish and could see Avalon's naked ass in his bed from here.

Heat slammed up the back of his neck.

Holy crap, this could count as a major fail on his part. He'd thought about Sage, but he hadn't exactly run through every level of consequences. Not that sisters were something a man *wanted* to think about before they were about to get dirty.

Fuck. Up. Hard-core.

Made a guy almost want to discuss his shitbird father and the illegitimate son he'd left behind.

"Where were you, then?" Sage laughed. "No. Don't answer that. Probably best if you don't."

She had no fucking idea. He scratched short nails over the back of his head, but couldn't put a dent in the tension-locked muscles there. "Was there something you needed, sis?"

"Yeah. Mom. She needs you to come by today."

"Really?"

"Well . . ." She hedged a little bit. He could almost picture the way she'd duck her head and thrust her jaw to the side. She'd done it as a teenager when conning fifty bucks off him. "More like I think she needs you to come by."

"I don't know." His gut churned. The scalding sip of black coffee he took only added to the burn. "I was thinking I should probably give her some space today. Let it go for now."

"Tanner Wright, you've given this family almost ten years of space." She sounded absolutely exasperated. A person had to push pretty far to get levelheaded Sage to that point. But then, he'd always had a talent for fucking up family. "You get your butt over here by this afternoon, bare minimum. And expect to stick around for dinner. You'll answer any questions either Mom or I have and you'll do so as honestly as you did last night. And everything will be fine in the end."

"Yes, ma'am," he snapped. But it was a sort of relief. Direction. A way to handle it. Though he found himself doubtful everything would be that easy.

Sage was a ridiculously determined optimist. It was one of the reasons she'd founded her own surfboard-making company at twenty-three. Because she'd never imagined that it wouldn't work.

They chatted a few minutes more, but Tanner could hear the strain under it, even if no one wanted to admit it.

He'd been right to keep the secret. It seemed that no one agreed with him, but he knew. The hurt was all there, in the way Sage *wasn't* laughing by the time they hung up. She'd been happier when she didn't know.

Tanner tucked his phone in the pocket of his pajama pants, then carried his coffee, the carafe and a second mug back upstairs. But Avalon was still completely racked out.

She looked stupidly gorgeous for being so knocked out. The apples of her cheeks had been sleep-pinked, and even her curves looked warm. She was lying face-down and he could see the bottoms of her feet and toes, which were surprisingly tender and delicate looking.

Better to let her sleep. He'd kept her up late enough, after all.

He smiled around a sip of coffee as he sauntered out

toward the balcony. French doors gave way to a deck. Half the size of the ground-floor deck, there was still plenty of space, which was filled with cushioned wicker furniture. And all of it looked out on the best view in the world.

Beach. Pure beach, ended with only a beautiful white-frothed left break. Tanner knew without even pulling up the surf report on his phone that the waves had to be at least three feet on the backside. Plenty thick enough to get some tricks in.

But he plopped down on the deck chair and set his coffee on the mosaic-topped bistro table.

There'd be enough time for surfing later. For now, he meant to let Avalon sleep longer. She was always so wound up and riding some knife's edge of energy. He got the feeling she didn't rest enough.

But he didn't have long to catch up on the surf reports and preliminary standings, much less hit his e-mail, before the door slid open behind him. He tucked the phone in his pocket, then twisted to smile at her.

She had her camera again. Raised in front of her almost like a shield.

Didn't help her much. She still looked freshly fucked, her hair a tangled mess. She'd pulled on her shirt, but the only thing covering her ass was her red bikini bottoms. And her lips looked as reddened and swollen as when he'd first kissed the hell out of her last night.

He reached for his cup of coffee and took a sip. He needed his own armor, it seemed like.

This moment was not exactly wrapping up like he'd imagined. Maybe a kiss or two in the morning, a few nice words. Regrouping later with him in professional-sports-star and her in professional-photographer mode again.

He didn't like the dense knot that lodged in his chest.

"Brought you coffee." He kicked his feet up to the railing and leaned back. "Didn't know how you wanted it, so it's black."

The waves were rolling in sets of six. Same as they always had at this break, his entire life.

Duh. The obvious didn't make for very good avoidance methods.

She hesitated for a second. The camera wavered and he spotted her dark green eyes as it lowered. But then she snapped off half a dozen shots anyway.

Tanner tried not to feel the hair at the back of his neck standing to attention. He was going to have enough unwanted publicity, because of Mako's article. He didn't want the privacy of this moment broken as well.

"Thanks," she said, finally lowering the camera. "Black's fine. I've gotten used to it."

She picked up the coffee and drank deeply, but she didn't sit. Instead she moved to the side of the balcony— though that wasn't far, only ten feet—and hitched her ass onto the waist-high railing. Sipping from her mug, she silently looked out to the water.

The message couldn't have been any clearer if she'd written it in permanent marker across her forehead. Not interested, move along.

Tanner ought to take the message. They'd gotten what they wanted out of each other. Last night had been more about forgetting a messy evening than starting something new.

But fuck that.

Second place had never been to his taste.

He set his coffee mug down with a click that could barely be heard over the roar of the waves. Coming out of his chair, he moved toward Avalon.

She knew he was coming, watched him out of the corner of her eyes. Her fingers tensed around the coffee mug until her knuckles went white. But she didn't flee. Didn't run, or try to fill the space between them with chatter. He liked that about her.

He framed her pixie-shaped jawline in his grasp for a fast, swift kiss. They traded bitter coffee tastes when her tongue took his.

Pulling back, he brushed her long bangs to the side, the better to see her wide-open eyes. "Good morning, Avalon."

She swallowed on a soft sigh. "Good morning, Tanner."

Chapter 20

Avalon wanted her camera in her hands rather than the mug of coffee.

But she didn't usually get what she wanted, did she?

It wasn't like Tanner's hands at her face was any sort of hardship. She'd find a way to endure. Somehow.

She had to bury the sudden smile in her coffee mug. Explaining that one might be a wee bit difficult.

Tanner didn't return to his seat and she didn't want to examine how happy she was. The sun peeking over the rooftops had nothing on the happiness beaming through her. He stood between her knees, though he lowered his hand to her knees. The tingle that went up the inside of her thighs was proximity and possibilities.

She couldn't resist the devil on her shoulder. The slightest move tightened her legs and her knees brushed his sides, along his ribs. The man had incredible lats, that was all there was to it.

The very thought brought back the rush of holding him. Gripping those very sides.

He could go straight to her head—and other parts. Especially with the steady way he looked at her. As if he could see right down inside her, and maybe didn't mind what he was finding.

The fear that prickled along her skin at that thought was more than she could bear. She hadn't earned that level of interest. The smile she forced to her lips felt unnatural, but she made it. "Do we have plans? And mind you, I'm asking as your assigned photographer. Not the pickup chick who won't go home."

His smile was pretty, though she'd never tell him that. And the scar only added a tiny dash of recklessness. "I don't kick my pickups out quite that fast, thank you very much. There's always time for a second round."

"Oh?" She wanted to kiss him again. Lose herself in him, tell him there wasn't anything she wouldn't do for another chance.

Which was patently ridiculous. She didn't have any time for the likes of him, not when they'd both be moving on so quickly. Not when he'd need so much from her. "Make them earn their keep, do you?"

"Of course." His hold on her legs was completely possessive and self-assured. She almost felt like she could settle under a hold like that. "I'm not kicking you out, either."

"What are you saying, Tanner?"

"I'm saying whatever you want to hear."

On the surface, Tanner seemed as solid as the shore. Unmoving against the pounding surf. But what people didn't realize was that shorelines shifted. Sand slid away. Currents took it to rest elsewhere. Even land couldn't be trusted.

He might be offering her more time, but that didn't necessarily make it a good idea.

She had a history of making bad choices. Look at Matthew and every other boyfriend she'd had, after all.

She shook her head. But looking down at her coffee

was the only chance she had of escaping him; he'd crowded in that close. Truthfully, she didn't want to get away. Not yet. She could give him up later. Or he would realize she didn't have *enough* to keep him intrigued.

"Schedule, then. As both photographer. And pickup." Her hands would have shaken if she'd given them half a chance.

He grinned at her. Then sank his fingers deep in her hair and tugged her mouth to his. That smile tasted as brilliant as it looked.

For the shortest moment possible, Avalon let her eyes flutter shut and let herself . . . go. Whitewater froth come to rest. Temporarily.

Miracle of miracles, he managed to hold her up.

When he pulled back, it was everything she could do not to throw herself at him.

He brushed a thumb over her cheek. Bad man, to tempt her so. "I was going to go for a run now. Surf a little after that." His gaze flicked away from hers, noticeable in its absence.

"And then?"

"This one's not really photographer or pickup territory." He looked back at her, at her mouth this time. His hands kept roaming over her, touching. Everywhere, practically. Down her arms, over her hips. Almost hypnotizing. But so definitely not calming at the same time. "But Avalon can come."

She tilted her head. "Who's left of Avalon if I'm not a photographer or the chick you laid?"

The laugh that rolled out from him was part comfort and part embarrassment.

"You. You're here. My sister's friend. Honest chick. Great sport. Decent surfer." A wrinkle drove between his brows. Confusion clouded his eyes. "Did you really mean that?"

She pulled her mouth into a smile. Took that kiss she'd wanted, because it was easier than being looked at. Her forearm looped around the back of his neck, but he wouldn't have moved if he hadn't felt like letting her. He was such a brick house of muscles; there'd be no taking him anywhere he didn't want to go.

"Course not," she finally said, after she'd battered herself on his calm for a minute. "The phrasing made me curious."

He studied her for a minute more, as if he could see further through her words. Her heart tumbled in her chest and bounced up to her throat as she reminded herself it wasn't exactly a lie. And beyond that, it was none of his business if she didn't know who she was beyond her goals. "So what is it, then?"

"Sage called. I'm summoned for the afternoon."

"And you want me to go?"

His hands finally settled at her lower back, thumbs curving over onto her waist. The drape of his fingertips at the top of her ass sent a wiggle through her that was entirely too naughty for the subject.

"I bet Sage would have insisted on it too. If she'd known you were here."

Wasn't that one subject she'd like to skim right by. She swallowed down a silly burst of adrenaline. It wasn't as if they were about to be caught right then and there. Or that Sage would really care.

But man would it make for one awkward afternoon.

Good thing her mother had taught her to lie like a pro.

Only problem with that plan proved to be her failure to check with Tanner.

Avalon sat in the back patio area, her seat carefully chosen to be the max distance from Tanner's. And she'd managed to keep her eyes off him for the most part, even though he sat with a stillness she found fascinating.

He wore an old dark blue T-shirt that did amazing things to the color of his eyes. Cargo shorts showed off his thick thighs and calves, borne from hours and hours of balancing on a surfboard. He looked so damn calm and focused.

She wanted a piece of that. Or she wanted to climb in his lap and shake him up. Either would do.

But Sage and Eileen sat leaning against each other on the padded swing. They looked flat-out miserable. No two ways about it. Sage's blond hair had been wound into a limp ponytail, and dark shadows ringed Eileen's eyes. The woman hadn't slept, that much was obvious.

"One more question."

He leaned forward, his elbows resting on his knees. His body became a thick curve. "Anything."

"Do you know what he said about me? To her?" She leaned into the arm Sage put around her shoulders. "I know Hank had to mention me for Mako to find us."

Tanner shook his head. Sympathy darkened his eyes. "No. I stopped talking to Dad, and . . ."

"And things went downhill from there." Eileen let her head fall back against the swing. Sunlight spun around her in a gentle caress, lighting her features and pointing out the delicately wrinkled skin at her jawline. She wasn't exactly a young woman anymore. "Neither of you have expressed any wish to involve yourself in the retail portion of the store."

Guilt pinched Sage's features, but she never stopped rubbing Eileen's arm. Tanner shifted back in his seat, his hands folding over the wrought-iron arms. "Not really," he said.

Eileen pushed up from her seat, then set her glass down on the table. She patted Sage's shoulder, left her hand there, but the move seemed empty. Her gaze was focused somewhere else. Maybe somewhere inside herself. "It was your father's idea to even open the store. Everywhere I look, I see him. I might sell it."

"Oh, Mom," Sage said. Her eyes widened and she grabbed at the hand resting on her shoulder. "You don't want to do that."

Eileen patted her again, then patted Tanner, as if they were little children. Avalon sat quietly on the other side of the patio. This was their moment, their time. She'd be intruding.

"I might," Eileen said. "No decisions now, but remember what I've always said about telling others how to feel."

Sage pulled a face, her nose wrinkling, but she didn't protest. And when Eileen walked away, toward the house, the brother and sister pair let her go.

Fear prickled along Avalon's forearms and wedged a hot rock under her ribs. Awful. Miserable. The thought of the store being gone, this family falling apart . . . She couldn't stand it.

The Wrights were all she had. Over the years, they'd given her more support and love than she'd known what to do with at times. This couldn't be allowed to happen.

Sage watched the door Eileen disappeared through, sadness etching her delicate features. Sage pulled her legs up onto the seat of the swing, curling them up under herself in her usual way. But she didn't look as relaxed as normal. The back of her neck was stiff in a way that Avalon had never seen before. "She didn't sleep last night. Kept going downstairs and making cup after cup of tea. I don't think she could have possibly drunk all of them."

RIDING THE WAVE 163

Her wide blue eyes fixed on Avalon. "I peeked in your room but you weren't there."

The rasp of Avalon's tongue over her lips didn't help much. Her mouth had gone dry as sand. The last thing Sage needed was to know exactly what Avalon had been doing last night.

Hell, it was already haunting her—but in the best possible way.

Halfway through their run this morning, she'd looked over at Tanner and seen a scratch on his knee. The very knees he'd been on while licking her.

She forced a smile. "I went for a walk. Sat on the beach for a while."

"Oh really?" Tanner's gaze flew to hers. His eyebrows lifted on a distinct air of challenge. And the smile that quirked his mouth looked decidedly smirky.

Naturally Sage didn't miss a thing. She looked back and forth from Avalon to Tanner, her lips parting more and more on each go-round. "What's going on here?"

Tanner smirked. No two ways about it. He leaned back in his seat, crossing his arms over that thick chest. "Avalon said she walked, then she walked."

The way Sage tilted her head sent the long sheaf of her ponytail spilling over her shoulder. Her small smile was at least related to her usual brightness. "Did you finally get some, Avalon? You've been a freaking nun since you moved back in here."

Hot embarrassment burned across her cheeks. She wanted to plaster a strip of duct tape over Tanner's smirk—which had only gotten bigger.

"I wouldn't have pegged you for the nun type." He was flat-out taunting her. No two ways about it.

Her mouth worked but sound refused to come out.

She shook her head. Okay. There had to be a way out of this. But it was damned hard with the way Tanner was looking at her. Like he'd like to strip her naked and start all over again—except he'd be laughing against her skin the whole time.

She locked her knees together against the sudden throb of her body. That wasn't a half-bad idea.

The cough she forced into her fist didn't clear her throat. But it did afford her an opportunity to flip Tanner off. Childish, maybe. Still satisfying though. "No. Nothing special last night."

At that, he choked back laughter. Thank God Sage was looking down at her nails, trying to pick foam out of them from making surfboards all morning, and missed it.

"You should hook up with Jack," she said in a voice that sounded a little strained. Probably from trying to maintain a happy conversation under the weight of discovery about her father. But that was Sage. A peacemaker down to her toes. "He was asking about you."

Tanner didn't seem to like that at all. The smile slid right off his face.

Avalon stretched her legs out, pointing her toes in their pink, sparkly flip-flops. She sent a smirk of her own at Tanner. "Maybe I will. He's not bad looking."

"It's the eyes, isn't it?" Sage spoke down into her hands, still without looking up. "He's got great eyes."

"He does." She was getting a hot rush of power off this; there were no two ways about it. After spending the whole morning feeling like she was only waiting for the other shoe to drop, she deserved it. "Maybe I'll give him a call later."

Except Tanner had apparently had enough. "That might be a little awkward. Especially if you call from my bed."

Chapter 21

The fact that Avalon was still annoyed with Tanner the next day didn't surprise him. What freaked him out to hell and gone was how much it bothered him.

"You sure you don't want me to smile and say cheese?" He knew it was the last thing in the world she wanted, but at least the question got a look from her.

The family surf shop wasn't a huge venue, but an hour before the place opened, its emptiness took over. The long, narrow place smelled of surf wax, salt, and a hint of coconut. Racks and shelves were filled with everything water-related. Shorts, bikinis, flip-flops. The back quarter was devoted to Sage's boards, a few demonstration pieces along the walls.

In the center of the room, toward the huge plate-glass window, sat the squared-off front counter. Tanner claimed a spot where the corner curved. His hand brushed the side of the register.

He couldn't even count how many afternoons he'd spent working that register, counting out change to tourists. It hadn't been his favorite activity.

Watching Avalon fling attitude around as she evaluated her cameras was almost enough to drown out the memories of a teenager affected with permanent wanderlust. The girl was certainly cute when she was annoyed.

With an impatient hand, she flicked her long bangs out of her eyes, then slanted him some decent side-eye. For all her irritation, she didn't seem capable of exactly ignoring him either.

He hadn't ever liked being ignored, so that was a definite win.

"You," she said, wagging a long, black lens at him, "are an asshole."

He grinned. "And you're not very good at maintaining the silent treatment."

"I wasn't giving you the silent treatment. I was keeping my mouth closed until I had something nice to say. Your own mother taught me that."

"Calling me an asshole is something nice?" Surprise lifted his brows. "I'm not sure I want to know what you're holding back."

She tucked lenses and cameras back into her bag with precise, sharp moves. Everything had a padded slot and little zippered compartments kept tiny pieces in order.

The slim T-shirt she wore rose up in the back as she bent to tuck her camera case beneath the counter. Her spine was a delicate curve, and her khaki shorts dipped enough to reveal the dimples at the base of her spine.

Tanner slipped off the counter, his feet slapping on the ground. He rested his hands behind himself on the counter. No matter how much he wanted to touch her, he couldn't. Not yet.

He had no doubt he'd get back in her panties before too long. If it hadn't been for a meeting he'd had with one of his sponsors, he'd have devoted his whole morning to Avalon.

God only knew she was a damned sight better time than practically everything else in his life.

Like the fact that his knees groaned in protest when he hopped off the counter. Old man. At thirty-one. It was beyond ridiculous.

But the five-mile run this morning had taken a lot out of him.

She stood up again, this time with the black camera curled protectively in her hands. The Canon, if he remembered right. She ran off a series of shots of him, ranging him in a half circle.

He ought to be used to it by now. The way she took photographs was something akin to breathing, like she couldn't shut it off if she wanted to. He doubted that she even realized what she did half the time.

The tiny acts, one by one, built a huge shield. He wanted to pick it apart, piece by piece, until he knew what was underneath.

But he didn't have the time.

He made himself rest his elbows on the counter, leaning backward. The smile he wore was his usual public-appearances look, and it did the job well enough to nail him plenty of sponsors. "Are you sure you want to stick around? I'm hanging out for a while. Not worth taking pictures of."

"Are you kidding? I'm not missing this one for the world." She wedged herself into the far corner of the counter, leaning on one elbow. He could reach out and touch her too damn easily. The soft cotton of her shirt would feel good under his fingers. "Big, bad Tanner Wright meeting and greeting? I'm not going anywhere."

"I'm not meeting and greeting." Something hot burned across the back of his neck. "I'm hanging out in Mom's surf shop for a while."

Darkness flitted across her eyes. She ran a surprisingly gentle hand over the black Formica counter top. "Do you really think she'll do it?"

"Sell the joint?" He couldn't help another look around. Despite the changes in clothing and colors and light fixtures, the place was still pretty much the same as when he'd been in school.

He and his dad used to stop by before morning surf sessions to grab whatever last-minute items they needed. An extra pack of surf wax, a new pair of board shorts. Tanner had always liked the dimness, as if they were wandering through a partly make-believe world. But his dad had always immediately flipped on the lights.

Tanner shook his head. "It's her choice."

"No way. It's more than that." A mulish pout took over her mouth. He wanted to bite her bottom lip. "This is your family business."

"What exactly are you implying?"

She turned her face down toward the digital display of her camera, but then looked at him from under the dark, thick fan of her lashes. He wondered what it would be like to feel them flutter against his skin. He coughed, as if that would have any effect on his half-awake cock.

"You could step in." She clicked a button on her camera, but she couldn't be paying attention to whatever it was. "Insist she keep it."

"No way," he said, but her words went somewhere down inside him and caught hold with wicked little nails. "That's not my choice. I can't make her do anything. And I can't keep the store myself."

Her mouth opened, but then she shut it on a little shake of her head. She slapped the counter lightly as she rounded it, heading toward the front window. "Come on. It's time to open up shop."

"That's not your job anymore." His hand flashed out, caught her by the elbow. "And it's not what you were going to say."

"You wouldn't like it." She ducked out of his grip. Camera dangling from one hand, the strap wound around her wrist, she keyed the alarm off the front door, then unlocked it. "And Krissy is still in back, putting the final touches on next week's schedule. She'll be out any second. Not sure we should start this now."

"Tell me," he insisted.

But then she did the oddest thing. Stepped near him. Not exactly close enough for him to lean down and kiss her, but nearer than casual contact. The girl knew how to work a man when she felt like it.

"Keeping it open would keep your dad's legacy alive."

"Jesus fucked, why the hell would I do that?" He stepped back fast enough that someone who didn't know better would think him almost scared. More like pissed as hell. Something hot burned across his shoulders and dove down his spine in a curved pinch. "In case you've missed it, I've been trying to duck Dad for almost ten years. Not to mention he seemed to have misplaced his dick at some point. I'm not really into his legacy bullshit."

She shook her head. The hand she set on his forearm was both soft and shaking a little. "Fine, then think of it this way: This store matters. That's the important part. There are people who rely on it. They come from an hour away to shop here. How crazy is that? Wright Break is an institution. I think your mom needs it more than she wants to admit right now too. I don't want her making any rash decisions while she's upset."

Fuck, he didn't want to have anything to do with it. But the way Avalon looked at him, with her huge eyes turned up and her lips barely parted, was proving to be pretty damn kryptonite-like. "I'll think about it," he said.

No way had he really said that. Had he? Crap.

She lit up. No two ways about it. The apples of her cheeks rounded until her eyes were almost squints and her smile turned huge. Lifting up on her toes, she kissed him. "That's good enough."

"Better be," he said, pushing as much grumble into his voice as he could manage. But truth was, he liked making Avalon happy a little too much.

Hell, he needed something to do once his career ended, didn't he? Scrubbing a hand over his head, he looked past Avalon's dark head. Could he do retail?

Probably not. More than a couple hours inside on a gorgeous day left him itchy at the edges. His feet would feel too confined in real shoes and he'd be eager to surf at the first opportunity.

That wasn't even taking into account living under his father's shadow. Definitely not his style.

Avalon brushed another kiss over his jaw. The girl was so definitely wound up. Not to mention, almost absurdly easy to please. He hadn't even agreed to anything definite, come to think about it. And she was fawning all over him like he'd won the championship. There was something relaxing about her.

His hands found purchase along the sleek curve of her waist. No point in letting an opportunity like this escape. He took her mouth and pushed the kiss deep, tasting the smile on her mouth. The only thing that stopped him was bumbling footsteps from the back.

Krissy took her place at the front register, but not before giving Tanner a sly smile and tugging down her bright blue Wright Break T-shirt. He only smiled in return.

So he was kissing Avalon in public. Not like she was his dirty little secret or anything, but he trusted the Wright Break staff to keep things under wraps anyway. Avalon wouldn't want too many people talking about them. In fact, he turned back to Avalon and brushed hair out of her eyes.

More like any chance he got to touch her was a very good thing. "If Mom wants to sell, though . . . She's incredibly stubborn."

"No, she's not." Avalon's chin took on a stubborn angle of its own. "She's incredibly sweet. Eileen doesn't deserve to lose everything because she's upset."

He felt that one right under his ribs, a hard fist of contrition slamming through him. "More like she's not your mom. She's never had to put the crackdown on you."

"That's what you think." Her soft smile made him curious what secrets she was hiding.

"Name one."

"Hmm." She nibbled on her bottom lip, then glanced up at him. Pink washed across her cheeks. "How about the time that I talked Sage into sneaking out of the house and going to a party at Ricky Talbot's house?"

"You didn't. All the way down in Newport?" Tanner laughed. Under his grip, her sides were sleek and smooth. He snuck his thumbs up under the hem of her T-shirt. "I knew Ricky's older brother."

"I know you did. You were supposed to be at the

party. First time you'd even been back in California after you stopped talking to your dad." But she shook her head, as if declining to head down that road. She dangled her wrists behind his neck, her ever-present camera strap grazing his back. The tips of her breasts didn't quite brush him. Damn it. "But your mom found out somehow. She was waiting outside for us. Never even made it inside."

"Probably Sage."

She gasped, making a pretty O of her mouth. "No way."

He nodded. "She was always a scaredy-cat in certain situations. She'd call me and talk about how you were going to get her in trouble, ask me for help."

Stunned shock widened her eyes and opened her lips. Avalon laughed, then wiggled her way out of his arms. "Did you tell her to rat us out?"

"Not that time, but I would have." He shoved his hands in his pockets and couldn't help his smile. "No way could I have my kid sister at a rager like that one."

"I was so upset that I didn't get to see you that weekend." She smiled around the words, but something dark wriggled behind her eyes. "Sage met you in Long Beach, but I . . . I didn't."

"You wanted to see me?"

She flashed a wider smile, then lifted her camera. Armored up again. "Didn't every girl in Southern California?"

Chapter 22

Two hours later, Avalon still couldn't believe what she'd almost admitted.

There was absolutely no reason in the world for Tanner to know she'd had a crush on him when she was seventeen. He'd been a world-traveling surf star already and twenty-three. When he'd stopped coming to the house, it had felt like losing a heart she'd never realized she had.

Tanner chilled out at the front of the store, looking every bit the gorgeous man worthy of a teenager's crush. In fact, the two blondes who bubbled and bobbed in front of him were probably still teenagers too. He smiled and joked with them, then signed a pale pink visor, of all things.

Much like she figured he would have humored her if she'd actually made it to that party. Tanner was a good guy. He wouldn't have taken advantage of her, even if she'd been young and dumb. He was too good for that.

Sage had shown up at the store for a while, but then she'd headed to the back, where music had heralded the beginning of her creative process. Avalon was always faintly surprised to hear heavy-duty rock leaking through the door, no matter how many times Sage explained she needed to "hit a deeper point of her subconscious" when she was working.

Avalon wasn't nearly as hippy-esque about her work. Checking her watch, she realized it was more or less lunchtime. She stowed away her cameras, then slid over toward Tanner.

He was still laughing and talking with the young women, but white strain at the corners of his eyes gave him away. He was certainly not having a good time.

She thought about leaving him to his own devices, but even she wasn't that cruel. Wrapping an arm around his waist, she tucked herself into his side. "Ready to go, sugarnibs?"

His eyebrows almost climbed into his hairline, but he tossed his arm around her shoulders in response. "Sure." He slid another smile toward the matched pair of blondes. "Sorry, but we've got to go."

"We've got a date," Avalon said, opening her eyes as wide as she could. "Matching pedicures."

The teenagers' gazes dropped instantly to Tanner's feet. But they were big and strong and not decorated with even a smidge of polish. The girl on the left caught on faster, heaving what looked like a relieved sigh and grinning at Avalon.

Five minutes later, they stood outside on the sidewalk. Holding back the smirk was too incredibly difficult. Putting on her sunglasses, she probably failed. Then she grinned.

"Sugarnibs?" Tanner echoed. "Seriously? Do I look like a 'sugarnibs' to you?"

No. Not at all. Wearing a pair of board shorts and a

white shirt emblazoned with WavePro's logo, his feet shoulder-width apart in an easy stance, he looked lickable. Fuckable.

And a little too much like her hero.

He'd only agreed to think about saving Wright Break. No promises.

She'd learned the hard way that even promises didn't mean much. Not without follow-through.

After a nano-quick check up and down the street to make sure she didn't see anyone she knew, she leaned up on her toes and kissed him. With her eyes closed, it was harder to paint him in rainbow colors. Not to mention dirty thoughts went a long way toward de-hero-fying.

Her head spun when he kissed her, every time. The tingling under her skin threatened to incinerate every speck of caution she possessed, but she was beginning to wonder if she really minded. Her fingers dipped underneath his waistband. The tiniest brush of manly hair reminded her how far she could go for him.

But a public street wasn't exactly the place to try licking his skin. No matter how badly she wanted him.

She pulled back, her fingers still twined in his belt loop. "I solemnly swear never to imply you get pedicures again. You forgive me?" She delivered the words with her best enticing smile.

His big paw curved around the back of her neck. Warmth and steadiness dove through her and anchored her. "If I say no, will you kiss me like that again?"

"No, not this time. But I *will* buy you lunch."

"I think you owe me anyway." He nodded solemnly.

"You're out of your mind. Again." They swung into alignment, walking down the street without having to consult each other. Most of the lunch options were closer toward the beach, the better to grab some of the tourist trade. "If anything, you owe me. Do you know how long I'll have to answer questions from Sage? She's going to drive me batshit crazy."

"Funny, she hasn't asked me a thing." He walked with his hand still at the back of her neck. A sun-worshipping beast, his face turned up a little toward the sky. If she didn't know how much he lived for the water, between his golden hair and prowling way of walking she'd call him a lion.

Who'd apparently decided to claim her for the foreseeable future. There was no way of telling how long the attention would last, but she'd enjoy it while it lasted.

They agreed on a sandwich place tucked behind two tourist traps specializing in souvenirs, even as Tanner teased her that she needed something a little more substantial to put some meat on her bones—along with a sneaky butt grab.

She swatted his hand off her ass as she stepped into the shadowy sandwich shop. To be honest, she didn't mind. What red-blooded girl would mind if a hottie like Tanner was paying her attention? Not her.

But then her feet jerked to such an abrupt stop, she almost slid out of her flip-flops. And Tanner ran smack into her backside. She spun, flattening one hand over Tanner's chest. "Go, let's go."

"What? What is it?" He looked over her head easily, and the golden cheer fell straight out of his expression. "Son of a bitch."

Cold, shivering fear wove through her bones. Jack and Mako sat a mere three tables away, each with subs and fries in red plastic baskets before them. He'd seemed fairly ordinary the other night, but today it was like seeing the boogeyman. Her stomach gave a disconcerting flip. She set her back teeth together, letting the slight pain of wrenching them tight hold her together.

Jack hopped up immediately, but Mako only rested his elbows on the table. He twiddled his fingers in a smart-ass kind of wave. His dark hair fell across his forehead. Wiry shoulders filled out a plain T-shirt.

She'd liked him better when she hadn't known who he was.

Nobody could help to whom they were born. If that were true, she wouldn't have been born to her mother, not by a long shot. She'd have picked a family more like the Wrights. Which meant she couldn't bear to watch it fall apart.

Really, if Mako was Hank's son, that meant he ought to have a place in the family too. It only made sense that he'd want to know them. Except he'd gone about it in absolutely the shittiest way possible. The Wright family guarded their privacy fiercely.

She urged Tanner back out the door. She didn't really want to be anywhere around Mako. Her skin would like to stop crawling anytime now. But she couldn't let Tanner start trouble in the middle of a public place, either. "You don't want to do this."

The fists at his sides said otherwise. His dark glower set his jawline in a sharp angle.

On the street, he turned and started to stomp away, but the slam of the mesh-screened door stopped him. He looked back over his shoulder.

Jack stood in front of the plate-glass window, his arms crossed over his chest. "Look, mate," he said, his Australian accent lilting. "I know you've always had a bit of a problem with me."

Tanner's shoulders bowed up. The man could work some intimidation when it suited him.

Avalon ought to be afraid, or at the very least a bit disgusted. Good guys didn't solve problems with fists.

The warmth settling between her thighs said otherwise. She wasn't exactly creaming her panties yet, but they were most certainly warm. Because Tanner wasn't exactly solving his problems with fists—despite his obvious frustration and anger, he was holding back. Every sharp line of his body popped with restrained tension.

The very promise of danger held back was enough to make her inappropriately happy for the situation.

She forced a cough into her fingertips but it did nothing to batten down the heat weaving through her.

When Tanner stepped forward, his arms thick, it only got worse. "You're damned right I do. You're a showoff, Crews. If the fancy cars and the interviews weren't enough, you're a showoff on the water too."

Jack lifted his hands, palms out, to his shoulders. Both men had blue eyes, but Jack's were vibrant. Avalon liked the pure calm of Tanner's much better. "I'm not looking to cause more problems. But you ought to know the bloke's not here for trouble."

"You have no idea what's going on here." Tanner's mouth twisted, the faint scar turning white. "So why don't you mind your own fucking business?"

Jack flicked a look at Avalon out of the corner of his eye. He rubbed one hand over the artful scruff covering his jaw. "I do know."

"Motherfucker," Tanner muttered. He wrapped a hand around the back of his neck.

Avalon couldn't stay away, not when he was so obviously upset. She wrapped one hand around his arm, but even his forearm had gone rock hard. The touch she soothed over his back didn't seem to make a dent. He was still hard as steel beneath the worn cotton of his shirt.

"Like it's not enough he talked to that fucking magazine," he said, somewhere between a grumble and a curse. He didn't sound happy at the idea at all. "Now everyone in the universe is going to know."

"Thanks, jackass. Nope, I've no idea of how to keep a secret. Lips like your turns in the last WavePro surf vid. Sloppy." Jack leaned back on his heels, his expression as sardonic as possible. His eyebrows knotted and his finely carved mouth quirked.

"Fuck you, Crews."

"Thanks. You're not my type."

"Jesus Christ, get you two together and it's like you're both in the UFC, not the ASP." Avalon kept her words light, but really she couldn't allow them to keep going down that path. "C'mon, Tanner, let's go. You owe me lunch."

"First, wait." Jack waved a hand. "Listen, Mako's in town for talks to buy a T-shirt line. It's no big deal, nothing to do with you and your family."

Tanner shook his head. "You might want to believe that, but I know better."

"But look, it can't hurt," Jack went on.

"What can't hurt?"

"Meet with Mako."

A few seconds ago, Avalon wouldn't have thought that Tanner could have gotten any more wound up. But she'd have been wrong. He rocked forward on his toes, his fists rolling. "I already did, against my will. Like fucking hell is it happening again."

Jack shrugged. "Fine. No skin off my nose. Figured it

was worth a try." He tipped a wave at Avalon, along with one of the devastating smiles he was known for. Everything else aside, she'd kill for the opportunity to photograph him soon. "Take care, Avvie." He slipped back into the sandwich shop.

She rolled her eyes at the nickname, but Tanner didn't. His brows lowered and hard-etched lines marked his mouth. "Avvie? You've never told me that's your nickname."

"Because it's not." She tugged him by the arm and at least this time he came along. Her stomach wasn't even in the mood for lunch anymore, but they needed *somewhere* to go. So she detoured into the nearest pizza place.

Dark ocher walls were draped with fake grapevines along the top. Tourists filled almost every table, and lined up at the aluminum service counter, looking both exhausted and exhilarated at the same time. Not to mention, sunburned. Most of them looked two shades short of melanoma burned.

At least none of them noticed the barely leashed fury of the beast at her side. Tanner focused his gaze toward the menu board, but he didn't seem to be seeing it. "If that's not your nickname, why did Jack call you by it?"

"Why does that guy do anything? To irritate and crawl under your skin?" She lifted an eyebrow even as she traced fingertips over the inside of his wrist. His pulse still pounded at a breakneck pace. "That's not what you're really annoyed over, so don't even try to make it a big deal. Understand?"

Chapter 23

Fisted hands at his sides, Tanner popped his jaw to the side once, then twice. He hadn't liked the way Jack smirked at Avalon. The sidelong glance he'd slanted at her had aimed straight at her tiny ass and right over her head. She hadn't even seen it.

Avvie. It was a stupid nickname. Sounded like someone who had seen *Avatar* twenty-five too many times.

His teeth ground together. "I don't like him giving you nicknames."

Her mouth tweaked into a knot that looked suspiciously like she was holding back a smile. "So many things wrong with that, I'm not even sure where to start."

The menu hanging on the back wall had been designed to look handwritten. Tanner rubbed two fingers over his temple. Pizza by the slice, calzones, and salads. None of it looked remotely appealing. "Are you even hungry?"

Avalon shook her head. "Not really. Wanna blow this Popsicle stand?"

Avalon led them to the pier. When Tanner had been young, the end had been topped with a full-sized restaurant that served bacon cheeseburgers worth ditching class for. Now a much smaller building had signs for an ice cream and slushy shop, plus a bait store. But the extra space made for plenty of room for benches with birds-eye views of the waves. At midday, there weren't many fishermen left but for a single crusty old dude bouncing between three poles hanging off the very end.

Tanner and Avalon staked out a spot to the south side, sitting quietly side by side.

"That guy's going to cream it." He pointed at a surfer in a bright yellow rash guard way below them. Wiry arms and the boy's relative height to his board said he was probably in his early teens. The grommet was about to get quite a dunking.

Avalon's head tilted a little. She rested her hand on his thigh as she leaned forward to look past the dark brown railing. A single finger trailed across his bare skin, below the hem of his shorts. The back of her shirt rode up again, baring tanned, creamy skin.

"Why do you say that?"

"Angle of his back foot." He slung his arm across the back of the bench, turning his face up to the sun. "He's a goofy-footer trying to ride with the wrong foot forward."

Time and place.

Though his hands practically curled in on themselves with the sudden need to touch her.

Two minutes later, the yellow-shirted surfer took a header off the end of his board.

"You called it." Avalon's face lit up with pure enjoyment. "I can't believe that one. We're like forever away."

He shrugged. "I like working with grommets. I figure it's the least I can do. I've been there, you know?"

The way she smiled at him went to his head as if he'd

run out of air under the water. "Yeah, but not everyone does. It takes time to teach someone to surf. Dedication."

"I don't know that I've taught anyone. Just given a few tips here and there." The wood bench was rough under his palm, still soaking up plenty of the afternoon's bright sun. "One thing my dad gave me was great surfing advice. Don't want it to die out, at least not that part of him."

She lightly touched and patted his thigh. Completely innocent and yet something that went right through him. Until she spoke. "You should meet with him."

"Goddamn it," he said, but without any malice behind the words. There was only a weary sense of expectation. He'd known things like this would happen once he finally told everyone. Avalon especially would think she should help. Or think she had more insight on what had to happen. "I've been there. Done that. There's no reason for him to be in town if not to cause trouble."

"You don't know that." A tiny wrinkle scored her forehead. He had the most absurd impulse to smooth it away. "Jack said it was business. If he's even a little bit in the surfing world—"

"He is." Tanner had followed Mako's progress with a sort of begrudging interest. He didn't want to know, but he didn't want to be taken by surprise, either. The man had bought his first surf shop only a year out of college, a tiny place in Brisbane. He'd only gone up from there. "He owns Burn."

"No way," she said on a breath. It was one of the biggest chains in the industry, pushed by innovative marketing and aggressive tactics. She seemed to catch herself, coughing awkwardly and snapping her mouth shut. "Right. Anyway, see? A store in San Sebastian makes sense. Business. It's totally legit."

"It would be if I hadn't already had a nice little run-in with him when I first got to town. Besides, I wouldn't even need that. I know him."

"You know a what, a fifteen-year-old boy?" She leaned a shoulder against the back of the bench, giving him a gentle smile. "I've heard stories of you at fifteen."

He'd been nineteen when she'd become friends with his sister. There had only been a few months' overlap before he'd left for the tour, but he remembered her. Huge eyes and a tentative way of folding her shoulders in, as if she were expecting to be yelled at any second. "You and Mom always were close. Straight off."

She nodded. "So you know I wouldn't do anything to hurt her."

"I do."

"So let your mom meet with Mako." She went after him like a determined shark, all teeth and intent. "She's a grownup. She can make her own choices."

"Why should we give in to him? He's doing shitty things to get himself noticed now that Dad's dead. Plus, I've got a family already." Sage and his mom had always been good to him. Always been there for him.

"You don't have room for one more?" Her gaze shifted back out to the lineup of surfers. "I figure everyone can take more family. What's a little more love?"

His knees bounced. He'd rather be surfing, that was a damned easy call. But he trailed her ponytail through steady fingers. "You'd do anything for someone you considered family, wouldn't you?"

"I figure the question's more why *wouldn't* I?" She tossed the words out lightly to skip across the waves far below them.

But the stiff line of her blade-sharp shoulders said she felt it more keenly than that. "How's your mom?"

She jerked her head to look at him. "Exactly what are you implying?"

He traced his touch down her spine. The muscles and ligaments there were practically twitching. She'd break if she twisted any tighter. "Nothing. Nothing at all."

She looked back out at the waves, but he could still see the line of her jaw and the tendon down her neck that stood out in stark relief. "Mom's fine. She took a cruise."

Time slowed as Tanner sat there, touching lazy circles over Avalon's back. Plenty went unsaid, but he didn't see a problem with that. If Avalon was living in a glass house, far be it from him to toss rocks around. Maybe he wanted her to not throw any, either.

Not unless he was going to stick around to catch the fallout.

No matter what he'd told Avalon, taking over the store was not a possibility. He'd no sooner do retail than feed his foot to a shark.

"Hey," he said, tugging on the ends of her hair. "You know what?"

She looked at him over her shoulder again. The apples of her cheeks went round. He'd give anything to know what she was thinking about. "What?"

"I can't stop thinking about the way you taste."

Her lips parted on a gasp and her gaze flicked to the white-haired fisherman at the other side of the pier. But he didn't even look in their direction.

Tanner hadn't spoken that loudly. He hadn't needed to. The only person whom he meant to hear him was Avalon, and he'd certainly gotten her attention.

"We said it was one night. Back to friends, remember?"

Maybe. But he'd been having a harder time than he'd expected getting her memory out of his head. Or making his dick focus on anything else.

For example, he ought to be studying the waves, the way they were breaking. The rhythm of the sets. He had a championship to nail down.

Instead, he had his gaze fully focused on the way her long bangs tickled and tangled in her eyelashes. The way she slowly blinked, her pupils blown wide. Most especially the soft bow of her bottom lip and the way he wanted to nibble on it.

There was something about Avalon that went straight past all the rest of the world and fitted into some ragged part of him. He felt more centered when she flitted around him.

He wove his fingers through the ends of her hair and tugged. The move was light, and if she'd tried to get away, he'd have let her go. Somehow. Even though his hands would mourn the lack of her.

But she leaned into him, her chin tilting up into his kiss. The way they worked together was amazing. She kissed him as if chasing off demons.

Before Tanner knew what had happened, he had a lapful of Avalon. He didn't mind it one bit. An arm low around her hips, he cupped her jaw in one hand.

Too soon, she pulled her mouth away. Her eyes were hazy, her lips parted and wet. He liked her like that. Wanted more of it.

Her mouth tipped up in a smug smile. "Man, I haven't made out on the pier in years."

"I'm not your first, then." Contentment settled into him like an old friend. Sitting on the pier, Avalon in his arms, beautiful waves at his feet. Yeah, that worked for him. He smoothed a hand down the length of her throat. Delicious. "I always knew you were a hussy."

She pulled a face, but the way she didn't shrink away from the hard-on poking her hip had to indicate at least some hussylike tendencies. He appreciated that in a girl. "My first kiss was here on the pier."

"No way." There was something about that idea that resonated through him: That he'd be the last man to kiss her on the pier too. But that was pretty damn ridiculous. She'd go on after he left, find herself someone new. Someone who'd take care of her and remind her to calm down once in a while.

The very thought sent acid through him. The skin over his shoulders chilled.

But Avalon hadn't noticed. "The old one, before they rebuilt it. Behind the restaurant because Jared was working as a busboy there."

"I always knew you were a wild child." He kept smoothing touches over her. He liked the way she felt, the way she settled under his hands. But he also liked driving her up and wild again. He nuzzled his face in her hair, touched his lips to the delicate skin behind her ear.

She shivered, her ass wiggling in his lap. Dude, that sent pressure straight through his cock. He had to grab hold of her. "Do that again," he said and his voice sounded raspy.

"What?" She was all fake-innocence, her eyes held purposefully wide. "This?" The slow-hipped grind she gave would make a stripper proud.

"Fuck, yes," he breathed.

"You're too easy." Her smile lit up her whole face. "You make a girl think she's the queen of the world."

Not all of them. Not by far. There'd been plenty of times when he'd been accused of not giving a big enough of a shit about the women he was with. Which had never made sense to him, because he'd always genuinely cared about them. Maybe not more than any other close friend, though.

Avalon, though. He had the feeling he could learn everything about her and still have that half-fascinated, all-confused feeling about her. Like she was completely unpredictable.

The only shitty part was that he didn't have it in him to delve. Couldn't take the time to figure her out. It was something his dad would do, worm his way deep in some poor innocent girl's life and then leave her, except for periodic booty calls. Tanner couldn't do that to Avalon.

Even the back of her knee was silky, delicate. He traced figure eights over the skin, relieved when she wiggled on another shiver. "If we get out of here, I'll show you exactly how to get crowned."

Her head tilted. "I think that might have been the cheesiest pickup line I've heard."

"Fine." He held back his laugh by pure will. "If we go to my place, I'll make you come so hard you'll scream."

"Now, *that* is how to pick a chick up."

Chapter 24

The thing about a small beach town was that walking everywhere was possible. Sometimes, that was awesome. Walking provided an extra level of connection to the town community; stopping and chatting on the sidewalk became the norm. Not to mention, in California the gorgeous weather meant extra feel good from the sun at any opportunity.

But when a four-block walk stood between Avalon and some record-breaking orgasms, she had a tendency to get impatient.

By the time Tanner had unlocked his back door, she had a hand plastered across his back. "In you go," she said with a nudge.

"Somebody a little greedy?"

She loved his smile. The pure enjoyment he seemed to take from the world at large.

And she especially loved the way his hands felt closing over her hips. She almost believed she could lean into him and those big paws would never let her drop.

When she gave a little hop, her legs wound around his hips. His hands curved under her ass. The khaki shorts she'd worn that day were sturdy, but they weren't that thick. His every fingertip seemed to burn through them, grazing the tender skin at the center of her cheeks.

Hot pleasure rocked her. He made her think wicked things, made her want to grab onto the possibilities. She'd spent so long in her own head, sometimes it was difficult to escape.

But the slow, openmouthed kisses he dragged down her neck were certainly doing their part.

Maybe it spoke to some little weakness of hers. Some depth unplumbed, that she wanted to lean on him so hard. Wanted him to pull her along with him and teach her how to claim that easy sort of center.

But hell, she'd claimed her own path in everything else. Sometimes it was easier to let go.

She wove her fingers through his hair. Even those gold strands seemed brighter and more vibrant than anything about her.

Would he claim her?

She'd always wanted to be flat-out *taken*. Slammed up against a wall and fucked dirty-style. But she'd never been with a man who'd taken those kinds of liberties. Or she'd never driven a man crazy enough to want it.

The way she held her mouth up to his was an invitation. And a test, if she were to peel back the layers she didn't often like to delve beneath.

Tanner passed with flying colors.

She'd barely lifted her mouth to his before he kissed her. Stroked his tongue over hers, then took her bottom lip between his teeth.

The whole time he carried her, hands still locked under her thighs. She wrapped her arms around his shoulders, grabbed a nice handful of T-shirt. He was a man on a mission and God forbid she even think about stopping him.

She obviously didn't want to.

The kitchen counter wasn't exactly what she'd been expecting but she'd be damned if she'd protest. The cold granite at the edge of her shorts sent a chill up through her skin. Nothing could suppress the deep heat curling through her or dampening her pussy.

"There," Tanner said, leaning back to look down between them. He fitted his pelvis carefully to her. Holy Christ, was he big. Hard.

She held down her shiver only by dragging her nails over the back of his neck. The feeling went through her veins like a hit of top-shelf prescription drugs. "What?"

"Been more than twenty-four hours since I've been between your thighs." He flashed another grin at her, this one completely unrepentant. "I'm thinking we can't let that happen again."

"You're a busy man," she said. Her fingers danced over his shirt, but that wasn't enough. "Got that dinner tonight, a meeting tomorrow. And I'll be in photographer mode."

A girl needed a little look-see now and then. She curled her fingers under the hem of his shirt and tugged it over his head.

He laughed as it went, but he let her pull the T-shirt off easily enough.

And then she had him at her disposal. All sorts of lovely muscle and heavy curves. The little fingers of connectors from his ribs to his abs were meant for licking. She wanted that chance. Wanted to climb all over him, exploring as she went.

The best kind of sex was a full-throttle experience.

She spread her hands wide over the ribbed divides of his stomach. Under her touch, they went from already-firm planks to individual boxes.

She liked having that kind of power over him. Knowing that her touch made his lips part and his eyes go a little bit fuzzy.

But when he wrapped her ponytail around one hand and tugged her head back she almost melted straight into the countertop.

She might have to look at how much she liked this feeling of being *owned*. That'd definitely have to be some other time though, because this moment was all about the liquid pleasure spinning out from his mouth onto her neck.

Or the way he didn't even rock when she locked her ankles at his ass and tried to tug him closer. She let her eyes drift shut, let herself float along.

She'd lose herself to him if she wasn't careful. Hand everything over, and it would hurt that much more when he left again. Or when she was forced to leave first, in order to *not see*. Tanner had been a force in her thoughts for so long, simmering beneath the surface. If it all went bad, she wouldn't be able to take it.

She'd much rather get him inside her. She tried to kiss him, but he seemed intent on other purposes. The hard grip of his hands as he skimmed her shirt off over her head said he was a man on a mission.

He cupped her breasts. Made her damned grateful she'd broken out the pink-and-white pretties. Her girls put in quite the showing in their fancy bra. The warm tan of Tanner's hands right next to her paler skin sent wiggling little tingles down her.

They only got stronger when he ducked his head and

slicked his tongue over the top of one swell. She'd always counted herself as pretty lucky in having responsive breasts, but this was out of control. He tucked his thumbs inside her bra cups, scraping roughly over her nipples.

Maybe it wasn't ladylike to scrabble off her shorts, but she was pretty sure she'd left ladylike behind. Years ago. She was only trying to grab onto what she still could at this point. Tanner let go of her breasts long enough to tug the material down her hips while she pushed up from the counter.

The tiny scrap of pink-striped panties didn't conceal much. And it was entirely possible that was a damp spot on the front of them. She didn't care. Because Tanner lowered one hand to cup her front, sending a whip-sharp crack of pleasure through her when he rubbed.

Her head dropped forward, her forehead resting on his shoulder. Still her hands didn't stop moving. "Oh God," she whispered.

"You like that?" There was a fair possibility that the curve of his mouth was another smirk. She hated those and loved them at the same time. Mostly, she wanted to be responsible for shaking them up. "I'll have to remember that one."

The words should have been a good thing, but they got her going in all sorts of unpleasant ways. The implication that any sort of again or future or once more waited on them. They had only each connection, each touch. Looking past them only meant looking toward pain when they moved on.

And she was realizing with every kiss how much of her had rolled over and shown its preciously soft underbelly. Tanner could take anything of her and she'd give it.

There was no way. She couldn't let that happen.

This was sex. Only sex. She'd deal with all the fallout later. It would all be in her own head—and her own heart—anyhow. He'd be gone by the time she realized there were pieces to sweep up.

Lost inside her head again, she scrunched her eyes shut, her head still leaning on his shoulder. At least he held her up so well.

She never expected him to notice. But he did. One hand wedged under her jaw, forced her face up to him. "Here. I'm here, and you're here." He flashed a huge grin at her. "And my hand is in your panties, making you wet."

She didn't expect the laugh, but at the same time she didn't know why she wouldn't. The guy could definitely lighten the mood. "Yes. It is." She gasped over a particular thrum he made over her clit. "That right there. Do more of that."

"So demanding," he chided, but it didn't sound at all real or concerned. Instead, he did it again. Then again, then more, until she was panting and getting sweaty at the edges.

If he quit, she thought she might freaking climb him and wedge herself down over his cock.

She needed more. A deeper, harder fuck. Something to drive away all these happy, cheery thoughts sweeping through her.

He seemed to be reading her mind again. Two fingers filled her, stroking a spot deep inside her that sent a breath-robbing pleasure streaking over her limbs. At the same time, he unbuttoned and unzipped his shorts, letting them droop to his hips.

There was no way she could let that go unnoticed. She filled her hands with his length. And holy Christ was there a lot of him to hold. She'd felt him the other night, of course, but that wasn't the same thing. When she curled her fingers around his girth, they didn't meet at the tips.

So *that* was why he'd rocked her socks so hard.

It was almost a relief. Simple biology, something that could be replicated with someone else.

Right?

Pushing the thoughts out of her head was easier this time. Better, with his fingers working magic inside her—heart-stopping strokes that had her mewling and rocking her hips up toward his touch.

A condom made its way into her hand, fished out of Tanner's pocket. She unwrapped it, then slowly rolled the latex down Tanner's shaft. It was very possible that she took her time for the sheer pleasure of hearing his inward-drawn breath.

"You're a fucking minx—you know that?"

She laughed into his shoulder. "Did you call me a minx? Does anyone say that anymore? Oh my God, I'm going to tell the world what a dork you are."

"You do and you'll regret it." He drew his fingers out of her, rubbing her wet juices over her clit. She had to bite her lip to avoid letting him know how hard that shook her or how good it felt.

She couldn't afford to give him any more ammo. He did plenty well on his own and she'd rather not turn into a puddle once he left.

"Why don't you try to stop me?" she said, but the words even sounded strained to her.

Because they were such an empty threat. He only had to pull her hips forward as he notched his cock in her pussy.

He slid in with one smooth thrust.

And fucked if she wasn't owned again.

She slammed her eyes shut, but as quickly opened them again. He was staring at her, staring in her eyes, as she'd expected. The cool blue of his was comforting and exhilarating at the same time.

On a hot surge of sensation, she bit her lip again.

"Still think I'm a dork?" His voice had dropped an octave and the very sound of it rasped against sensitive nerves.

She shook her head. He gripped her breast, deliberately letting the rhythm of his strokes in her rub her nipple over his palm. "Keep doing that and I'll call you anything you want."

"Is that right?" He kissed her then, swallowing the noises she seemed to be making without even realizing it. Little gasps and moans and even one or two squeaks when he hit a spot inside her that turned her knees to jelly.

With little grasping slides along his back, she pulled him closer. Buried her face in the crook of his neck.

She didn't even have to try for the orgasm. It came with the hard slam of his cock in her, the pleasure that racked her.

One huge, roaring wave that broke over her, like getting slammed by thousands of pounds of water.

It was that devastating.

Tears prickled her eyes. But still she couldn't give him up. Wouldn't. Her arms wrapped around him, she waited out the last strokes he slammed into her. Rode the wave a little longer.

Because every wave eventually came to shore.

Chapter 25

"Goddamn it, Avalon." The sun burned Tanner's eyes, he was sweating his ass off, and he was about ten feet away from some of the best waves he'd seen since hitting California.

He was nowhere near being able to surf them.

"You'll cope." She circled him, the camera lifted to launch point. The woman wasn't the least bit put off by his grumbling.

He pretty much dug that about her. That he could get loud and blustery was no surprise. He'd run off plenty of chicks with too much smack talking. Avalon stood her ground.

Or rather, forced him to stand his ground. She touched him abruptly, taking hold of his wrist and draping it over the WavePro-printed surfboard next to him. He lifted an eyebrow. "Seriously? This is how you're posing me?"

"Look casual."

He rolled his eyes.

"It's part of your contract." She lifted the camera. The lens clicked in a near-steady whirr. "So suck it up, Princess."

"I can think of other things that need sucking."

She dropped the camera and peered at him over the black body. "Really? That's the line you're going with?"

He shrugged. She looked too gorgeous for words. They'd spent every moment of the last three days in bed. When he wasn't training, that was.

Or at meetings or making appearances or signing surfboards.

It probably made him a shithead, but he didn't like this part of the gig. If it all came after the event, that might be different. But he wanted to put that goddamned trophy on his shelf before he dealt with all the little bull-shit.

Not to mention, Avalon looked good enough to eat. She shook her head at him, then lifted some little device that measured . . . something. He'd never really paid attention to the photographers who'd swarmed around him before.

None of them had worn bikinis to their shoots, either. The little red halter one again, he'd been glad to see when he met her on the beach that morning. The expanse of her waist looked delectable. He wanted to dip his tongue in the small divot of her belly button.

Come to think of it, the photogs he'd dealt with before had all been male. Might've been a little off-putting if they'd worn bikinis.

"Pick the board up. Hold it behind you."

He rolled his eyes again, but he did what she'd asked. This Avalon was brisk. Mostly businesslike and definitely a woman in her element.

Major turn-on.

But he had to stop thinking about that, or in a minute he'd have to be holding the board in front of himself. He hadn't been that out of control since he'd been twenty-two and realized that being on the circuit pulled more tail than a bunny rabbit could shake. The way Avalon looked at him—when she wasn't ensconced behind a camera—was pretty damn intoxicating. Considering his pre–Sebastian Pro clean living regimen meant no drinking, she was as close as he could get to a rush.

And she gave mean rush, that was for damn sure. The night before, they'd been up against the sliding glass door in his bedroom, their only audience the sand and midnight-gleaming waves.

He'd still been out on the water at dawn.

But he wanted to get a piece of these waves, too. That was part of it. No ride was ever enough. He had to push harder, go faster, catch more air. Even if the trophy never came with it all. He'd made plenty of money over the years. At this point, he was in it for the love of the waves and for the pride of the wins. "You've got ten minutes, Avalon," he warned her. His gaze was fixed on the whitecaps. Burning down the left, they made a nice front he could slice down.

"Take your shirt off, then."

"What?" He jerked his gaze back toward her. "Why?"

She wasn't even looking at him. At the beach grass that lined the far edge of the beach, she knelt next to her kit, switching out lenses. "Beefcake shots."

"No way," he said automatically.

It wasn't that he'd never taken shirtless pics before. They kind of went with the territory of being a beach sports star. But . . .

Well, to be honest, he'd never taken them with a woman he was banging on a regular basis. It almost felt like it had a tawdry kind of edge, taking borderline appropriate pictures.

"C'mon," she said. Her tone had gone cajoling, her eyes wide. "No biggie, right? Don't tell me big and mean Tanner Wright has a problem taking his shirt off."

With a mental shake at his own momentary stupidity, he yanked the silky rashguard up over his head and tossed it on the sand behind him.

"Oh yeah," she breathed. She lifted the camera in front of her face, but not before he got a good look at her wide pupils and the bright pink rolling over her cheeks. She was completely affected.

He laughed, looking off at the pier. Scrubbing his hand over the back of his head didn't break the spell.

And it really didn't help when she said, "There. Don't move. Hold that a minute more and . . . Yes. Perfect."

He'd heard that breathy tone before. The last time he'd been cock-deep inside her, the sheer perfection of her hold on him making him lose every shred of his control. She'd taken him away by pure enthusiasm.

He almost wished she'd go back to that businesslike tone.

At least then he'd know which version of Avalon he was dealing with.

"Well, well, well," purred a male voice.

Mako stood behind him, a board under one arm. The man's skin was dark, with a whiskey gold tone to it, attesting to his mother's origins. But that mouth was all Hank Wright and it made Tanner want to plant a fist right in it. Especially when he smiled with smarmy intent, then flicked a gaze at Avalon.

"It does seem like this is a small world." Mako's hair was jet-black in direct contrast to Tanner's and Sage's golden tones. "I do promise I'm not a stalker . . . *brother.*"

The very word sent such strange, mixed emotions

through Tanner. He wouldn't have minded the idea of a brother—especially one who surfed. But Mako's very existence had become bound up in nasty run-ins with his dad.

No grown man liked to beg his father. Yet that's what Tanner had done, asking him to please, please, fucking put it all in the open. Hank had refused, leaving Tanner to deal with this wreckage after his death.

Some fucking surf god Hank Wright had proven to be.

Weariness suddenly sucked the power right out of his bones, draining into the sand. The years had put too much weight on his shoulders and he probably ought to get rid of it before the Pro. Or he'd be fucked.

Avalon edged nearer to him, but not quite enough to touch. That was a damned shame. He needed her reassurance for some reason. "Haven't you done enough?"

Mako let the tail end of his board droop toward the sand. A green-and-yellow fish, the thing looked like it'd be *almost* too short for the tall, slender man. But if he could get it to work, the thing would carve like nothing else. He shrugged. "With the way our father left my mother dangling for years and years . . . No. Probably not."

"I assume it'd be too much to ask you to withdraw your statements. They'll pull the article if you said you didn't want to talk." Tanner knew a few people at *SURFING*. Not enough to get it yanked entirely, because some old-school journalists worked there. But enough that maybe if Mako said he didn't want the publicity, either, they'd at least soften the angle.

"Not likely. Plus I thought you should know I'm considering buying Wright Break."

"Like fucking hell." He hadn't even *wanted* the place, but that didn't mean he wanted Mako to take it, either.

His hands fisted. Goddamn it, he'd take his toys and go home and, yes, he knew exactly how fucking absurd that sounded. He didn't give a shit.

He snatched up his board, pivoting on one foot. The days of fistfights were long behind him.

So close to the World Championships, he couldn't afford the bad publicity. But he'd be damned if he was going to stay around for the antagonism, either.

Mako's voice drifted over the sand toward him. "Guess this isn't the best time for me to be surfing this break."

Tanner flipped the bird over his shoulder. Bullshit. He didn't need this kind of stress right before the Pro.

The cool water came up to his chest before he realized Avalon wasn't behind him. A look back up the beach showed her bending over her camera case. Of course she couldn't leave that expensive equipment behind. He wouldn't want her to, anyway.

What he didn't dig in the least fucking bit was that Mako still stood over her.

Tanner's ears roared and it wasn't all the crashing waves so much as his furious blood pumping in his veins, blocking out any semblance of rational thought.

So he did what he'd always done. Paddled out, dove through the break. Let the ocean slam down over his head and drive out all other thought beyond purity. Peace.

There were three other surfers bobbing in the lineup, but they all nodded to him with the genial laid-back chill of stereotypical surfers. He sometimes envied people who could surf like that, for the perfection of each individual wave. Who didn't have to push themselves to fucking win and take and be on top.

That all came from his father, anyway. Hank thought

nothing was worth doing if it wasn't done to win. He might've worn tie-dyed shirts and kept his hair long, but underneath had sliced the soul of a diving, cruel hawk. Who'd had Tanner in his sights most of his life.

The first years of his coaching had been solid and nice, until Hank realized that Tanner had world-class potential. When he'd made the world circuit, he'd been told he should have made it the year earlier. When he'd won his first championship, it should have been done with more flair. A fatter lead. The first sponsorships hadn't been nearly big enough.

Fuck that noise.

Tanner caught wave after wave, waiting only now and then to give the other, older men on the water a chance. But if he had to be honest, once or twice he snaked waves right out from other surfers. Pretended like he didn't see them poised for takeoff.

And when he sliced a pretty turn, then caught air and did a motherfucking Superman move, letting go of the board in the air, then grabbing on again, he knew it was the right choice. None of them would have hit anything half as hard.

Feeling plenty smug and not a little worn-out, he was able to smile when he saw Avalon swim out to his position. Her camera was wrapped securely by the strap around her wrist, housed in a plastic waterproof housing.

He grinned. "Don't suppose you caught that one?"

"Actually, I did." Her grin was almost as wide. "Should be a nice one."

She gently paddled, floating next to the board he straddled. The water made her hair cling to her scalp and her ponytail was almost invisible with the way it had plastered to the back of her head. But she was still the most beautiful girl he'd seen in an unbelievably long time.

He leaned down to kiss her. A fast one, but she pulled away even more quickly. Her gaze slid to the left, where only one of the other surfers looked back at her. "Not in public."

Every bit of annoyance came crashing back. The soles of his feet tingled and his back curved down into a calculated angle. "You didn't mind kissing me on the pier."

"That was different." She slicked her tongue across her bottom lip, visibly searching for the words. "It was public, but it wasn't. No one from our world around."

"Fine. Never been someone's dirty little secret before. We'll have to see if there's some kind of bonus that goes along with it. Maybe a little head. Haven't gotten any of that yet."

A cold splash of water landed right in his eyes. "Shut the fuck up, Tanner. You don't get to be an asshole to me."

He showed his teeth in a near approximation of a smile. "So, tell me, Avalon. What was Mako saying to you?"

Chapter 26

The lie had been almost instinctual. Tanner had asked what Mako wanted, and she'd meant to answer, but when she opened her mouth, lies had poured out.

By that afternoon, she was pretty much a wreck.

That she wasn't a wreck immediately after she'd lied didn't sit well with her, either. She'd kinda thought that Sage and Eileen had turned her into a better person than that. Yeah, her mom had instilled the value of a well-placed distraction, but Eileen had abhorred liars. She always said they weren't being true to themselves.

Well, she was pretty much right, wasn't she?

But it didn't really matter, not in the bigger scheme of things.

She'd tell Tanner later. He hadn't been in the place to hear anything like that at the moment. It had been obvious he'd been barely holding on to his cool.

And seeing Tanner shaken up wasn't right. It was proof how desperately the whole family needed some help from her.

She wasn't going to pretend she was a disinterested negotiator, not by a long shot. She loved the Wrights way too much for that. But she did have at least a little extra distance.

So she agreed to meet Mako that afternoon. When she knew Tanner would be in a meeting with WavePro.

The deception was making her sick to her stomach. Even walking along San Sebastian's streets during the midafternoon siesta lull wasn't enough to break through her tension.

At the back door to Wright Break, she turned in. Sage's music blared with heavy guitar riffs. White dust flew through the air, the only snow this place would see for years and years.

But it wasn't really snow. It was foam sanded off the polyurethane blanks used for the boards.

"Hey, Sage," Avalon yelled, her hands cupped around her mouth to amplify the sound.

But the blonde still didn't hear her. She had respiratory gear covering the bottom half of her face, and protective glasses, because God only knew what Eileen would do if she came back here and her only daughter wasn't protecting her health. But the wrinkles of concentration on Sage's forehead were pretty obvious.

Avalon yelled her name again.

This time, she must have heard. Her head came up. But getting everything set in order to have a conversation was a bit more complicated and one of the reasons why she really tried to never bother Sage at work.

Avalon knew the disasters that could come of interrupted creativity.

She thumbed off the power sander, then tugged her mask down. The sander went down on the white foam blank that would eventually become a surfboard. Then the goggles slid up over her ponytail. Worry creased the corners of her eyes. "Everything okay?"

Avalon smiled. Her hand curled around the strap of her camera bag, strung across her chest. "No one's dying, if that's what you mean."

Sage rolled her eyes. "Once. I throw a diva fit exactly once and no one ever lets me live it down."

"Why should we?" Avalon slipped her bag off and set it down next to Sage's drafting board. On the floor, though. There was no chance of finding room among Sage's normal clutter and disarray. Post-it notes scribbled with fin designs, cutout pictures of waves—none taken by Avalon, she was quick to note—diagrams of board cross-sections. None of it made sense to Avalon, but all of it worked for Sage.

Pretty well, in fact.

Sage had already made a name for herself as a maker of crisp boards that slid over the water with the efficiency of skim boards and the maneuverability of fish. But the extra little kick and grip was all her own. Surfers could simply *move* on one of Sage's boards and they were willing to pay well for the privilege. Tanner regularly riding Sage's boards didn't hurt, but she'd kept her operation artisan-level small.

Reaching into the half-sized fridge she kept in the corner, Sage pulled out two waters and waggled one in Avalon's direction. She nodded, then caught the bottle in the air when Sage tossed it.

"Out back?" There was a worn silver picnic table kept out there for breaks for both the store and Sage's shop.

Sage nodded. "Sure."

Avalon hopped on the top surface of the table, her

feet on the bench. She leaned her arms on her knees and curled down into herself. Almost as if to underscore Avalon's failure to find her calm center, Sage stretched out. She planted her ass on the bench, hitched her elbows backward onto the tabletop and cranked her incredibly long legs forward.

The table under Avalon had sucked up the warmth of a hundred suns, and gave back in a steady comfort. She'd always liked it back here, even though it was mostly a tiny courtyard of stucco walls. It was clean and quiet. Eileen wouldn't have it any other way.

Sage cracked her bottle of water open and drank a third of it in one swig. Avalon sipped at hers.

The weird tension gripping her limbs wasn't going away. But then, she didn't know why she'd expect any different. Sage could ride out silence without worry; she'd always had that gift. She let go and took what was coming.

Sometimes it drove Avalon batshit crazy. Sometimes she wanted to be like her.

The tiny plastic top of her own water snapped open with a twist as she fidgeted with it. She bounced her heels on the bench.

Sage swatted at her calf. "Quit that."

"Sorry."

But Sage didn't take the opportunity to open conversation. Of course. Any other woman would have been curious why Avalon said she needed to talk.

So she'd have to start the conversation herself.

Fuck, she hated this.

She swallowed down the anxiety, willing her heart to beat calmer. It didn't work. "Where will you move your shop if your mom sells Wright Break?"

Sage shrugged. She still had white dust clinging to her

sweaty shoulders and thin-strapped tank top. "There's a place down on Seventeenth that I was looking at yesterday. It's got good light, excellent ventilation."

Avalon couldn't help but gasp. It felt as sharp and hurtful as betrayal and it didn't make one speck of difference that it wasn't logical. This whole situation was leaving her flipped upside down. Even the fact that she'd been stupid enough to agree to meet with Mako made her sick to her stomach. But he'd hinted there'd be possible consequences if she didn't. Sudden tears burned at the back of her eyes. She forced her gaze down to her knees. "You're going to give up?"

A thick wash of confusion twisted Sage's clear features. "Give up? What?"

"Your mom can't close this place. She's not old enough to retire. What will she do?"

Sage smiled. "China, apparently."

"What?"

"She said last night—when you were out, *again*, mind you"—Sage waved the bottle of water at Avalon in mock chiding, a disappointed schoolmarm look on her face—"that she's always wanted to go to China."

"No way. She's never said that before." A dull shock went through Avalon. She set the bottle of water to her side, the better to twist her fingers together.

Sage shrugged. "Apparently she's always felt silly for wanting it. When she traveled so much with Dad, you know? Like she should have been Zen and enjoyed seeing what she did. Lots of places with extensive beaches."

"While she sipped mai tais on the sand. Not such a hard gig."

"Except when it is." Sage hitched her elbows out a few inches, the better to lean back. Her hair brushed against the table, golden strands snagging against rough wood. "Except when you'd rather be drinking . . ." She sat up abruptly. "I don't know. What's something authentically Chinese? Not Panda Express–style?"

Avalon shrugged. "Coca-Cola? I think I heard it's huge over there."

Sage's toes poked Avalon's thigh. "Very, very funny."

"You keep me around for a reason." God only knew it was the truth. Would become more so the truth too, if she could iron out the situation with Mako. Make sure that even if not everyone was *happy* that things were at least improved.

That was kind of her gig, after all.

Her mind tripped a hundred miles an hour. No decisions had been made yet. And there was nothing that said Eileen couldn't both own the store and go to China. People took vacations all the time.

"Has she made up her mind?"

Sage pulled a face. "Of course not. This is a huge thing. And half the time, I think she's still in a fog from . . . the other stuff."

Something sharp and weepy lanced behind Avalon's eyes. The man she'd loved like a father—the man she'd thought better than anyone she'd ever met—had done something horrible.

Even worse than that, he'd kept it up.

One of her brightest memories was standing on the shore with Hank's arm around her shoulders while he explained that everyone made mistakes. But what set good people apart was the willingness to own up to mistakes and make them better.

Not hide them for decades. Not forcing his son to hide for him.

She chewed on the inside of her bottom lip. If she was meeting with Mako this afternoon, she needed all the pieces. To know exactly what she was dealing with. "What about you?"

"Me?"

"Have you thought about buying your mom out of the store?"

Sage shook her head in denial. "Nope. Got enough on my plate."

She was tempted to invite Sage along to the meeting, especially since the other woman had always been better at staying steady. Avalon always felt like she was pinging along at supersonic speed. But Mako had asked to talk to Avalon, saying that he wasn't getting anywhere with anyone else. He'd earned the stonewall treatment, but Avalon knew people like him. Knew the trouble they could get up to. Sometimes the Wright family was too *good* for their own good. They couldn't imagine anything worse than the article that was already on its way out. Thanks to her mom's world, Avalon knew how shady people could get.

And Sage, for all her calm, seemed to feel things on a deeper level. Took them more personally.

Avalon wasn't about to expose her closest friend to more pain than needed. That was half her mission in the family, after all. To be a buffer, to make things *work* in the best possible way.

"What about . . ." She took a deep swallow of water, which chilled her throat but couldn't cool her worry. "Mako. Does your mom want to meet Mako? Have you thought about it?"

"I don't know about Mom." Sage sighed. "Me . . . I think I'll want to get to know him sometime. Eventually, you know? Even if he keeps being an asshole. Better than someone unknown." Her fingers closed around the water bottle, until the plastic crinkled under the pressure.

Sage set the bottle to the side, flashing a weak imitation of her normal smile. When she laced her fingers together, her knuckles popped white, but she drew long, slow breaths. Intentionally, it seemed.

The Wrights were good people. They deserved a good life. And she'd do anything in her power to make it happen. Even if that meant acknowledging another Wright. They'd thank Avalon in the long run if it tempered Mako.

But even if they didn't, it'd be worth it to help them after they'd done so much for her.

She slipped off the table, then brushed off the back of her thighs. Sand clung to everything given the first opportunity. "I'll catch you on the flip side, babe."

Sage pulled her long blond hair out of its ponytail and ran a hand through it, flipping it to one shoulder. "Wait a second. I thought you wanted to talk to me."

Avalon wasn't exactly content, but at least her stomach had quit doing backflips. She already had her answer. "I did." She smiled. She'd always been good at teasing a smile out of Sage. Considered it one of her duties, in a way. The girl was prone to hitting a point at that steady calm where nothing could shake her. "Didn't you notice my mouth moving? Voice coming out?"

"Sure, but mine was running way more." She flashed a devious look from under her lashes. "Tanner. Please tell me you wanted to talk about Tanner."

Avalon shook her head almost frantically, then had to scrape a piece of hair away from the corner of her mouth. "No."

"C'mon," Sage wheedled. "Tell me what's going on."

"I am *so* not talking to you about him."

"Any other guy you would. And it's not like I want details." Sage shuddered. "Not at all. I want to know where you guys are headed."

Looking off at the plain stucco wall, Avalon bit the tip of her tongue. A sharp tingle of pain worked its way up her jaw, but she couldn't seem to center. Nothing ever worked for her. "I'm not sure we're headed anywhere. We're having a good time." She grinned at Sage. "Summer fling. You should try one. When's the last time you got some?"

Sage lifted from her seat in a show of grace that was this side of levitation. "No way. I don't need some."

"Your girl parts are going to wither."

"Then let 'em." She redid her ponytail with a couple quick snaps of a rubber band. "Everyone I have the *time* to know lately is a surfer. And the absolute last thing I need is a surfer."

"Oh, but I need one?"

"Sure." Her eyes lit up. "In fact, you should *marry* him. Oh, that's brilliant. Marry him, let him go off on the circuit and then you'll be my sister for real! I'm a genius."

"Oh, fuck no," Avalon said automatically.

But she didn't want to admit how damned good that idea was starting to sound.

Chapter 27

Tanner really tried not to get a big head about all the bullshit surrounding his surf career. He had skill and determination and he'd been lucky enough to get his start both young and well. For all his faults, Hank Wright had been a pretty damn good surf coach.

But the way the WavePro staff treated him when he walked in the offices could almost convince him he shit rainbows.

As if seeing his own face life-sized on the walls wasn't enough, they ushered him into a fancy boardroom with a black marble-topped table.

The chairs were some miracle of chrome and black webbing that felt really good after the five miles he'd run that morning and the three hours he'd spent on the water when the tide was up. He didn't have time to screw around. The San Sebastian Pro was right around the corner.

After an hour-long meeting, he was pretty much zoned. His manager and his accountant rattled on at length with almost half a dozen reps from WavePro.

Normally he'd be all over a meeting like this. He liked to understand the figures they were working with and what kind of responsibilities his people were signing him up for. But with everything else that was going on in his life, he kind of figured that WavePro was lucky he could still keep his game on the surfing.

Avalon had been up to something. The way her gaze flicked away when he'd asked what she'd been talking to Mako for . . . It had lying written all over it.

If they actually had a future, he'd have made something of it. Not let her duck and weave.

While he couldn't deny they had a relationship anymore—and he wouldn't want to, either—neither of them had discussed any sort of continuation.

Though he didn't want to admit how much that bothered him. There was no reason to think why they couldn't at least give it a shot. If the spread for WavePro did its job on Avalon's behalf, there was every chance she'd soon be traveling the world as a *SURFING* photographer. Or under the employ of one of the bigger sponsors. There was no guarantee she'd follow the circuit, though. She could just as easily focus on the big-wave surfers and stick to the North Shore of Hawaii. Or follow free surfers to less traveled locales.

He thrummed a rhythm on the tabletop, chin propped in his other hand. The real problem was that Avalon had never shown any sign of wanting more than some orgasms from him.

At least he'd made sure they were freaking awesome comes. That should keep her around a little while longer.

Though her propensity to lie to him made him a little bit nervous.

Not much of a relationship foundation, as far as habits went.

He'd have to get the truth out of her.

Maybe he'd fuck it out of her. Get his hands all over that tidy little body, get his cock in her, watch her cheeks go red as she came all over him. He had to curl his hands over his mouth to hide the smile.

Good fucking times.

Pun intended.

"Tanner?" Mike Wolchoky, the brilliant man who made sure that Tanner's money kept growing no matter how many surfboards he bought, waved a pencil in his direction. "Do you approve?"

He scrubbed a hand over the back of his head. A tiny bit of heat burned across his neck. Not embarrassment, though. He'd have to be caught at a lot worse than thinking dirty thoughts about Avalon to admit to being embarrassed.

More like disturbed to not be paying proper attention to the meeting.

He grunted as he shifted in his chair. Thankfully Edwin Timbersand sat to his right. Tanner lifted his eyebrows toward his manager. "Best choice for me?"

Ed nodded, then folded his hands over the files he'd brought along. "By far. Advantageous to WavePro too. We ought to get this locked down."

The faith he had in his manager had always been worth it. Ed would explain everything afterward, once Tanner needed to know.

The man's job was to keep Tanner's head in the water, so he might as well let him work.

Tanner nodded, then spread his hands flat across the glossy surface of the table and levered up. "In that case, I'm going to leave you fine gentlemen to it."

A quick round of farewells ended with Tanner standing alone in the foyer. He shoved his fists in his pockets while wondering where he needed to go.

What he wanted was an easy call: to see Avalon. Make her smile, make her laugh and relax. Then make her come, so her lips would part on a gasp in that special way they did.

But then, Avalon had lied to him. So his first stop would be figuring that tangled mess out.

And that didn't sound near as good as making her come.

A tiny, pretty blonde sat behind the receptionist's desk. She smiled at him even as her chest managed to raise another inch. Amazing, considering how far silicone had already artificially lifted 'em.

There was no way the girl surfed, not like Avalon.

She gestured back over her shoulder. "Don't forget about the goodie room."

As if he were some wet-behind-the-ears noob who'd never been to WavePro before. But he only nodded. "Thanks."

Might as well do with a stop, anyway.

The size of a small office, the room was packed with shelves and Tupperware bins stocked with every goodie WavePro had ever made. And some, Tanner realized as he picked up a key chain/beer koozie combo, that had been made purely for promotion. Usually giveaways at the pro events.

Tanner wasn't the only person in there, either.

A skinny-necked teenager crouched in the far corner, digging through a box of grips. Long, floppy brown hair fell in his eyes when he looked up at Tanner. He broke into one of the widest grins Tanner had ever seen as he bounded up.

"Yo, man, I can't believe it's you." The kid was really all mouth, it seemed. If he smiled any bigger, the top of his head might pop off. "I knew there was a shot you'd be here, but I didn't think it was that likely."

Tanner stuck a hand out. The boy shook like a puppy— and he had the lanky, oversized paws of one too. He hadn't fully grown into his body.

"Ethan Bells," he said. "So stoked to meet you."

Tanner couldn't help but laugh. Hell, this was half of why he did it. Because he'd been that bright-eyed, enthusiastic kid once, and more than that, still remembered it as if it were yesterday.

"I think I've heard of you," Tanner said. He had to scan way back in his memory, but it was there. He liked to keep an eye on the up-and-comers. "Junior Pro two years ago?"

"Yep, that was me." There was no way it would have seemed possible, but his grin went even bigger at being acknowledged. "I qualified for next year's world circuit."

"Congrats, man." Tanner leaned one shoulder against the doorjamb. "That's huge, you ought to be proud."

"I totally am. My dad's even more stoked. He's meeting with all the bigwigs and all."

"Your dad your manager?" Tanner remembered those days. His first year on the circuit. Having his dad at his side had felt like the right thing to do. That had been before he'd known the truth.

Ethan nodded. "They sent me down here to, like, get out of the way." But his grin said he didn't mind at all. He flashed a handful of gear. "I was looking for a new set of fins."

"What ride are you gonna be on?"

But when Ethan told him, Tanner shook his head. He

popped open a different box, held up a set of fins that were longer, with less hook at the tip. "No, you need these."

"You think?" The kid had pale eyes, but he squinted a lot. Probably avoiding glasses or contacts since wearing them in the water became awkward. Probably didn't help that his long hair was barely shy of tumbling into his eyes and he was constantly brushing it away. "I saw footage of your air in Indo. You were climbing with the long rakes."

Tanner moved past him and went to a knee next to the trunk. "Nope. I've got three inches and forty pounds on you. You need different stuff."

He paused for a moment, but then shrugged and tossed the grip back in the stack. The boy knelt beside Tanner, eagerly looking to him for advice. "Yeah? You think I can grab like you did?"

"Well, it depends." Tanner rocked back on his heels, knees rising.

"On what?"

"Lot of factors, of course."

That easily, they dropped into the back-and-forth. Ethan would go places—that much was for sure. He had the eager enthusiasm the circuit needed and the willingness to unbend and listen to outside opinions, which were invaluable. But at the same time, he didn't agree blindly. He asked pointed questions about technique that Tanner sure as hell wouldn't have thought to ask at his age.

Tanner liked this part. The little rush from knowing he was giving good guidance. The feeling that he'd done the right thing and let loose a little more knowledge in the world. Good stuff, every bit of it.

They ended up back in the lobby, still talking technique. Ethan had some vids of his surfing on his phone, so Tanner watched them to figure out if the kid was slipping on his back foot.

"No, right there," he said, tapping the screen. "It's actually your shoulders. You're not twisting far enough."

"Yeah, you think?"

He nodded. "Betcha anything. I tell you what, why don't we meet up? After the Pro, though, if that's cool."

Shaggy dark hair wagged as Ethan nodded. "Sure, yeah. Wow, man. I thought all the old guys on the circuit would be rougher on me. Make me earn my place or something."

Tanner winced at the implication he was washed up. In a way, he almost was. If he didn't win the Pro, he'd be in a rough spot. It was entirely the reason Ed had maneuvered WavePro to today's meeting. The money was in the bag. WavePro paid well, and Tanner had invested well. There was no chance he'd ever be hurting financially. But there would be face lost if he didn't put together a World Championship win after being this damn close. His pride would take a beating.

And really, if he was going to be washed up at thirty-one, he might as well put the rest of his time to use.

Coaching was as good a use as any.

Hell, it sounded good. Damned good. A way to be out on the water and help out grommets at the same time.

Maybe he could work with that.

He rubbed a hand across the back of his neck, grinning. "Oh, don't get me wrong. I'm sure there'll be someone who tries to feed you to the sharks. Or snakes wave after wave off you." He shrugged. "But it's never really been my style."

He liked the younger set. The best way to shape the future of surfing was by getting his hands on them.

They traded phone numbers; then Ethan's dad came to collect him and Tanner was left alone in the lobby. He slipped his hands in his pockets and leaned back on his heels.

He'd have that kid blowing so high, he'd be competing with the seagulls for breathing room.

The thought made him smile. Straight on the heels of that came the impulse to tell Avalon. Maybe while he was kissing along her neck.

When he hit that certain spot high on her shoulder, she practically became putty in his hands.

That settled it. There was no way he was letting that girl go, not that damn easily. He'd never been so obsessed with a woman before. He wanted to know every thought in her head.

He'd always loved a challenge.

Chapter 28

Avalon tugged down the hem of her skirt. Futilely. The bright green tissue-paper silk thing would barely cover a sneeze.

But damn did her legs look awesome.

When Tanner held out a hand to assist her from the car, she put her fingers in his. The warmth of his gaze never left her face.

Unlike the two dark-red-jacketed valets who stood at the nearby podium while their buddy dashed around the front of Tanner's car. Their eyes were firmly glued to her legs.

She smoothed down the fabric again, thankful her nerves hadn't yet extended to sweaty palms. The marks would be impossible to get out of the silk.

Tanner squeezed her fingers. "You look gorgeous."

She resisted rolling her eyes, but still tucked her hand under his elbow and aligned her body with his. That part always came easily. "I know I look good." Her profession meant hours and hours of exercise as a matter of course. The rest was just a great haircut and carefully applied makeup. "The question is whether I look appropriate."

For the WavePro meet and greet, she'd have picked a pair of black slacks along with a top that drew minimal attention. After all, she was essentially an employee, as far as she figured. No need to draw extra attention to herself.

But Tanner had said hell no. That she was talent, not employee. That he'd never seen any of the male photographers keeping themselves in corners. More than that, the bigwigs wouldn't want their pictures taken when they were busy getting lit and hitting on surfer chicks.

And then he'd demanded a fashion show. Sprawled over her bed, he'd insisted she show him every possible party outfit she had, which ended with his face hanging off the bed while she stood above him, trying to hold the bedpost to stay upright while he licked her into another huge come.

In the end, her head still swimmy with what he could do to her, she'd given in. Figured he knew what he was talking about.

She'd drawn the line at letting him pick the outfit, though. He'd have wanted the tiny green skirt paired with an equally tiny shirt. Instead she'd worn a high-necked black cotton shirt that draped low in the back, showing off a long, bare expanse. Not a bra in sight.

A fact that Tanner was taking intense interest in. He rested a hand low on her spine, the brush of his thumb over her bare skin sending calming ripples through her.

But at the same time, she couldn't relax. Not too much. There was too much on the line.

She had to impress everyone tonight. Her photos would have to hold their own merit, yes, but this was playing with the big boys. No room for error, no room to come off as the little sister who'd wandered into the big kids' party.

And what a big kids' party it was. The ballroom of the San Sebastian Wave Club—where the rich people in town congregated when there was no land for a golf course—was an absolutely gorgeous place. Tiny white lights twinkled as the primary decoration, matching white flowers their only counterpoint.

She wanted to relax into it all. Have a great time. Let everything go.

But she still hadn't told Tanner about her meeting with Mako. About what Mako threatened.

Her bones felt like lead as they stepped down the tiny stairs that marked the ballroom's entrance. Heads turned to watch Tanner. Of course they did. In black slacks very similar to the ones he'd told her not to wear, paired with a white-on-white-striped shirt, he looked this side of a god. Since she'd watched him get ready, she knew his hair hadn't been styled into that careful-looking tousled mess.

She'd done it. Weaving her fingers through, trying to grab hold of him, while he kissed her into oblivion.

They'd almost been late.

The smile was absolutely irresistible.

Her chin rose an inch to go with it.

"There we go," Tanner's voice purred, right above her ear. If he wasn't careful, everyone was going to know about the two of them.

The question remained whether she'd mind. "What?"

"I thought you might crack from nerves. You've been a wreck all day."

He smiled down at her. The warmth that flowed through her helped her get as close to a calm center as she'd ever thought herself capable.

She didn't even know how to classify what she felt for him. More than a friend, less than forever. Because forever was too painful to try to grab hold of when it never even existed.

The moisture in her mouth dried and fled. Suddenly every tiny worry about impressing the company bosses scattered.

She pushed her lips up into a smile. "You're a good guy, Tanner."

He laughed softly. "Yes. You wanna make something of it?"

"No." She shook her head, ignoring the tiny prick at the back of her eyes. If she didn't give in, the tears didn't count. "Just pointing it out."

"Remember that one for later. I figure it should give me some points." He tugged her around to face the rest of the ballroom. "Now, chin up. The bosses are on the way. Remember, this isn't your opportunity, it's theirs."

Her gaze flashed to him, but it was too late. The Mutt and Jeff pair of bosses walked up, both carrying two glasses of champagne. Mr. Wakowski handed one to Tanner at the same moment Mr. Palmer handed the other to Avalon.

In an absurd flash of amusement, she wondered if they'd practiced the maneuver. She bit down the giggles and took the fluted glass with a tiny murmur of thanks.

Mr. Wakowski grinned, his gray hair actually catching a ray of the light. "Here's to a great year."

"And another upcoming," added Mr. Palmer, though with decidedly less grace than his counterpart. He'd been the one who hadn't wanted Avalon to catch the assignment, so it made sense.

Tanner smiled, but by now Avalon knew him well enough that the whitening of his scar gave him away. Something was wrong.

She wanted to take his hand, but that would be a level too far. She couldn't afford to flaunt their relationship. She wanted her pictures to be able to speak for themselves.

Instead, she flashed a smile at the other two men. "That's a toast I'll always agree to."

Tanner shook off whatever it was that had grabbed him and added in his own smile. He lifted his glass. "To highly productive partnerships."

"Indeed." Mr. Wakowski's cuff links gleamed silver as he downed half his glass. "We at WavePro are thrilled to have you with us another year."

The shorter man's eyes narrowed with a pernicious interest. "Are you sure there's no chance you'll be hitting the circuit again? You've qualified. The opportunity is there."

Tanner rubbed an idle hand over his thigh even as he shook his head. "No, I don't see it."

Avalon paused with her wineglass at her lips. Effervescent bubbles tried to counteract the sudden clench in her chest. Tanner wasn't even going out on the circuit next year? That had never been mentioned.

"No matter, no matter," chimed in Mr. Palmer. The two were reminiscent of a fast-patter comedy act. "At least WavePro has the opportunity to be in on your new venture."

Tanner waved a hand, slanting a look out of the corner of his eye at Avalon. "If it happens, of course. It's only in the planning stages."

"Still, it'll be great to have you local. San Sebastian could do with a really top-level surf school. The local talent is already top-notch. Polishing can't hurt."

"A surf school?" The words spilled out of her.

Pride made Tanner's shoulders lift. "An idea I had the other day. How I might spend my time after I leave the circuit. And I'll buy out Mom's store, like you wanted. I've already talked to a couple investors, plus Ed's looking into it. Could be a viable idea."

A bright splash of hope made her eyes widen and her lips part. But just as quickly, it was doused with a stronger wave of something Avalon didn't even know how to describe. The absence of hope was an emotion all of its own, wasn't it? Something sickly and tense and living in dark tendrils that wrapped around everything.

Tanner hadn't said a word to her.

Mr. Wakowski nodded along with his partner, absolutely oblivious to what was going on in her head. "Plus, with the high-income communities in proximity, there will be plenty of students who are more leisure based rather than career intensive."

That easily, the pair of them were off on a discussion on the socioeconomic responsibilities of surf companies toward bringing lesser privileged surfers to the beach versus the need to woo those with disposable income.

Avalon's fingers pinched her wineglass. A sick knot churned in her chest, while her heartbeat rushed out of control.

Tanner flashed her a little smile, inviting her to laugh with him about being left out of the conversation. But when she didn't smile back, confusion clouded his eyes and made him frown.

She managed to endure awhile. An hour or two. She faded in and out when the conversations didn't pertain to her, watching the roll of the waves through the giant westward-facing windows.

Tanner kept darting glances at her. Eventually he must have had enough. Pulling her through open French doors didn't prove difficult. She went as if walking through sea spray, slightly lost and foggy.

The cool breeze coming in off the ocean cooled her overheated cheeks and shook the cobwebs out of her head. She couldn't afford to be ridiculous about this. The family as a whole was her concern.

What she and Tanner had been sharing was like happy bonus land. Not the main game.

By the time she curled her hands around the railing that overlooked the beach, she'd managed to smile. "Who makes a beach club, fences off the beach, and then doesn't even pay attention to it during a party?"

"Very rich people."

Tanner nestled up behind her, the full and solid weight of him at her back a reassurance. He grabbed the fence around her, caging her in, but she didn't feel trapped. She felt relieved. His chin brushed her temple, then his lips. The way he nuzzled her gave her back those tender feelings.

The ones she couldn't indulge. Because he obviously didn't mean them, not the way she wanted him to.

"Are you okay?" His voice sent another whisper of temptation through her.

What she wanted was to turn and bury her face in his chest. Rub her cheek over the warm expanse of his shirt. Instead, she blinked down the burn of tears that threatened and stared at the water. Dark and glimmering at the same time.

At least the ocean never changed. Never went anywhere.

Even if she could never quite capture what the water meant to her in her photographs, she could try forever. Over and over again. Because age didn't matter.

Unlike Tanner.

In the past week, he'd made plans. Big plans. Ones that apparently didn't include her at all, even though she'd been the one to suggest he take over his mom's shop.

Sure, she'd meant continuing retail, but it's not like she'd have been totally closed to other possibilities. Not so long as the Wright name stayed stamped over the door.

By the time she twisted inside the gentle trap of his arms, she'd managed to push it all away. If now was all they had, then she'd make sure it was memorable.

He might be able to put her away, but she wasn't going to let him do it as easily as Matthew had dropped her. She wasn't going quietly.

She trailed her nails over his shirtfront. "I'm fine. Why would you think otherwise?"

"Back there. About the school idea . . ." He cupped her shoulders, his big hands shoring her up. "It's still exactly that. An idea."

"You already went to WavePro."

"I had the idea while I was there, that's all. Bullshitted it out with a few of them during contract negotiations."

She pushed up on her toes. Kissed him, softly. There was one way to make sure a man's mouth didn't run anymore. And she didn't think she could listen to any more of this without her heart breaking.

Which said really, truly scary things about the state of her heart.

So she kissed him harder. She shouldn't have, considering the doors right behind them, and how they could be spotted at any moment, but she couldn't resist him. Not when she didn't have any other choices at the moment. She swept her tongue into his mouth, taking all she could. All he was willing to give.

Because she'd wanted him too hard and too long to give up now.

Chapter 29

The way Avalon kissed him made the blood in his veins perk up. As well as his cock. He kept his hands locked over the caps of her shoulders by pure will, and the reminder that there was an entire party behind them. Music and voices and the plenty of oh so sophisticated laughs poured out through the open doors.

But Tanner's world had become only the soft plushness of Avalon's bottom lip. The way her breasts brushed against his chest.

The tiny, softly pleading sound she made when he pulled his mouth away.

He kept his hands on her shoulders, more for the chance to keep touching her than anything else. But she was straining toward him still, a tiny bit, with her chin tipping up and her eyes half-lidded. Enough to puff his ego higher than the Rockies.

"Look, I'm sorry I didn't tell you." He wanted to make sure she understood that. "It was a timing thing. I didn't think it was a big deal."

Not to mention that after ten years pretty much on his

own, he'd gotten out of the habit of consulting others about every little detail.

"It's not." She smiled, her cheeks going round. But the skin at the corners of her eyes wouldn't quite relax. The touch he soothed over her temple did nothing, either. "It's your business. I wouldn't dream of intervening."

Now he knew something was really wrong. Avalon was a meddler, born and bred. Years of Sage's stories backed that up.

But before he had a chance to pick that apart, she'd come up on her toes and wound her forearms around the back of his neck. Forceful as she took his mouth again.

Fuck, she was like a drug. One he was rapidly becoming dependent on. He framed her face and pushed her back a bare inch. "Not here, Avalon. We can't do this here."

Her gaze flicked over his face. Each glance was like a touch and as evocative. Her lips were glossy. "Where?"

There was an entire party of people behind him. And he couldn't give a shit for any of them. "Down the rocks, to the water."

She looked left and right, then laughed when she spotted the gate. "Escape. Blessed escape."

Escape was ridiculous, since they'd been at the party barely two hours, but there they went. Hand in hand through the metal gate, then down the rock-strewn path. In this portion of San Sebastian to the north, the beaches were ringed with low cliffs and the shoreline scalloped into small coves.

When they hit the sand, Avalon took her heels off, grabbing onto Tanner's arm for balance as she wiggled and bent. The look she flicked from under her fringe of bangs said she knew exactly what she was doing to him.

Then she wandered off ahead of him, shoes dangling from her fingers. Her ass twitched as her hips swayed.

He pushed his hands in his pockets, the better to not get grabby. If she wanted to tease, who was he to stop her? "You know, that thing deserves a medal."

She looked back over her shoulder, but didn't stop. The quirk of her lips carried everything mysterious. He wished the dark didn't obscure the dark green of her eyes. "What's that?"

"Your skirt."

"A medal?" She laughed, a single huff of humor. But it didn't sound as husky as her normal laugh.

He nodded, then captured her hips from behind. She gave a little shimmy. Something had certainly gotten into her. But at the same time, it was like she rode on the surface.

"Yup." He rubbed his cheek over hers, the silk of her hair brushing his temple. She felt amazing, anywhere he touched her. Always did. "For valiantly maintaining its position in the face of such extreme fabric shortages."

Finally, she laughed for real, tossing her head back and offering her gifts like a pagan's gifts to the gods. "That doesn't sound much like a complaint to me."

He skimmed his hands over the back of her leg, up the gentle curve of her ass. "Not at all. I wouldn't even think of it. In fact, if your skirt would like to retire for the rest of the night, I wouldn't mind that, either."

She laughed again, this time a little more quietly. But there was still something dark about her expression.

Around the curve of some rocks, she darted out of his hands. Arms out, she spun with her face toward the darkened sky. The half moon couldn't do justice to her beauty, though it sure tried. The shadows lengthened and draped.

Tanner had never really been one to look away from the ocean, but this time he couldn't help himself. The landscape of the tiny cove made the space their own world. Steep-sided cliffs with tiny scraps of green clinging to them hid them and protected them from outsiders. Hard-packed, damp sand indicated that at high tide this entire place would be underwater. But for now it was a couple sticks of driftwood tucked at the base of the rocks.

And Tanner and Avalon. Together.

She tossed her shoes to land at the base of one of the jagged rocks, then turned back to him. The crook of her finger was a siren call that he didn't mind answering. Breaking open on her rocks didn't sound so awful.

But when he stepped to her, caught her hips again, she waggled the finger at him. "Uh-uh. I've got a plan."

She'd pinned her hair up for the party, in one of those supercomplicated girl styles that took almost an hour to do but made her look like she'd been freshly fucked. Dark strands framed the angles of her cheeks. He hooked one with a finger and stroked it back. "Do these plans bode well for me?"

"Of course they do." Her hands skimmed over his torso, quick flashes of promise. They hooked his belt, her eyebrows rising in one of those unmistakable signals.

Her smile became everything wicked, but he couldn't shake the feeling that they were skimming over the surface. She hadn't moved an inch, but it was almost as if some frantic buzzing zinged under her skin. It was as if she'd fly into motion at any moment.

Normally, he liked her energy. Loved it, even. But this felt off. Strange. The manic glint in her eyes could sink them both.

He cupped his hands around her face. The delicacy of her bones was distracting sometimes, an unwelcome reminder that she was surprisingly fragile. He could hurt her if he wasn't careful.

But that was absurd. If anything, she'd been the one more firm about holding to their expectations. That this was nothing but fun.

Still, he couldn't stop his mouth. "You don't have to do this. We don't have to."

The second he said it, he could almost kick himself. Because really, what normal-in-the-head red-blooded man turned down a blow job—and he hoped like hell that was where this was going. But he didn't want it from some weird place or some . . . odd sense of daring.

He wanted Avalon. That was all it came down to.

He wanted more time with her. More opportunities to figure out what was going on in her head.

She laughed a little bit, her teeth flashing white in the dim light of the moon. Her head tilted. "We don't have to what?"

He opened his mouth, but then shut it again as quickly. Looked past her head to focus on a tiny bush clinging to the rocks fifteen feet up the cliff. Then he looked back down at Avalon. Her eyes were huge, and they seemed to be asking him for something that he didn't quite understand.

The skin over her bare upper arms was softer than down. He couldn't stop touching her, it seemed. "I'm sorry I didn't tell you about my school idea."

Whatever she'd been looking for, that was the wrong answer. Her lips pulled up into a smile again. A false, plastic smile. "It's okay," she said. He didn't believe her. "It's not a big deal, really."

She stepped even closer, into his space and breath. So close they were almost one. She rose on her bare toes, until she skimmed over his chest. Her lips brushed over his jaw. "More than that . . . I don't want to talk about it anymore."

He didn't know how to explain the tumult that had him so confused at the edges, so he let it go. Felt the mixed-up words tumble through his head . . . then opened his mind and let them fly away. His worries piled up one on top of the other. He had her for now. That would have to do.

Their kisses were always intoxicating and gave him an extra rush, like floating a barrel twice. The extra bonus no one had expected.

He figured it was her enthusiasm, which was out in spades tonight. Her grip wound through his hair, only to change directions. He sucked in a deep breath when her touch dove down again. Straight for his cock. The pressure was dulled through his slacks.

She ended the kiss only to skate her lips over his neck. "Someone wakes up quick."

"Vitamins." He swallowed the hard rock that had wedged in his throat and looked up toward the top of the cliffs. Nothing. No one watching.

For now.

A hard shudder worked through him and only got worse when her wicked little fingers went to work on his fly. Two seconds later, warm sultry air brushed over his exposed shaft . . . and her fingers wound around him. Hot brands of intent.

His fists locked at the base of her spine. He wanted to grab and take and snatch.

But she'd do this all on her own if she wanted to.

Like the siren she'd seemed a few moments ago, she sank out of his grip with eternal grace. Her bare knees went to the sand and she looked up at him with a mischievous smile. The curve of her cheek had always seemed innocent to him, a reminder that no matter what they did together, she was still a good girl at heart.

Until she rubbed the head of his cock against that curve.

He bit the inside of his cheek as a hard jolt of lust went through him. Jesus, she looked dirty. Kneeling in front of him, all perfectly styled and beautiful . . . but ready to suck him off.

The first flicks of her tongue over his head were almost enough to undo him. A hot rock of pleasure jolted down his spine to lodge behind his balls. He'd give up anything for her, for this moment, if she only realized.

But she didn't know. She glanced up at him again as she opened her lips over the tip. Wet and heat had his heart thumping into a ridiculously fast rhythm. The power she had over him at that moment could have levered the world into a different orbit.

She sucked him deeper. Laved over his whole length. The tips of her fingers played low on his body, adding in an extra thump of pleasure he hadn't expected.

She knew exactly what she was doing. The looks she aimed up at him were half laughing at him, her eyes glimmering. He didn't care. She could laugh at him forever if she kept making him feel that way. Like his body was going to flip inside out. He wasn't even sure what she was doing, some flickering action of her tongue over the underside of his cock, but then she did it again.

And Christ, he was going to lose it. Soon. The bone-stomping rush had started in his spine and was promptly sweeping over every bit of him. His orgasm gathered. Grew imminent.

He wrapped his hands around the curve of her neck, the angle of her jaw. Her cheeks had hollowed with filthy intent. He tugged, which was about as close as he could make himself come to giving up watching her swallow him down. She wouldn't be put off her prize. Even as she shook her head, making his shaft rub over the tender roof of her mouth, she took him deeper.

He brushed across the back of her throat and goddamn, but that was all he needed. Let go. The orgasm tingled down his cock in a hot rush and he'd be damned if she didn't take every bit.

She eased back on her heels, delicately wiping at the corner of her mouth. "Now, that," she said around a bit of a happy sigh, "is how to wrap up a party."

Chapter 30

By the next morning, Avalon had almost managed to convince herself that it didn't matter that Tanner had failed to include her in his plans.

She'd also almost made it out the front door when a creaking stair made her look back over her shoulder. She smiled weakly. "Hi."

Tanner stood at the top of the stairwell. Wearing only a pair of boxer briefs that clung to his narrow hips, he looked delicious. He had his arms crossed over his wide chest, and it only made him seem bigger. More impressive, with the way it bulked up his shoulders and made his biceps stand out in lovely relief. He lifted an eyebrow. "Going somewhere?"

She leaned backward against the door. She only had her tiny clutch purse, which wasn't great for fidgeting with. Her trusty camera bag was at home since the party last night had been a nonpress event. Even if she had been hired by WavePro.

Which meant that coming back to Tanner's place last night had been all booty call.

She'd never been one to feel shameful about sex, but

something sickly and chilling wove through her guts. She flattened her hands against the cool wood behind her and made herself shrug. "Home."

He smiled. The hand he held out was big and strong and she wanted to feel it on her. So she held still. "The sun's barely up."

True. A skinny window next to the front door didn't have much hope of lighting up the room at this hour, not when the sun was still struggling to get its head up over the houses across the street. The foyer was shadowy, the light of the sun only sending a couple tiny tendrils of yellow across the tiles.

It only made it more apparent that she shouldn't be there. She had no purpose. Nothing she was doing there, beyond putting out. Without her cameras, she was no one. Not to Tanner, at least.

Not the way it was rapidly becoming apparent she *wanted* to be someone to him. Someone special.

Because he was special to her.

She made herself smile and hoped the dim dawn light didn't give away the tiny prickle of tears in her eyes. "Don't you have somewhere to be soon?"

He leaned a nearly bare hip against the railing, then ran a hand through his hair with a sigh. "I'm meeting my trainer in an hour."

"I thought so." She wanted to go to him so badly, it was an ache inside her chest. Wanted to bury her face against that wide expanse of chest and let her tears go. Let everything go.

But it had become increasingly apparent that wasn't what he was in for.

She'd known this would happen. Somewhere during the last few weeks, she'd lost her heart. Dropped tiny pieces of it into his hands, bit by bit. Until she had nothing left for herself.

Her breathing was shallow, rapid. A wispy darkness licked at the outside edges of her brain and she tried to make herself calm. Focus. Find that Zen place she'd always been seeking.

She failed miserably. Of course.

Her insides were as tumbled as her mind. "See?" she said, carefully modulating her voice. The fierce rush of pride that she managed to keep the tears away almost drove off the fear that somewhere she'd fallen in love. "It's best that I go. I have to go get my cameras." She ran a hand down the side of her tiny skirt. "And get changed."

"You've got clothes here."

She did. When the hell had that happened? So gradually, she'd lost sight of what she was bringing to their half-assed relationship. It had been easier to keep stuff here than explain why she was making six a.m. walk-of-shames into the house she shared with Tanner's sister. And mother.

God, what had she done?

Her heart tried to kick its way into her throat. She'd lost her mind. That was the only possible option.

Because holy Jesus and the seven sacraments, she had to be freaking *nuts* to get herself in this situation. In love with a man who didn't love her back. Whom she'd have to see again and again for the rest of her life. Because his sister was her best friend and his mother was her biggest source of support and love. Have to see his face in theirs over and over again. Never get away from him.

Her fingernails curled into the tender meat of her

palms, sending a short spike of pain up her forearms. She forced a long, slow breath out. Maybe she wasn't screwed.

The way he was smiling at her certainly went a good distance toward calming her.

On impulse, she darted up the stairs. Her hands went right to the warm skin over his sides, the steady thump of his heart under her fingers spread over his chest.

She kissed him, hard and fast. Taking his mouth was like throwing herself into a huge wave and trusting she'd make it through. Exhilarating. His arms wrapped around her back and she felt as close to steady as she'd been in years. When she ended the kiss, she dropped her forehead to his bare chest. He smelled good, like a little bit of last night's cologne but even more warm male.

She let out a shuddery breath.

His hands rubbed over her back. "You okay?"

Though she didn't look up, she shook her head. "No. Not really."

His touch rose, smoothing down the back of her hair. He nuzzled her temple with his chin. "Is it something I can help with?"

Considering that he was the problem? Not likely. "I'll be fine."

They stood there, wrapped together, for a long moment. Until Avalon felt almost like the version of herself she knew. The one who'd earned her place in the world. She didn't trust extra gifts.

When the back of her eyes didn't feel like they were burning with the pressure to cry, she pulled away. "I'll be back in a little bit."

He looked deep in her eyes for a moment, his hand still wrapped around the back of her neck. The way he studied her, she could almost make herself believe he cared as much as she did. But that was virtually impossible if he didn't even think of her when he was in the middle of life-directing changes.

But then he smiled. That quickly, he was all flash again. The gentle charm that had effortlessly seduced her was also shallow. Changeable. And a little more comforting because she knew it so well.

"I guess that'll have to do," he finally said. He tugged on a lock of her hair. "But if you don't show up, I'll come looking for you."

She smiled. If only she could believe that. "We can't have that. You're too close to the Pro to be screwing around hunting me down."

He winced slightly. "God, don't remind me. There's so much shit to do, still."

She lifted up on her toes, the better to look him in the eye. "You'll be fine." If nothing else, she needed him to believe this. "All you have to do is keep your head in the game and surf the best you're capable of. You'll nail this and you'll take the championship home."

"You make it sound pretty damn easy."

"You forget I've spent the better part of the last month doing nothing but watching you train and surf." Her mouth brushed over his jaw. The tension there could almost be tasted. "You own this. It's already yours."

He laughed, the husky sound comforting her even more. Nothing got her out of her own head more than helping someone else. It was what she did, after all.

His touch ran over her back, reminding her she still wore the backless blouse from the night before. "You're good for me, Avalon. I hope you know that."

That remained to be seen. She brushed another kiss

over the corner of his mouth. From this close, the scar over his lip was more noticeable. She traced it with one finger, half expecting him to pull away from the intimacy. "This was from that reef in Indo?"

He nodded, then licked the tip of her finger. She yanked it back on a giggle.

"Way too shallow a wave to spill out on," he said, brushing off what had by all accounts been a pretty bad wipeout. Eileen had immediately flown out to Indonesia and Tanner had been in the hospital for three days.

He didn't even realize the risks he took. The way he harnessed the ocean's power was everything impressive. Obviously he'd swept away her heart.

She made herself smile again. "I'll be back before your afternoon surf session."

"You better be." He kissed her again, this one long and lingering in exactly the kind of way she couldn't risk. And couldn't turn down, either.

Five minutes later, she was out the door with a gentle swat to her rear. When she turned at the street, she saw him still lingering in the doorway. In his boxers, for all the world to see because he was that self-assured.

And she loved the arrogant ass. She waved as she turned the corner.

God there'd be a mess to deal with later. But for now, she could ignore her feelings. She'd have to, or go nuts. If she was already sunk, she might as well enjoy the swim.

The soft trill of her phone jerked her from the task of busily compartmentalizing her life. She muttered to herself as she dug it out of her purse, figuring Sage had called to check in, but she didn't recognize the number. "Hello?"

"Have you talked with him yet?"

That voice sent a cold frisson of fear over her skin, manifesting in goose bumps. Her feet stumbled to a halt, her ankles wobbling in the high heels. Uselessly, she turned to look behind her. But she was out of sight of Tanner's house and even if she hadn't been, it's not like he'd have been able to hear who was on her phone. "I haven't had a chance."

Mako sighed and it sounded genuinely rueful. "Look, I know it was a lot to ask of you. If you can't handle it, I'll go—"

"No, no," she spluttered, cutting him off. "You don't have to do that. It'll be fine. I'll talk to them. Leave Eileen alone."

"I can't promise that." He'd made that more than clear during their conversation. He was pushing for a meeting with Eileen, and if he didn't get it, there was apparently more trouble he could make. "I bet *SURFING* would be really interested if I called them back and mentioned how the first time my mom met Hank, she was only fifteen."

Avalon shuddered so hard that her stomach cramped. She didn't know if the insinuations Mako made about Hank were true, but no one in the Wright family would want them to go public anyway. "I'll work it out."

She didn't like this. Hadn't liked it when she'd met with Mako and still didn't now. Tanner had so much on his plate and Eileen was still reeling from the discovery that Hank was Mako's father. They needed Avalon to act as intermediary, even if they didn't know what she was doing. "Are you sure it can't wait 'til after the Sebastian Pro? Tanner's got so much on his plate."

"You know what, Avalon?" Mako's voice zipped over the line with perfect clarity, as if he were talking right in her ear. "I was never Hank Wright's little bitch and I'm not going to be Tanner's, either. I'm meeting Sage and Eileen one way or the other *and* I've got a flight out the morning of the Pro. I'll leave this one up to you. Call me when you think he can handle it."

The line went flat as he hung up.

Avalon blindly shoved her phone in her black clutch purse.

So yeah. This had become one giant clusterfuck. Somewhere she'd gone from the Wright family's protector to the one who'd have to derail Tanner before his big moment.

It would be worse than saying *I love you*.

Chapter 31

Two days left. Tanner could feel the weight of the up-coming Sebastian Pro like a two-by-four to the back of the neck. All his tension clenched down there in a heavy throb that he couldn't shake.

The surf was thumping, big, heavy six-footers that would provide plenty of rail time and let him get his fins in the air. But he'd already spent four hours out there in the morning and then another hour at the gym after lunch. Tanner swirled the thick mass of protein shake in his iced glass. There was such a thing as getting too over-worked before a big competition and he couldn't put himself at risk of that.

Sitting on his balcony, feet up on the railing as he watched the surf, probably wasn't helping. His head might still if he found some way to disconnect, but he couldn't help but think that wasn't what he needed.

So he studied the waves. The curl, the fronts. Looking for the pattern that would sink the championship or win it. The second and fourth waves out of each five-wave set were the best. For today. He'd keep scoping until the morning of the competition.

Hell, if he were honest with himself, he'd keep scoping until the moment he had to report in, pretty much.

Just the way he was built.

Nothing could be taken for granted in the face of the water's strength.

The sliding glass door behind him wooshed open. Tanner craned his head backward to peer at Avalon. From the sort of backward, sort of upside-down angle, she still looked cranky. Her mouth had pulled down into a frown and her green eyes looked even smokier and darker than usual.

"Well?" he asked. She'd had an important conference call with the WavePro marketing, public relations, and creative directors.

She sighed and leaned back against the glass door, sliding her hands behind her ass along with her iPad, as if she were unconsciously trying to hide it. He tried not to notice the way the position pushed out her tits or made her stomach one sleek curve that he wanted to lick. Nope. No way. She was obviously having a moment and to notice such things would make him a shithead.

And he'd realized the night of the WavePro party that he didn't want to be a shithead. Not to her. He generally avoided the designation, but he wanted to go the extra mile with Avalon.

"It went fine," she eventually said. Or lied, probably. She squinted into the afternoon sun, looking at the water. Supposedly. If she were actually taking in anything, he'd eat his sunglasses.

The drooping line of her shoulders said it hadn't gone the way she'd expected, at the very least.

Tanner set down his shake, then stretched his arms behind his head. He could hook the loops of her tiny jean shorts with the tips of his fingers. One tug, two, brought her reluctantly forward, until her belly ran into the top of his head.

"Tell me."

She leaned over to put her iPad on the table next to his protein shake. Her fingers combed through the sides of his hair. She dredged up a weak imitation of her usual smile. "You like the view."

He made an exaggerated examination of her face. There was certainly nothing to complain about. Up the long stretch of her smooth stomach, to her breasts, then her beautiful face bent down to smirk at him.

"I do. I certainly do." But it was obvious she needed more than goofy. So he pulled her around to the side of his chair, then down into his lap.

"Oh, c'mon. It's over ninety degrees, the sweat'll glue us together."

She pushed at his chest, as if she'd get up, but he wrapped his arms around her hips. And she wasn't protesting that hard, not really. Avalon spent hours in the water, daily. She could put a lot more oomph into wiggling out if she wanted.

Instead she gave another sigh and leaned back against his chest. One long leg dangled over the arm of the chair still, but the other rested across his thigh. Her ponytail trailed across his bare chest in a silky swish.

All in all . . . right. Avalon was exactly where she belonged.

Everything in its place. A warm feeling that had nothing to do with the afternoon sun melted Tanner from the inside out.

He spread one hand flat across her bare stomach. The

muscles under there were still slightly tense, as if she couldn't quite relax. "Now spill it."

"They said everything was fine." Her voice was quiet, but this close he couldn't help but absorb every nuance. He wouldn't want to miss a thing anyway. "Every picture I sent them was useable and good. The spread in *SURF-ING* will be five pages, with at least one double-page included."

"That all sounds awesome." But the muscles under his fingers still hadn't eased. He kneaded lightly, stroking down her skin. She was gorgeous, every inch of her. But she was about as tense as a newly strung guitar.

"It is."

He slipped his fingers under the line of her jaw and tipped her face up, forcing her to look at him. "If you don't tell me what's wrong, I'll be forced to take drastic measures."

Her mouth finally started to slip out of the smile. "Oh? What would that be?"

"I'll have to fuck it out of you."

She laughed, giving an extra little wiggle of her ass. "In the first place, crude much? And second, I don't think that's much of a threat."

"Why Ms. Knox, are you implying you like the dirty things I do to you?"

Her eyes drifted shut and she made a humming noise in the back of her throat. The slinky move of her arms up over his shoulders rubbed her ass across his lap. "Like? No. Love? Oh hell yeah."

There had been occasions where the word *love* had struck fear in Tanner's stomach. Once or twice it might have even sent him running in the opposite direction.

Maybe not the best thing to admit, but he'd always been on the up-and-up with the women he got involved in. Never went in without letting them know he wasn't looking for anything permanent. Not yet.

Not then.

But with Avalon sitting in his lap, he certainly wasn't going anywhere, now was he? "You're not getting up until you tell me. So you might as well give in."

She sighed. "You're kinda stubborn under all that laid-back charm, aren't you?"

He laughed a little bit. "Um, yeah. World Championships don't come free."

"No, that's not what I meant." She kept her face trained carefully toward the view. It almost felt like she was avoiding looking up at him. But it gave him the freedom to drink in her fine features and the roundness of her cheeks and her snubbed nose. "People. You don't give them up. Your opinion of someone can be hard to shift."

Under her words was something he couldn't read. Something he wasn't getting. "Is that good or bad?"

"Both?" She almost seemed to shake it off. The grin she flashed up at him was entirely cheeky. "Depends what you think of me."

"I think you need to talk."

She rolled her eyes. "It wasn't the more I hoped for."

"The more?"

"The spark was missing. Everything was fine, but no more. No one was totally in love with my pictures." She sighed. Her fingers fiddled with the hem of his shorts and though her gaze had dropped, she wasn't really seeing him. "It's greedy, isn't it?"

"What is?"

"I've got everything. What I said I wanted—a spread in a major surf magazine. A huge campaign's going to be run off my shots. But I still want more."

Something within Tanner stilled and coiled. Leashed energy waiting for the word *go* or a wave before cresting. He'd been bulling his way through life, but all of a sudden, he pulled up short. Ready to wait if needed. The hand he stroked over Avalon's hair trembled the tiniest bit. No one would ever know, not even her, but he noticed. He felt it. "What is it you want?"

The moment hovered. Three waves crashed into shore in the meantime. Finally, she sighed. "Everything. But I've got no freaking clue how to explain it."

"Try."

"I want to make people care about my photos. Not because they're contracted and perfectly decent and show a killer sweep through a barrel. Though they do." She patted his thigh and looked up. "You look awesome."

"Not the concern right now, but I'm glad to hear that," he said, lifting an eyebrow.

"You know what I mean."

"I think I do." He kept stroking over her hair as he gathered a few thoughts. There was a track to grab somewhere along there, not the one he'd almost got lost down. "It's the difference between technical proficiency that gains me a couple more points in a heat . . . and finding the perfect ride. The perfect moment where wave and board go together."

She nodded. "Exactly the way they were meant to. I want that. I need it. There's a technically good picture, and I think I do that just fine, but there ought to be emotion and feeling behind it. I didn't hit that. I can tell by their voices on the phone. All fine, but . . . no one fell in love. The pictures are 'appropriate' and 'sufficient.' Exactly what I hate." Her sigh almost drifted away on the ocean breeze.

"Did you send them everything?"

"Not exactly." Her cheeks hollowed as if she were suddenly holding back a smile.

Suspicion narrowed his eyes and had him bending his head to look at her features. "What does that mean?"

"I didn't give them certain ones." The held-back smile burst into a full-fledged grin that was as bright as the sun. She wiggled over and grabbed the iPad. A couple flicks opened the photo-viewing program. "Like, oh I dunno. You drinking coffee in this very chair the morning after we slept together. Or this one. You have a fine ass."

The picture showed Tanner in bed, completely racked out. He was naked except for the pale gray sheet covering his ass. She'd focused on the small of his back, and though his face was in the picture, turned to the side on the pillow, he was fuzzy and gently out of focus. He groaned, pressing his eyes to the warmth of her hair. "Thank God for small favors, I suppose?"

"More like more of me being greedy." She wiggled a hand under his hips, fingertips grazing the ass in question. "I want to keep it all to myself."

"It's more than that, isn't it?" What he really wanted to ask was if *they* were more than that, but he also wanted to be able to look other men in the face now and then. Asking such a chick question would leave him terminally embarrassed.

She craned up to look at him, one eye slightly squinted. "Maybe? I don't want . . . us wrapped up in my career any more than we already are. It's one thing if I can still take a brilliantly awesome picture of you catching air. It's another if I make my mark with something pretty damn intimate."

He curved his hand over the back of her neck. "That's us. You and me. We don't need anyone else looking in on it."

He slicked his fingertips across the iPad, moving to the next picture. In this one, he sat on the beach. His knees were up and his wrists drooped between. He'd been grinning at Avalon, teasing her about what they'd do later that evening, and looking at the photo, he realized every single thought was in his eyes. He blazed with dirty intent. He swallowed. "Thanks for not sending these ones in. They're ... Christ, they're too much."

She nodded, her head tucked under his. "Yeah. I ... These are more snapshots than anything else." She tilted her head back enough that she could flash him one of those naughty smiles. "For my own personal consumption."

Part of what he loved about Avalon was how complicated she was. Serious depths one moment, cheeky and dirty the next.

That quiet part of him shuddered to a stop again. The wave that had gathered earlier broke open. Wild. Uncontrolled, like a freak swell from some far-off storm that couldn't even be seen over the horizon.

Did he love Avalon?

More than that, if he did, where did that leave them? If anything, his career was ridiculously in flux. The next two days would leave him either a reigning champion or the sad sack who'd given up something epic to a fluke missed wave. Anything was possible.

A ten-year span of history waited to be marked down

in the rule books. And here Tanner was, more worried about the woman in his lap.

The special, amazing woman who shared his sense of focus but took it up a notch with a life-affirming energy that lit him up.

His hands clenched down on her hip.

"Us," he echoed. There wasn't much else he could say, not until everything else was settled. Not until he had the smaller details worked out. Then he'd be free to chase Avalon. And he'd chase her all the way until the ocean froze and she ran out of surf to photograph.

Chapter 32

Avalon loved the way Tanner kissed her. The absolute perfection of it. The way it made her feel both calm, as if everything were right with the world, and incredibly bubbly at the same time. An effervescent joy that could sweep away everything else in its path, if she let it.

So she did. She tossed all her worries away. Let herself be overwhelmed by the strength he poured into her. The way his mouth moved over hers was a benediction and an endorsement. She'd given nothing of herself away that couldn't be taken back later.

They were friends. Very good friends who frequently got to rub naked bits. And friends talked about the setbacks of work and career. There was nothing unusual there.

Except she'd felt safer in his arms. Telling him her fears while sitting on his lap had taken so much of the pain out. He probably had no idea how difficult it had been for her to share. She and Matthew had never gotten to this point. Though she'd always blamed him for being too closed off, maybe it had been her all along. Years with her mom had taught her how dangerous opening up could be.

She'd reached a new level in relationship land by exposing the vulnerable part of herself that feared simply not making it in her career. Never rising the way she needed to.

Part of her almost resented that she felt so exposed. He'd already been champion once; this extra round was a bonus. Though she knew he had pressure riding him, it wasn't exactly the same. The part of her that was so frightened wondered how much he could really understand.

But then his hands slid over her back and she managed to forget altogether. Letting herself absorb the strokes was entirely tastier. She had to pull her mouth away long enough to twist and straddle him.

Her knees dug past the cushion to the poking wicker back of the chair, but she didn't care. Not when she could get closer to him. The warm, achy core of her was only barely appeased by straddling. She rocked down over the hard ridge of his cock.

Tanner looped her wrists in his big, rough hands. "Hey now," he said softly. His voice was deep and rumbly and vibrated her nipples. "We have time."

She rubbed her entire body up against him. Absolutely shameless. "My schedule's yours, after all." Until he was gone again.

Or not exactly gone, but not hers anymore. How hard would that suck, to see him all the time and not have the right to touch.

She ran her fingers through his hair, down around the back of his neck. "I love what you do to me. Love the way you make me feel." It was as close as she could come to putting words to how she felt.

But she wanted to believe he heard her anyway. That he knew at least how important he was to her.

His hands under the curve of her ass, he stood in one fast swoop. The blood rushed out of her head, down through her body. Naturally it pooled in her dampening pussy.

She locked her ankles at the small of his back. "What happened to having time?"

That grin of his sent its own set of tingles through her. "We've still got time." He laced openmouthed kisses along her neck. Nibbles that made her melt across her chest like some kind of wanton strumpet. "We're going to spend that time in my bed."

And God, wanton strumpet was so much better than messed-up neurotic pile of goo.

She could deal with slutty. She could *be* slutty. That was all body and sensation. No biggie.

But when he tossed her onto the bed, he stood at the edge. The bounce jostled her brains for a second, but she blinked rapidly to find him looking down at her. With his hands on his hips, he looked every bit a man.

Her man.

The dark blue board shorts barely dipped over the blades of his hips and above them were those deliciously angled V-lines that pointed to the promised land. With his elbows out, he looked half marauding pirate.

His bright grin only confirmed it. "Now there's a picture a guy could get used to."

She lifted up on her elbows, suddenly a little anxious. "What?" She ran a hand over her stomach, caught by the sudden worry that she had a huge old smear of dirt or pudge that had popped up from nowhere. No, she didn't always claim to be rational.

If a girl couldn't be a little bit crazy inside her own head, where could she break out with the nutso?

But he shook his head. "You're so fucking sexy. Do you know that?"

When he looked at her with that hot glint, he could make her believe it all the way down to the soles of her feet. She ran those very toes over the hard plane of his abs. So fucking tasty. Sometimes she was tempted to push him down and rub herself all over him. A perverted game of tag, maybe. To get her hands all over him. "So come here and show me what you think's sexiest."

That quickly, he was on the bed, stretched alongside her. A blessed sort of magic. "I'm not even sure where to start. Here?" He slid a kiss over the end of her shoulder, dipping down her arm. "Here, maybe?" This time it was her ribs, the bottom edge that stood out in stark relief from her leaned-back position. "No, this." He ringed the shallow well of her navel with his tongue.

Avalon melted into the rumpled bedspread. Let him take her away. Let him worship at her body. She could cope. One way or the other.

She bit back the grin, not wanting to explain.

Tanner's head continued lower, leaving wet tracks of attention all the way across her lower stomach and along the band of her shorts. But his long, blunt fingers tugged them down with no trouble, especially when she gave an extra hip wiggle to help him along.

The way he licked her was a freaking miracle. If she weren't nearly so selfish, she'd insist that every woman should get a chance at his licking, sucking, blessing of a mouth. Her eyes rolled back in her head as she clenched fingers through his golden hair. The sweeping tingle was almost enough to send her over, and she only wrenched higher when he thrust two sure fingers in her pussy. The

fullness was enough to make her want to hand over anything. Everything.

But he apparently didn't have her orgasm in mind, not
yet at least. When she got close, the leashed pleasure inside her tingling through her insides, drawing her nipples
tight, he pulled away.

When he lifted his head, the wet gleam of her juices
limned his mouth.

And she didn't feel the least bit guilty over that. She
grinned. "Where the hell do you think you're going? Get
back down there."

He laughed and swiped the back of his hand over his
lips. But then he stuck the two fingers he'd had inside her
into his own mouth. The pink of his tongue slicked over
the mess she'd left on him.

The hard thump inside her chest was half turn-on and
half owned. He could have so much of her, if he only
took.

"You're kind of bossy." He dipped his head, rubbing
his mouth over her sternum. His tongue curled around
the center string of her bikini top; then he took the strap
between his teeth. Tugged. Goose bumps washed out
over her flesh. "You're lucky I dig it."

"You dig lots about me." She wanted to believe it.
Needed to hear it a little more.

"Lots and lots and . . ." The last word was lost as he
sucked her nipple into the wet heat of his mouth.

Avalon moaned. Her fingers found purchase across
the back of his head, and they didn't even know if she
wanted to pull him closer or push him away. She pretty
much could listen to him forever, but the way he made
her feel would do as well. He was drawing tiny layers of

sensation from her, layering it all together like some sort of sex god. The whisper of his fingers over her hip, the push of his rough thigh against the hot center of her pussy. The licking, nipping delight of his mouth.

It almost became too much. She thought the hard-edged pleasure would shake out her bones and fly away if she didn't grab hold. Her hands dove between them, pushing down his shorts.

He snagged a condom from the bedside table, from the most recent box they'd been zooming through. A minute later, he pushed inside her.

He was hard and big and exactly what she'd needed. More of him, more sensation. And he didn't stop touching her. His hands were everywhere, his mouth at the bend of her neck. His tongue along the top of her chest. A special, wet kiss to the knot where she'd broken her clavicle at eleven.

The way they moved together was enough to make her forget everything else. She needed nothing but him. She lost track of how long, until she needed something more. A little harder.

The pushes on his shoulders weren't missed. Wrapping one arm low around her waist, he flipped them over so she was riding. Speed made her gray at the edges with dizziness. She put her hands flat on his chest, reveling in the hard strength thrusting up into her.

Part of her wanted to scrunch her eyes shut to get what she needed. But the way his eyes almost seemed to glow couldn't be denied. Tanner couldn't be denied.

He was such an elemental force of nature. And she was only riding along until she was shaken free.

But Christ, what a ride it was.

Her hips worked over his, the burn in her thighs more

than worth it for the rubbing, blunt thrusts. She needed more of that. Sweat pooled at the base of her spine, trickled down in another wet lick. More sweat beaded across his chest, and she curved down to lick at him. The new angle of her pelvis stroked the head of his cock against some throbbing, clenching place inside her. Blunt-edged perfection.

Her orgasm came first, blasting her off her rocker. The hot flushes of tingles swept over her body from her pussy first, then down her legs. And it was all even better with Tanner's shell-shocked expression as her sheath clenched down on his cock.

She collapsed in a heap, first on him. Then when the heat and the sweat stuck their skin together in a clammy mess, she slid to the side. "That was my idea of an afternoon workout."

Tanner laughed, running a hand over her side. "Don't even think this'll get you out of this evening's surf."

"I wouldn't think it." Her jaw cracked on a yawn that almost felt like it spun her eyes inside out. "Maybe a nap first."

"Yeah?" His mouth brushed over the top of her head. "You think you've worked hard enough for a nap?"

"Puh-lease." She sighed. She was striving for smartassed but the pure bone-melting pleasure of her orgasm had replaced every bit of smart-mouthed she owned with plain tired. "I rocked your world. You should be thanking me."

"Thank you, Avalon." His quiet voice encouraged her eyes to drift shut.

Even the soft trill of her phone couldn't make her eyes open. "Get that?" she muttered. It could be Sage. Or maybe even one of the WavePro reps who she really ought to give a shit about. But all the care had been fucked right out of her.

Tanner fumbled across the nightstand and grabbed her cell. "Avalon Knox's phone. How may I direct your call?"

At the very last, absolutely too late second, the bottom sank out of her stomach as quickly as if a shark had taken a chomp. Her eyes snapped open. And sure as shit, it was a shark on the other end of the call. From her position nestled against Tanner's chest, she barely heard the tinny voice. "Tanner? Is that you? Well, well. Now I see Avalon's problem."

Underneath her very grip, Tanner's muscles locked hard. His body went still. Stiff. Steady in a new, cold way that she'd never seen or felt from him before. "Mako?"

Chapter 33

Cold. Tanner felt himself go as cold as snow. The sultry air felt like an arctic breeze cooling the sweat on his skin. His blood slugged to a halt in an absent roar of sound.

Mako still prattled in his ear. Going on about . . . something. Words Tanner couldn't grab hold of. Because he didn't really want to. A rattling, horror show of destruction bounced around in his skull. His chest wrenched and pinched on something that was supposed to be air, but fell far short. This was . . . bad. Fucking awful.

Because Avalon was scrambling to her knees on his bed. She'd lost her shorts and bikini bottom but the dark blue strings of her top were still tied in place. As if they hadn't been crawling all over each other. Wrapped up as if nothing else could get between them. But that wasn't exactly true, now was it.

Her eyes were absolutely huge. Giant and glimmering. Begging him silently for understanding. But the color in her round cheeks was long gone. Guilt if he'd ever seen it before.

Tanner's fingers gave a numb tingle. He was clenching

her phone entirely too hard, the metal edge biting into his fingertips.

Still watching her, he uncranked his fingers one by one. The phone fell, but unfortunately it landed impotently on the bed in a soft bounce. Avalon grabbed it, then lifted it to her ear.

Half of him cringed at the added betrayal. The other half felt like it was watching from miles away.

He'd almost drowned once. The same time he'd sliced his face open on the reef. The blow had disoriented him, twisting up from down and flipping his mind inside out. He'd lost himself.

So many factors would have kept this from wrecking what little emotional balance he'd been able to achieve. It wouldn't have been nearly so devastating if she hadn't talked to the one person he couldn't stand in the world. Or if Avalon didn't mean so much to him. Or if their afternoon hadn't already been so . . . right.

She lifted the phone to her ear, offering him a weak smile. "Not now."

He didn't hear the response but it wasn't like it mattered. He raised an eyebrow. Challenge met. How she thought of him was more than obvious now.

Her tongue slicked across her bottom lip. The fast flutter of her pulse at the base of her neck said she was beyond anxious.

He ought to care. He didn't. Instead there was the chilled wasteland inside him.

Rolling off the bed, he scooped his board shorts from the floor. At least they weren't clammy as he stepped into them, then tugged them up over his ass. He wasn't about to have this conversation with his junk hanging out. Small favors, right? He obviously wasn't getting any big ones.

"I can*not* do this right now," she said into the phone in a half whisper. "No! Don't do anything. Don't go anywhere." A pause, then her eyes managed to go even bigger as her gaze flew to Tanner's. She scrambled off the bed, tugging her bikini top back into place. "Do *not* come here."

Tanner pointed at her. Cold, hard fury rocked down his spine, pushing everything else out of his way. At least if he was pissed, he couldn't be mopey depressed over chick shit like getting his feelings hurt. So he let the anger come. "Tell that fucker if he shows up here, my fist will finally land in his goddamn face. He's not a teenager anymore."

She blanched even more, her cheeks going seafoam green. "Don't fucking do it." And then she hung up on him. Finally.

"What the hell is going on here, Avalon?" He yanked open a dresser drawer and grabbed the first T-shirt his hand touched: Tahitian Bureau of Tourism. Fuck that noise. He yanked it right back off over his head again. Plain black worked. "What? Cat got your tongue? Fucking shark got your tongue, maybe?"

She grabbed her shorts and pulled them up over the sweet curve of her ass without even hunting down her bikini bottoms. He looked away. He needed to focus on being mad, on being angry. He couldn't think of their fucking, or the sex, and absolutely couldn't think about the way he'd started hoping for more.

The hard yanks she raked through her hair left finger tracks in the dark mess. "I'm not even sure what you think is going on, but I'm damned sure I don't deserve this."

"No?" He folded his arms over his chest because he'd be damned if he could figure out what else he could touch. Not her, because he almost wanted to throttle her, and if that wasn't an old-fashioned idea, he'd never heard one. He'd obviously lost his goddamned mind over her. "Then explain. Were you or were you not talking with Mako behind my back?"

"It's not like that." The lush line of her mouth set into a hard pout. "You're making it sound like I've been doing something shitty."

"You fucking have been. Or you wouldn't have been hiding it."

"I'm trying to figure out how to help. He didn't really give me—"

He cut her off with a hard slashing motion of his hand. "You fucking hid it. How is that at all okay to you?"

"I just wanted him to stop making trouble."

A dulling roar of confusion washed over him, starting at the top of his head and shaking down to his churning guts. "What the fuck? What are you talking about?"

Over the past couple weeks, she'd taken to bringing along a bag when she didn't have to be home by a certain time. She fished a tank top out, then tugged it down over her head. Her shoulders bounced on a heavy breath. When she turned around, she seemed calmer. "If he didn't get to meet Eileen, he was going to go back to *SURFING* and tell them that Hank first met his mom when she was underage. I don't even know if that's true, but would it matter? The Wright name doesn't need to be dragged through the mud."

He shook his head. Hard. But nothing put the brains back in order. "Threats? Why didn't he tell me?"

"Because you've been so friendly to him?"

"Mom doesn't need trouble from him."

"I know! That's exactly what I was trying to avoid." Avalon's eyes flashed bright, and her lips parted as if she'd say something else. But then she swallowed it down with a shake of her head.

"Say it."

"No."

Something hard and mean rose up. The little boy who was so pissed at the father who'd slipped out of his grasp. There was nothing he could do about that, but he *could* make Avalon say whatever she was holding back. That would be child's play. And maybe he'd have someone else to be mad at. "No, say it. I insist."

Her neck was marble. Tendons in stark relief, like she'd shatter at any moment. "You're not in charge of the family. You don't get to choose like that. Last I checked, we didn't elect you as dictator."

"Last I checked, you weren't a member of the family."

She flinched. More than that, she withdrew. Pulled down into herself as her eyes dulled out. "I see."

He ran a hand through his hair. Only Avalon could make him feel like he'd disemboweled a puppy. "I'm sorry, but you're not." If she were, they wouldn't be sleeping together.

She waved a hand as if she didn't care, but the line of her spine said otherwise. It screamed hurt in its stiffness. "No, I get it. I was only trying to help. He wanted to meet with Eileen and Sage, and it didn't seem like that big a price to pay to get him to withhold insinuations. It's not like paying blackmail or something."

"I know he did. And I told him to fuck off. It's shitty that he tried to use you to get to them."

The stance she took seemed almost like she were prepared to go into battle. "Not tried. I arranged a meeting between Mako and Eileen. Like an hour from now."

"And you let them?" The rage came back, full force. A heart-thumping takeover of his body that sent his brain black. "For fuck's sake, did you even think about that at all? Do you have any sort of idea what he could say to her?"

"I did what I thought was right. I'd have done the same for my own mom."

"Except she's not your fucking mom. She's mine." Something sharp and mean twisted him from the inside. His voice dropped sharp and low. "How far will you go, Avalon?"

Confusion clouded her eyes. "I don't know what you mean."

"How far will you go to be part of the family for real?" Christ, he'd put so much of himself out there already. But if she'd been hiding something that she had to have known would hurt him that badly . . . "Do you actually even want me? Or were you hoping to marry in?"

Her head jerked back as sharply as if she'd been smacked across the face. "You bastard."

"No answer? Kinda suspicious."

"You really think I'd sleep with you for . . . What? Some archaic sentiment? Because I like your mom and sister a lot? If that's the case, why don't I bang Sage, hmm?"

She snatched up her bag from the corner and started shoving the odds and ends of her belongings in. Her tiny bikini bottoms from the end of the bed. A bottle of lotion from the nightstand.

Every move screamed her fury. Well, good. Because Tanner was as pissed as well.

"I don't need this shit two days before the Pro."

A bitter smile twisted her mouth as she tossed a glance over her shoulder. "Funny. That's pretty much what I figured. You know. When I decided to go behind your back. It was the primary reason I didn't tell you and all."

"Oh, so sorry," he said, sneering. "I didn't realize there was a good reason for my girlfriend to lie to me. It's all good now."

"Was I ever your girlfriend, Tanner?" She slid the zipper of her bag shut and it was a wonder he could even hear it over the harsh rush of his breath and the pulse that still slammed inside his skull. "Or was I one superconvenient fuck? If you've got to have a photographer hanging around, might as well take extra bonus points for nailing her."

"Don't make this my fault."

Her shoulders curled inward. A glassy sheen spread over her eyes and her lashes fluttered against quick blinks. But somehow she dredged up a tremulous smile. "It doesn't have to be anyone's fault." Her throat worked over a clench. "Come over to your mom's with me. Mako will be there soon. We'll all sit down and talk."

And that almost made it worse. Because she was still making nice. Smoothing over the family. The family that wasn't even hers. He wanted her to keep fighting for herself. To be spitting mad at him. She'd almost been there, so close his breath had caught.

"I want you, Avalon. You, not any of the other shit. Can you say the same about me?"

Her expression shuttered down. The soft pink of her lips opened, but then slammed closed again. The battle against her tears was lost and one went skating down the curve of her cheek. Misery on the wing.

Seeing his girl crumple so suddenly rocked Tanner down to his soul. He wanted so badly to grab her, to hold her close. Keep the two of them locked up until the rest of the world fell into the ocean. But he couldn't afford that right now.

And to be honest, he wasn't sure if he could. He wasn't going to fight for something that wasn't actually there. The relationship he'd thought they'd been building could have as easily been nothing more than hormones. Because it was obvious to see where her loyalties lay.

So he didn't touch her. Not even when she walked by close enough for him to smell her sea-salt sweetness.

Instead he kept his arms crossed over his chest and his chin tucked down. The door shut on the silence of the room.

And she was gone.

Chapter 34

Avalon had to get her shit together. Standing on the front step of the house she shared with Tanner's sister and mother was not exactly the place for crumpling into a tiny ball and sobbing until her lungs fell out.

She'd wait for that until she got upstairs.

But first, she had to breathe. Her chest felt like it was fifteen inches smaller than it had been just an hour ago. But that wasn't any excuse.

She blinked, turning her face up toward the palm trees lining the street and the breeze that did absolutely nothing to ease the hot ache behind her eyes. That was all pending tears. Nothing to be done about it. At least she'd managed to beat back the few that had fallen as she'd left Tanner's house.

This shouldn't have been any surprise. And yet it was. A tearing, gasping-for-oxygen sort of surprise.

The stairs had never seemed quite so steep or long before. For regular suburban construction, they were fairly Escher-like. Never ending. But she was eventually in the quiet of her room.

Alone.

She shut the door quietly behind her, the soft *snick* of the latch holding no bearing on the violent tumult of emotions inside her. This was where she belonged. Where she should be.

And where she'd always known she'd end up. Keeping Eileen and Sage happy was easy. It was everyone else, men particularly, who became so twisty and confusing.

She wanted to tell Tanner to go to hell.

She'd also wanted to tell him that she needed him, desperately. That she'd do anything to keep him happy and, hell, to keep him. But that hadn't been what he'd meant. And she'd had no idea how to separate him from the rest of it. Everything was so badly bound up together.

The right thing became more difficult to tell when she'd fallen in love. There was only Tanner in her mind and she'd thought keeping everything quiet until after the Pro would help. But she'd been so damn wrong, at least in his eyes.

When she put her back to the door, she melted as if her bones had turned to liquid misery. She slid down, down, her knees folding in front of her. The moment her ass hit the floor, it was like she unlocked.

A harsh sob racked her throat with tiny knives. She shoved the back of her hand into her mouth, but it was too late. The tears burned.

She'd known it was coming. There shouldn't have been any surprise. Yet there it was, a raw hole inside her chest that refused to yield. This was more than simple hurt. It was open and cruel and flat-out hideous.

And it all came from inside her. She'd earned this. She'd known what could happen and she'd flown head-first into the fray. Didn't care.

Another sob choked in her throat, swallowed before

it could ever find voice. She sniffled but nothing could hold back the tears. Candy hadn't ever liked drama that she didn't cause herself, so Avalon had learned to cry quietly. But it didn't make it any easier.

A knock on the door at her back made her twitch. The heels of her hands made poor tissues but she swiped the wet away from her eyes anyway. "Who is it?"

"Me." Sage's voice was quiet. "You okay?"

"Fine." Christ, talking was hard. The very act shoved more sobs up into her chest, clawing their way out. She gritted her teeth. She didn't want to worry Sage. "No problem here."

"Are you sure?" The doorknob twisted but obviously Sage wasn't getting very far with Avalon's butt planted in front of the door.

"Fine. Sure." She swiped at her eyes over and over, but they wouldn't quit leaking. "You can go, it's no biggie."

There was a long pause and for a moment, Avalon thought Sage might have gone away. And to prove she was as crazily neurotic as ever, she had a painful flash of resentment that Sage would take her word so easily.

Something poked her in the ass, a bare quarter inch above the floor. She scrambled to her knees. A pencil.

Sage had stuck the eraser-end of a pencil under the door and was poking at Avalon. "If you don't let me in, I'll pester you 'til you come out. You do realize that, right?"

"Okay, okay." Avalon took one more useless swipe of her eyes, this one with the back of her wrist, as if that would help. But she was still a mess.

She kept her face averted as she opened the door, then immediately grabbed a handful of tissues and went face-first across the bed. Warm lavender and vanilla filled her head, but it wasn't enough to drive away the pure spun sadness. If anything, it made it worse.

Sage dropped to the floor on the far side of the bed, where Avalon's head had landed. Her long legs folded underneath her butt, she stroked Avalon's hair away from her face. "What happened?"

The sobs Avalon had been holding back so well finally won the battle. A harsh, painful drag up her throat, then her chest collapsed in on its own black hole of hurt. All because she couldn't even explain. Didn't have the words.

Saying she and Tanner had broken up wasn't exactly true. Because they hadn't ever really been a concrete *thing* in the first place. And only in his absence did she realize how much she'd invested in him. How much she'd wanted to believe that they could be something. Nothing fancy. Not forever. Just to . . . *be.* With Tanner.

She shook her head, squeezing her eyes shut. But the tears wouldn't even stop. "Tanner and I are done."

"I didn't realize you cared about him this much."

Face buried in the comforter, she shrugged her shoulders in a stupid gesture. "Maybe I didn't realize, either."

"Does he know?"

Another shrug. "Doesn't matter. I screwed up."

"Mako?" Sage's hand ran over Avalon's head in a soothing gesture.

"Yes." Her mouth crumpled around the word. She dissolved into another round of tears.

But Sage didn't go anywhere. She sat next to the bed, providing the comfort Avalon had always absorbed like a greedy sponge.

This, here. This was why she'd been willing to balance

everything on a knife's edge. Because Sage had always been there for her. And she knew without a shadow of a doubt that Eileen would be patting Avalon's back if she knew. This was home. This was where she ran when her wounds bled too deeply.

If she'd gone to Candy, she'd have gotten some advice on not crying too long because it would ruin the Botox—and what did she mean she didn't use Botox? Candy would have tried, but ultimately always failed when it came to the kind of comfort Avalon needed.

Sage's easy peace washed over Avalon, eventually calming her. When Avalon pushed herself up to a sitting position, her joints felt as weak as seaweed. She'd completely exhausted herself.

In a way, she felt better.

The inevitable had happened. Now there was nothing to be done but deal with it.

Sage stayed where she was, but folded her hands on the edge of the mattress and rested her chin on them. "What are you going to do?"

She grabbed a handful of tissues from the box on her nightstand and mopped at her face. "There's nothing to do. One of those easy come, easy go things."

Sage's pale eyebrows twisted into a knot of disbelief. "Bullshit. People don't sob their brains out over easy come, easy go. You care about Tanner."

"Of course I do." It wasn't exactly a lie. She couldn't love him if she didn't care for him. But she didn't need to tell Sage every single dirty detail either. "But I've got to put my big-girl panties on. It's over. End of story."

"You could try talking to him."

Tanner's cold, hard face rose in her memory. She shuddered. She would do anything to never again see that level of disgust on his face. Even if it meant playing pretty and polite to keep the surface smoothed over. "No. No way."

"It's not worth a shot?"

"Why?" She made herself laugh a tiny bit. "Because Tanner's such a paragon of rationality and he's open to discussions?" If he'd broken with his father for almost ten years, there was absolutely nothing to keep him by her side.

It would be bad enough to love him from a distance. Having him nearby, knowing that she felt for him so strongly? No, thanks. She'd already had him in her head for years. Going back would be like walking on ground glass.

And she wouldn't do that, not even for Tanner.

She could only apologize for being herself for so long, and she couldn't try to fix everything. Because in the end, she was starting to realize she needed to be needed for who she was. Not because of the things she could do for others.

When she'd made the right choice, she didn't deserve this level of shit. It wasn't as if she'd intentionally introduced a serial killer to someone who met his victim's profile. She'd arranged for a man to speak with the other half of his family.

She knew that she shouldn't have gone behind his back, but ultimately, what she did was right. She couldn't let Tanner be a dictator. He didn't get to make those choices for someone else.

Not for her, at least.

She blinked, realizing Sage was still sitting there. The smile she pulled up didn't feel like much, but at least it made the worry fade from Sage's eyes a little.

Avalon wiped at her nose again. "Look, it's not really that big a deal. Not . . . as things go. I think I'm a little overwhelmed. I have to shoot the Pro, and I turn in the final round of WavePro stuff in less than a week. It's a lot, you know?"

Sage's head tilted. She didn't seem to quite believe Avalon's line, and, well, she shouldn't. Every word was both lie and truth at once.

Because really, in the end, only one thing mattered. Avalon's heart was broken.

Putting the pieces together would have to wait for another time because the doorbell pealed downstairs. She scrubbed her wrists over her eyes, wiping away what she could of her tears. "Showtime."

Sage sat up. "Is that him? Mako? He's early."

Except it wasn't Mako at the front door. It was Tanner. He stood with his back to the entryway, looking at a middle-aged woman who was walking a small Chihuahua, as if he didn't even want to be there. The late-afternoon sun gleamed off his blond hair. It was hard to believe it had been less than an hour ago that she'd been in his arms. She willed him to look at her.

Avalon swallowed the knot that had found a permanent home in the back of her throat. "I didn't expect to see you here."

His mouth was pressed into a flat, hard line. When he finally looked at her, she wished she could have taken back her need to see his eyes. There was nothing there, at least not for her. "Where's my mom?"

"Probably out back."

He stared at her for a minute more. The sun beat down on them, making her eyes sting against the tears that had already burned her out. "He's not here yet, is he?"

She shook her head. She clenched the doorknob, and it was cool against the throbbing heat of her blood in her palms. "No. Not yet."

Tanner's gaze shifted past her to Sage. "Did you know about this too?" Sage didn't answer in words, but she must have nodded because Tanner gave a small nod as well. "Fine. Then let's do this."

Chapter 35

Tanner didn't know what to expect when he walked through the kitchen door out to the patio. The sun was at the right spot in the sky to light up the courtyard. His mother was at the far end, her head bent over a trellised plant. In contrast with the shot-silk blouse she wore with a dark blue skirt, which was subdued as far as Eileen-wear went, she had on worn gardening gloves that once had been red. They were now closer to the color of mud.

If Tanner didn't know better, he'd think they were the same exact gloves she'd worn years ago, when he was in high school, before he'd left for the circuit.

Tanner approached slowly, and Eileen didn't lift her head even though she had to have heard his steps. He crossed his arms over his chest, but he suddenly worried that he might look too confrontational. It wasn't his mom's fault that he'd just had such a giant fight with Avalon.

Because shoving his hands in his pockets felt awkward, too, he settled for picking up a small clay pot. An herb sprouted in it, looking too weedy for basil. A fragrant and earthy scent wafted up from it. "Do you want me to leave, Mom?" The words were hard to wrench out.

She shook her head, but didn't look up. Her neck was graceful. The blond hair that pooled at her shoulders was shot with gray. "I want this all to have happened ten years ago." She gave a quiet huff. "No. I want this to have happened twentysomething years ago."

"Dad should have told you."

Her head snapped up. Her eyes flashed and the grooves around her mouth flashed white. "*You* should have told me."

Tanner felt the insides of his elbows wrench tight, along with the base of his spine. "It wasn't my place. I was twenty. How was I supposed to go to my mom and tell her that I'd met my half brother. And his mom too?"

"I'm an adult and your mother. Please don't treat me like a child." There was no anger in her words. Only soft, chiding disappointment that scraped his skin off. It hurt almost worse than the argument with Avalon had. Her hands kept moving with quiet efficiency, cutting back dead flowers and dropping them into a basket.

He pinched the bridge of his nose. The pain there was subtle, but demanding. He breathed deep. "I never meant to."

Eileen set the basketful of withered purple flowers on a side table and stripped her gloves off. "I know that. You've always had a good heart, Tanner. You get a little bullheaded at times, but it's part of the magic of your makeup. You're a world champion and you're going to do it again. You've made the life you want for yourself. I only wish you'd given me that same agency."

He shifted from foot to foot. His flip-flops stuck to him. "Mom . . ." He sighed and shook his head. He should have done this a long time ago. So many should haves; they stacked up like surfboards behind a team house. "Fuck, Mom. I'm sorry. I got so pissed at Dad that I let it get into everything else, didn't I?"

She gave his cheek something that was a little more than a pat but way less than a smack. "You watch that language, mister. But otherwise, yes. You stepped outside the bounds, Tanner."

Tanner scrubbed both hands over his face, then through his hair. "I was trying to do the right thing, Mom. I loved you, and I loved our family, and I wanted to keep you safe."

"I'm the parent here, Tanner." She patted his cheek more softly this time. "Even though you're a grown man now, I'm still your mom. I make choices around here, especially the ones for me."

He folded her hand in both of his. "I'm sorry. So sorry, Mom. I won't do anything like it again."

"God, I hope not," Eileen said with a wry smile. "I hope there are no other secrets left to keep. I'm about done with them. Tanner, I'm so sorry I snapped at you, though."

He shook his head immediately and squeezed her hand. "Mom, I get it. You don't have to apologize at all. Not even a little bit."

Tanner wanted to be able to accept things like his mom did. He wished he could be that sort of optimist. But that was another element of his father within him, most likely. The asshole side of him. He'd spent years *trying* to do the right thing, only to realize too late that he'd screwed up. And screwed up badly.

An hour later, the guilt had frothed into a level of upset that had him on edge. Eileen puttered around her courtyard, Sage had taken up residence in the living room with the TV remote in one hand, and Avalon was upstairs. She was probably hiding from him, and as well she should. He didn't know what he'd say to her. The tension in the house was riding higher and higher.

It kind of figured that it would. This wasn't any sort of happy reunion. Avalon had arranged a meeting with all the so-subtle tension of a meeting with North Korea.

Tanner leaned against the archway between the living and dining rooms. His arms didn't feel comfortable any-place except crossed over his chest. He glowered at the TV, which was running racing footage from Germany. "Why are you watching cars go in tiny circles around a track?"

"They are not tiny circles," Sage replied without look-ing at him. "Albert Park is a street course. And if you're going to be so negative, you can take it outside. I don't need your crap."

He huffed, but he stalked outside anyway. Sage had a point. She didn't need anything from him.

None of them did.

Seeing Mako walking up the street was almost a blessing. His anger found a target. The other man wore tan cargo shorts and a bright green polo shirt with the collar lifted in the back. He drew to a halt at the foot of the walk. "Are you here to stop the meeting? I thought I was . . . invited." His mouth lifted in a smirk.

Tanner's fists locked. "It doesn't count as an invitation if you're blackmailing people into it."

"That's the difference between you and me, Tanner." Mako propped one foot on the stone of the front step. He leaned an elbow on his lifted knee. "I take the expe-dient route. I don't have time to dick around for a decade before capping off my career."

Tanner narrowed his eyes. The ups and downs were

hitting a ridiculously erratic level. Like riding a roller coaster that seemed to go in an eternal loop. "You were five years younger than me. Dad missed my first day of kindergarten for your birth, didn't he?"

Mako's dark hair slipped into his eyes when he tilted his head down. "I wouldn't know. Being only a day old and all makes the memories a little fuzzy."

"I didn't do the math until the night I went to your house." Standing in the middle of that dinky hut, with the screams flying around his head. "I wondered what else Dad missed or skipped or didn't show up for because of you. And it wasn't like he'd told me where he was going. So every time, it was another lie."

"That's the way lies work." Something dark and angry flew behind Mako's eyes. He shoved a hand through his dark hair. "They keep adding up like that. The beginning gets lost in the mess."

"I wish you'd get lost."

"Why so mean, Tanner?" Mako drawled. "What have I done to you?"

Tanner couldn't help a step toward the other man. He was younger than Tanner, but he wasn't a kid anymore. He'd filled out through the shoulders and his face had lost the roundness he'd had as a teenager. "The magazine article isn't enough? And more threats about my dad? No one's going to believe he's that scuzzy."

"You're right." Mako's teeth glinted in a sharp smile. "I'll have to do better next time."

Tanner couldn't take it anymore. He snapped. His fist was up and back, then flying through the air. He punched Mako. His half brother's head snapped back. His hair flew.

Mako staggered back a half step, but then he threw

himself at Tanner. He swung. Tanner blocked it. They staggered off the step, locked together. A punch to Mako's gut had him doubling over with a groan.

The door swung open behind them. Two feminine voices rose in protest. Through the blood pounding in his ears, Tanner couldn't tell who they were. Soft hands wound around his biceps—and yanked hard. The unexpected strength threw him off balance. He stumbled backward two steps, and quickly righted himself.

But the small interference was enough. Sage pushed herself between Tanner and Mako. She had her back to Tanner and her open hands raised in front of her. "Get out of here!"

"You don't know who you're fucking with," Mako growled.

"No," Sage snarled. She seemed about as far from her usual calm self as possible. "Your mistake is thinking I *care.*"

Tanner tried to suck in a long, calming breath. He figured out the long part of it, but calming was something far, far away. Even the fact that Avalon had her hands on him contributed to the mess in his head. He didn't even know which way was up, much less what to do. A low, grinding noise bubbled up from his throat.

Avalon spread her hands across his arm, then pushed over his chest. "Stop it. Stop it right now, Tanner. You have to surf tomorrow. What are you going to do if you're injured because you're fighting?"

Pain shot from the bridge of his nose toward his temples. His fists balled. He hated that she was right. Absolutely hated it, all the way through him, but he couldn't deny the truth of it. And more echoed in his head, about the conversation he'd just had with his mom. What she deserved. How he shouldn't try to interfere in her life anymore.

"Get Mom," he managed to bite out.

Avalon looked at him with wide gray-green eyes. Her lips were parted enough that he could see the delicate pink skin of her inner lip. "Tanner . . ."

"I can behave myself." He shot a look at Mako, whose features were set in a steely edge. The skin over his cheekbones was tightly drawn. "I can't speak for others."

Avalon slipped away, darting into the house at a flat-out run. She was back with Eileen faster than Tanner expected. Red splashed over Eileen's cheeks and across the back of her neck. "What is going on out here?"

"Mako, say what you need to." Tanner managed to grit out the words. His knuckles were starting to throb, but he'd had worse before from a run-in down in Mexico. "Say it fast, before I lose my temper."

Mako's eyes narrowed. "Fuck you."

"You better be talking to me and not my mom, or I'll make you regret that."

"You ought to be *thanking* me. I didn't tell *SURFING* everything that I could have about Hank." Mako stood straight, running both hands through his hair. It stood up in disarray. "You don't know what kind of trouble you're sowing here. I've got enough for a whole series of articles. Maybe a documentary."

Eileen came off the front step, but she didn't step between Tanner and Mako. She balanced herself evenly between them, and pointed a sad smile at Mako. "I don't really care, Mako."

"He was your husband. You were the one he picked as his real family." Mako sneered, his eyes narrowing.

"Real family?" Eileen stepped closer to the younger

man, her hand lifting toward his shoulder. But he flinched before she managed to touch him. "Is that what this is about? You're so angry with us, with the whole world. You can't live like that. It'll eat you up inside."

Tanner felt himself holding his breath. This was what his mom was so good at, what he'd gotten the benefit of all his life and particularly through the antagonistic teenage years. Mako didn't realize how damn lucky he was to get a taste of it.

"What am I supposed to do?" Mako snapped. "He practically abandoned me. My mom lived and breathed for his rare visits. I'm supposed to just forgive him?"

"Eventually I hope you can. Your father was a flawed man. I'm going to have to work hard to be able to see past that. But I'm going to try."

"Why?" He swallowed hard. There was something in his chest that he couldn't seem to breathe past. "What's the point of trying so hard?"

Her mouth curved into something that was near a smile, and yet miles away. She stepped forward again, curving a hand over his cheek and patting. "Because I don't want my anger and my fury to color everything else. Whatever else I have to work through, your father gave me at least two children whom I adore. I have that much, at least. Do you think we could spend some time together? I'd like to get to know you too."

There were tears shining in Mako's eyes, but Tanner did him the favor of pretending he didn't see anything. "I'm not sure if I can stand to look at you yet, but my mom's a much better person than me. Take her up on it, bro. You won't regret it."

*   *   *

After everything was said and done, Tanner surfed for the love of the ride. That perfect moment when man and board actually came close to conquering the monster ocean. Grabbing hold of something so distinctly elemental it became a level above ordinary. A truth.

The entire event came down to him and Jack in the last heat. Jack actually went in two points ahead, having nailed a sweet spot on his second heat. But Tanner ... Tanner took the finals.

And he had to admit that having Avalon watching him had something to do with it.

She was in the water, her hair skinned back into a severe ponytail, clutching her camera in its waterproof housing. Everything they'd said to each other over the last three days spanning the Sebastian Pro competition had been nothing but business. So polite, there could have been a shell made of dried salt over them each. But her dusky green eyes watched him.

Not that he tried very hard to get away. He needed her, in a way.

But every time his palms burned with the need to grab her, he also remembered how damn bad her betrayal had hurt. It was that much worse that she believed that she had been doing something good for him. Made him wonder what else she failed to understand about him. How much else she didn't see.

For the last heat, it was him and Jack on the water and the photographers barely out of the way, on the far end of the swell.

He had to push everything away. Not a scrap left in his head but him and the water.

The only thing he had to beat was the wave. He waited

on his board, the water soothing and swelling. On shore, the beach was packed. In the water, he owned both the power and the calm of the ocean.

He'd already had one excellent wave, barreling out in a maneuver that was both clean and technically perfect. For his second score of the heat, he wanted something bigger. Fancier. He spotted the swell he needed. Felt it surge under him. Paddled as hard as he had in his life, trusting the magic would happen. And it did. The wave took him. He popped up, standing. Belonging.

He took the wave in return, poured in every bit of his frustration and upset. Slammed down the front, dug in a rail. Flipped a sharp turn at the bottom and rode his momentum up. Up and out until he was floating over the moment. He hovered in the air, his heart rising to the back of his mouth. He was a god.

But a god without a destiny.

His arms spread for balance, he slammed back to earth, cut across the top of the seafoam as the wave broke. Slowed. Dropped back to his board.

He knew he'd done it. Won. He felt the immediate rush of perfect wave plus perfect ride.

His eyes cut to Avalon first. Behind the housing of her camera, he couldn't see her, not the way he'd wanted to. Not the way he needed to. The way her eyes lit up for him on practice runs, he knew this one would be epic. She'd fucking explode.

Or she would, if he hadn't fucked all that up.

After he rode the wave all the way in, the throngs of people rushed toward him from the beach. It was something to put down in the record book—two championships, during his first and last competitions, and exactly ten years apart. The odds of it ever happening again were slim. He might not be Kelly Slater, but he had this year. He had his place.

As Sage and his mom slung their arms around his wet back, he couldn't help himself. He looked past them both, over their heads.

Avalon walked out of the waves. Water clung to her curves, even though she wore a pair of unrevealing board shorts and a dark green, silky rash guard. The camera dangled from one hand. From some deep depth, she pulled out a weak smile. The two fingers she tipped to one eyebrow were a salute, but it didn't feel mocking.

It felt right. There was no reason in the world why she shouldn't be a part of the best moments of his life.

He missed her.

He wanted her back.

On some level, he'd have to admit that he'd flipped out about the Mako thing because he'd been beyond scared. Cut-his-balls-off-and-bury-them-in-the-sand-level scared. Avalon was strong and brilliant and fascinatingly creative, while Tanner could be her rock. Be her calm in the storm. He'd just been too damn afraid he'd turn into his father and put his own ego and wants ahead of his relationships.

And he didn't know if he could get over that.

Then he didn't have any choice but to pay attention to the crowds. Sage laid a big, fat kiss on his cheek, and his mom did the same in quick succession. Mr. Wakowski was right there, grabbing his hand in a hard shake.

Avalon slipped away. Her narrow back wove between two beach bunnies in tiny suits.

And he didn't stop her.

Something sick took up residence in his stomach, even as he thanked everyone and accepted their congratulations.

Jack appeared in front of him. He held his hand out. Dark blue eyes narrowed at him in direct opposition to the wide smile. "Congratulations, man."

Tanner shook, though they kept it fast. "Thanks."

"About everything."

Tanner held his hands up, palms out.

"I wanna say I'm sorry. You deserve this win."

Tanner nodded.

Really, he was fucking exhausted. His brain had short-circuited right about the same time he'd spotted Avalon on the sand. His knees were weak, his thighs hard-sprung with leftover adrenaline, and his back felt like it needed to pop back into place. He wasn't a young man anymore. The win couldn't have come at a better time.

Part of that had to mean letting go of the things held on to by the younger version of himself. He nodded, clapped Jack's wet shoulder. Hard, of course, so the other guy staggered under the blow. Certain male things couldn't be left behind altogether. But he smiled. "It's all good. Water washes it all away. We're even."

Because hell, if he couldn't be the bigger man when he was flying high on a win, when the hell could he?

A few minutes later, he found himself high on a podium. He hefted the golden cup over his head. Thousands of people looked up at him.

He owned the moment.

Even if Avalon had managed to hide herself out of his line of sight.

The press went first, spattering questions at him. The release of that perfectly timed magazine article meant that plenty of them were about Hank Wright and his hidden family, as well as the young age of Mako's mother. Tanner ignored those questions as if they'd never been asked, and answered the ones about how it felt to win. How it felt to be the champion.

Speeches came next. Most of them slid by in a blur. He wasn't even sure what he said during his own except that the words *thank you* echoed a lot. Repeatedly. As in over and over again, until he figured he pretty much qualified as babbling, because he was afraid if he stopped talking he'd cry.

There was no way he'd cry on stage.

But when they hustled him to the staging area in back, he sucked in a harsh breath as he stepped down from the stage. The press of bodies was gone. Mostly his manager and a few WavePro people remained. Plus his mom and sister, of course.

He pressed cold, tingling fingers to his eyes to stave off the pressure there.

He wished his dad were there to see it. And not in some fucked-up, revenge-tinted way. But really, truly wanted him there. Hank would have gotten such a kick out of a random, record-book kind of moment like this.

His dad had made mistakes. A lot of them, it seemed. The anger he'd left in his wake was overwhelming and almost epic. But he'd been just a man, and he'd been Tanner's father. The dad who'd raised him and taught him to surf and ingrained the drive to win. Things had gone downhill later, but Tanner had been lucky enough to get that much of him. He wished Mako had gotten more of Hank, seen his good side.

Under the wish, a decade of anger sloughed off.

Only one thing would make this moment actually perfect. Avalon.

Chapter 36

Avalon had always liked her bedroom in the Wright house. When she'd left her mother's tiny apartment, it had felt like moving into a castle—one almost on the beach, to boot. Coming back after school and Matthew, it had been a safe haven. The pale blue walls always made her feel better and the high four-poster bed had that touch of whimsy that every teenage girl lived for.

Of course, back then she'd decorated the walls with cutouts from every surf magazine ever published. Now the walls were covered with prints of her own action photographs.

Except the biggest print, the panoramic she'd labored over, was simply of the waves—the ones that were less than a quarter mile away. The same ones Tanner had dominated to seal the championship two days ago.

And she hadn't seen him since.

The ache had gotten worse when she had to pick through a month's worth of photographs of Tanner too.

God, he was such a beautiful man.

She paused on a shot from a day trip they'd taken to San Onofre. Tanner had a wetsuit on, but he'd peeled it down to his waist, and he was holding a bottle of water as he stared out at the waves. Thick slabs of muscles etched him with the solid strength she'd known up close and personal. The sharp line of his lats, arching over the side of his ribs that she'd grasped as she exploded. Those heavy arms that had wrapped around her in the dark of night.

And also the steady trust in his eyes. He knew the waves and he knew himself and he let everything else *be*. She wanted that. Needed that in her life and in herself.

But it didn't mean she was wrong to have tried to help, did it? After all, the visible proof was in Eileen. She didn't look happy, not exactly. But she wasn't walking around as shell-shocked as she had been.

This morning she'd greeted Avalon and Sage with a smile, then made them whole-wheat pancakes. She'd made her mind up on selling the store. Said she was done with it, that between what she'd make and Hank's life insurance, she could take early retirement.

With slow, deliberate clicks, Avalon shut the picture on her screen. She put the last pictures meant for Wave-Pro on a disk, then added the last batch to the external drive she'd been gathering for Tanner. He deserved his own record of the win.

Plus she had to admit she had an ulterior motive. A tiny, petty part of her wanted to make sure Tanner never forgot her. If he picked one of these pictures, framed it maybe, kept it as a memento of his ten-year-span win? She'd be part of his memories forever. A fixture in his life, even if he eventually forgot the rest of what they'd had.

Because Avalon was pretty damn sure she'd never forget Tanner. What he was to her would never fade into the background of their other truths. Friend, brother of her best friend, coworker—and the man she'd always love.

The disk slid out the side of her computer; then she snapped it in a case and marked the dates spanned. The drive she slipped in an outside pocket of her smaller camera bag.

Downstairs, the house almost echoed with quiet. She put her stuff down on the island counter, then set about refilling her iced coffee. Eileen had left the air conditioner off and opened every door and window, so she couldn't have gone very far.

Swirling her coffee so the ice could do its job, Avalon stood in front of the sink and looked out at the back patio. The afternoon sun wove between latticed vines, leaving a dappled pattern across the flagstone. A pair of feet stuck out from the lounger, with sandals dangling off the end.

Avalon slipped through the back door. "I'm going into the WavePro offices."

Eileen didn't open her eyes, but she smiled. Her face was tipped up toward the sun, but Avalon knew she'd have already slathered on SPF eleventy million. "Will you be home for dinner?"

Something fluttered deep in Avalon's chest. Home. Yeah, this was home. She'd made the right choice. "Yep."

"Good. I'm making pesto pasta."

"My favorite." She managed to keep the thickening out of her voice, but there was no doubt her eyes watered a little.

"That would be why I'm making it." Her hand flew out and wrapped around Avalon's wrist in a gentle grip. "Hey." She tugged Avalon around and down, then kissed her cheek. "Everything happens for a reason. There's no such thing as chance."

Avalon shook her head. "I don't like this one. It hurts."

Eileen sighed. Her eyes were the same color as Tanner's. Avalon hadn't quite noticed before and it hurt. Badly. "Tanner is so much like his father. I always knew that was why they stopped talking. The excuse doesn't matter. And for all his faults . . . for all his mistakes . . . Hank always made me feel special."

Avalon's eyes burned with the force of the tears she held back. She shook her head again, as if that would matter, then shrugged. "It doesn't matter. Done is done."

Eileen patted her cheek. "You'll always be a daughter of my heart. The rest is details."

Avalon wrapped her arms around Eileen and squeezed. The older woman rubbed Avalon's back. The warmth that spread through Avalon was as close to comfort as she'd gotten in the last few days. But at least it was better than nothing.

She felt sort of traitorous for wanting Tanner's arms. The feeling wasn't at all the same.

Finally she wiped at her eyes, then pulled back. "See ya."

Eileen gave a wistful smile as she waved.

But getting out of the house wasn't near that easy. An atom bomb waited on her in the kitchen.

Tanner.

He looked so good, it shouldn't be allowed. The charcoal gray pants and green button-down made as nice an outfit as Jack could have picked out, but Tanner wore it with aplomb. With his hands spread to each side of his hips, curled around the tile edge of the counter, he leaned back. The length of his legs stretched out before him, crossed at the ankles. A pair of metallic-sheened sunglasses covered his eyes, but the curve of his mouth was soft.

Everything relaxed. Not a care in the world. Because he was the motherfucking world champion.

Avalon's movements became sharp, her steps like

mincing through a pool of pudding, every step a slog. Fucker. Bright, hot anger rushed through her.

Anger was easier, after everything.

She slapped the flap of her camera bag shut, then slung it over her shoulder. The pain arrowing up the back of her head would give her an awful headache soon.

"Avalon." Tanner's big, warm hand curved around her shoulder. With one tug, he turned her around. The heat of his hand burned into her flesh. Part comfort and twice that much pain. "You're not even going to talk to me now?"

"I need a little distance." At least her voice came out steady and calm. Nothing of the mess inside her. "Besides, I've got to go to the meeting."

He glanced down at her, taking in the slim pencil-cut skirt that stopped below her knees and the red silk blouse. "You look amazing."

She managed to snort. The strap of her camera bag dragged the blouse all out of alignment. And she didn't want to admit how good it felt to hear it from Tanner. She still wanted him. Which meant she wanted him to want her as well, as convoluted as that might be. "I clean up nicely."

"No." He caught the side of her face in his cupped fingers. His gaze bore into hers with an intensity that zinged all the way down to her toes. "You look gorgeous. Don't blow it off."

Her breath caught in her chest. But it wasn't enough. That gaping, angry place within needed something more to hold on to. "What exactly are you saying, Tanner?"

He shifted on his feet. When he shook his head, it looked more like he was trying to shake free of some confusion. But he still didn't remove his hand from her cheek. Instead, he flipped it over and trailed the back of his knuckles over her jaw. "I'm not sure. I know I miss you."

She swallowed down the threatening tears. Part of her wondered why this wasn't enough. This, right here. The moment when Tanner came to her and said that he missed her.

But the truth was: It still wasn't what she needed.

She needed to know he wouldn't let her down. Maybe the expectation of an end was part her own problem, but goddamn had it hurt when he'd just started in on her, and he'd assumed she'd been operating from the worst possible motives. He'd been quite ready to let her walk out, hadn't he, without even a word of protest?

She needed someone who'd make life better for her. Who didn't assume she'd be the one to make everything better for *him*.

More than that. She *deserved* someone who'd have her needs in mind.

Maybe her mom hadn't and maybe Matthew hadn't, but that didn't mean she shouldn't get someone who would.

She shuffled around in the outside pocket of her bag until her fingers curled around the chunky hard drive. Pulling Tanner's hand from her face was one of the hardest things she'd ever had to do. Winding her fingers through his would be entirely more natural. Instead she spread them open, so his hand was held up.

Setting the drive in the middle of his palm, she folded his fingers over it. He watched her with a fine line of worry between his eyes, like he didn't exactly understand what she was doing.

That was fine. She didn't know, either.

"I'm not going to lie and say I'm not glad you miss me." She smiled a little at that. "But it's not enough. Call me if you figure the rest out. Or don't. And we'll be friends again in a little while."

"Avalon . . ."

She lifted her brows, waiting for him to finish. Instead his voice trailed off. All gone. She didn't get him after all.

And damned if that didn't hurt a little bit all over again. That somewhere within her had been a tiny well of hope that he'd fight for her. Fight with her.

She stretched up on her toes, until her calves strained. She meant only to brush a kiss over his cheek, but at the last second Tanner turned his head. Took her mouth.

Flash-fire incendiary. Everything they'd been together. Exactly how they'd ended up in this tangled mess in the first place. Avalon's lips clung to his, trying to drink in a last measure of his calm. But there was no more to be had, at least not when his kiss also made her want to cry.

She pulled away. There was a tiny smudge of red lipstick across his bottom lip. She wiped it away with her thumb, her fingers folded over his sharp jaw. The line of his scar pulled. So damned stubborn. Why couldn't part of that stubbornness be *for* her?

She wanted to say something else, to put a point on the moment. A statement that would end things with a good flounce.

But in the end she only walked away.

Tanner's gaze burned into her from behind as she slipped out of the kitchen. Her heels clattered on the tile, making the only noise in the house.

The bright, sunny day she found outside sure didn't feel right when compared to the mess swirling around inside her. Birds even had the audacity to chirp and sing as they swooped down the street.

She didn't slam the front door. No point. Everything was said and done.

Chapter 37

Tanner bounced the external drive in the palm of his hand. Avalon was gone.

He'd have to decide for how long.

He found his mom out on her patio. She spent uncountable hours out there. When he was younger, Tanner had never understood why anyone would hang out somewhere that was practically walled in when there was an entire beach a block away.

She was lying in the hammock, but to Tanner's eyes she didn't look particularly relaxed. There was still white strain at her knuckles, curled around the edge of the net, and the tendons along her throat were as sharp as he'd ever seen them. Even the time he'd been caught sneaking out of the house at three thirty to catch the front wall of a storm surge.

"Hey."

When her eyes opened, she smiled. "It's nice to have you here."

"You've said that before." He tugged a chair up beside the hammock and dropped into it. Sun-warmed metal still didn't come anywhere close to warming up his flesh after that moment in the kitchen.

He knew what that had been. Avalon saying good-bye. Yeah, maybe they'd see each other here and there, including at the WavePro meeting in less than an hour, but that wasn't the same. She wasn't going to be *his* anymore.

He didn't know if he could take that.

"It's still true." Eileen laced her slender fingers behind her head. "It's nice that you feel able to come and go. That's always been one of my biggest goals. To have a life where my children were comfortable with me. Happy and well adjusted is a bonus."

"Am I well adjusted?"

Eileen looked at him out the corner of her eyes. "Nope. Not really."

He cut his gaze up to the pale blue sky. A tiny cloud peeked out over the roofline. "Thanks, Mom."

His mom shrugged, but then she pushed up to a seated position, her legs dangling over the edge of the hammock. For a moment, in her tiny white Keds and pale pink shorts, she looked surprisingly like a teenager. "Son, you're the one who won a worldwide championship two days ago. But you look like your favorite toy got broken in half by the schoolyard bully."

It was more like he missed Avalon already. He could still taste her on his mouth.

Half that choice had been his, though. He'd known what she wanted. Some declaration. For him to own up to his part in their fight.

"I care what you do with your life. And whether you're happy."

"Of course I'm happy." He was the freaking world

champion, and he'd won in an epic way. What was there to be unhappy about?

Except he was missing part of himself. The part that had walked out the door in Avalon's wake.

"Certainly." Eileen patted Tanner's shoulder. "I'm sure you are," she said in a tone that said she was convinced of anything but.

Pushing out of the seat, he pulled the tiny jump drive out of his pocket. He knew without looking what it was, a fat file of pictures. But he had a feeling that baseline knowledge wasn't the same thing as the effect.

Avalon had done him one last favor, because that was the type of woman she was. It was obvious that he'd hurt her, but she'd given him a file full of pictures so that nothing would take him by surprise at the meeting.

He had to track down a computer first.

He ended up perched at his sister's desk. Her room was a disaster zone, which he didn't remember at all from when they were growing up together. Her place used to always be neat. But he had to sit on the very front edge of the desk chair because the back was entirely stacked with clothes.

He took another look around. All the mess seemed to be clothes, as a matter of fact. "Swear to God, if I put my hand down on a bra, I'll burn it."

Sage stood in front of her open closet door, where a full-length mirror hung. As if the tiny halter-top dress she wore wasn't enough of an anomaly for her, she bent at the waist and fluffed her hair, then tossed it back. She looked distinctly beach-bunnylike. "You better mean you'll burn your hand, because my bras are seventy-five bucks each."

"Dude, are you serious?"

"Completely." She bent over him to grab up a tiny thing with a clasp on top that he supposed was a purse. It wouldn't have held anything more than a lipstick and some cash. "You better behave if I leave you in here alone. Don't go digging in my files. You might not like what you find."

"What, the cute cat vids will scratch my eyes out?"

"More like I don't want you in my porn."

He shuddered. "Oh Jesus, Sage. Don't even joke about that."

She swatted his shoulder with her minipurse. Clutch, maybe? "Your sister has sex. And sometimes I don't, and then I need the porn."

"Go away and stop talking about that stuff."

"What, porn?"

He plugged his fingers in his ears and hummed. Sage would always be his baby sister. The two should never, ever come together.

"Where are you headed, anyway?" She looked a little more tarted up than he was comfortable with. The sheer red gloss was a little much, but she'd have a shit fit if he tried to wipe it off.

"On a date." The grin that spread across her face said way too much about troublemaking and was probably a result of Avalon's influence. "Hopefully to get laid so I don't have to come home to *porn*." She put extra emphasis on the last word, as if insisting he notice.

He clapped his hands over his ears again. He was playing it up, yeah, but this was sort of fun. Letting Sage tease him . . . It spoke to a level of intimacy that they hadn't always had. "Can't hear you—did you say you're a virgin?"

"Sure. Yeah. Virgin." She snickered, then gave a tiny

wave of her fingers as she sashayed out of the room. "See you, brother."

"Don't do anything I would," he called.

But he still waited until the door was fully shut before popping the external drive into a USB slot. This was a moment he needed to keep exclusively to himself.

Because Christ if this wasn't going to hurt.

She had organized the files. There were two little blue folders to start with. One was labeled WavePro, The other said "Private."

He stared at the computer screen, his fingers running lightly over the flat top of the mouse. This was . . . surprisingly difficult. A little, burning kernel of emotion flipped around and around in his stomach.

He didn't want to think about the tingling tremble that made directing the cursor difficult. He clicked on the WavePro folder first. This was a piece of pie compared to winning a World Championship—and yet it still felt as if his whole life was tilting.

The file held lots of shots of water and breaking waves. Plenty of him shredding pretty damn hard for an old man, if he did say so himself. Her shots from shore were minimal. She'd preferred to be out there in the water with him, ducking flying boards for the perfect shot. As a result, most of them were wet and Tanner didn't look too bad. He deserved the win he'd nailed down. The pictures showed that in their technically clean exposition.

They were spare and sparse. It worked, in a way, because it pared the visual impression down to the bare necessities. But it left the overall impression of something slightly cold. They were pretty much on par with the photos he'd seen in her portfolio almost a month ago.

He swallowed when he came to the last file in the WavePro folder.

The photos in the second folder were something more. Something special. The very first was a predawn shot of him waxing up his board, staring out at the waves. The light made him look a little bit old, a little bit weary. Like he'd reached the end of his journey.

He remembered that moment. There had been negative stuff in his head, but he'd still held out and paddled through the waves. Avalon had managed to capture it. His throat locked at the idea of anyone else, anyone at WavePro seeing that moment.

Even more so with the next series of pictures, the ones that had been taken when he was back out of the water again. He'd been exhausted. Weary lines circled his mouth, and his jaw looked hollowed out. But he'd been stoked about a particular change-back turn and he hadn't been able to stop grinning. He looked like a fool ... and he looked happy. Staring straight at the lens. Staring straight at Avalon.

She'd also captured *them*, from her viewpoint. The pictures of him sitting on his balcony, a cup of coffee curled in his hands. Even the steam showed up in the shot. His shoulders were relaxed, and the tilt of his pelvis said his spine was nearly melted into the deck chair.

And also the way he'd looked at her. Half-awed, half-fascinated. A little bit wary, too.

Had he loved her even then?

He folded his arms, staring at the monitor. Something both uncomfortable and reassuring settled in his chest.

Yes, he probably had. There was something about Avalon that simply fit within him. The rest of it could all be worked out later.

She wasn't going to show anyone the second set of pictures. That was obvious from the label. Keeping them under wraps would be foolish. She'd finally found that extra spark that she craved, that she needed to break through the pack. But she'd hide it all because she thought that was what he wanted. What he needed. That was Avalon, the curious blend of creativity and self-sacrifice.

Part of him twisted uncomfortably at the idea of exposing their most private moments. But if that was what it took, he'd do it gladly This gesture would make Avalon's career, but most important of all it would get her back in his arms. She needed to know he was behind her, no matter what.

But he had a feeling he'd better hurry up.

Chapter 38

The meeting was one of the most uncomfortable things she'd ever sat in on. She didn't want to be there. The pictures were what she had, and they'd have to be enough. There were no words in the world that could talk WavePro into taking photos that were subpar.

She tapped a pen across her knee. She'd rather be doing it on the black-marble tabletop, but she'd gotten a nasty look from the head of public relations around twenty minutes ago for the very same thing.

A quick glance up from under her lashes said the picture on the projector was from Tanner's second week of preparation. He'd followed up a two-hour surfing session with a five-mile run. Like a freaking boss.

She felt weak for being so stuck on him, even when he wasn't there. The warm, heady feeling she got all through her stomach . . . there was nothing to be done about that. She guessed she should enjoy the ride while it lasted.

It took monumental effort to get her head back in the conference room where she belonged. She'd done her part already. But Mr. Palmer had asked for her input. The change from his piss-poor attitude about her at the first meeting had been too good to turn down. Beth, the attorney, had sat in as well, and their chat in the hallway had been nice. If Avalon's mood had been even a fraction better, she'd have invited the other woman out for a girls' night out with Sage. Only problem was that Avalon didn't feel like she'd be in the mood for drinks anytime soon.

Finally, things seemed to be drawing to a close. They'd settled on a handful of shots for full-page ads, including a double-page spread, and the rest would be sent on to *SURFING* for selection. Surely something would make the cut for this year's special edition on the world champion.

At least Tanner would have given her that much.

She took her time stacking up photos and gathering up her backpack. If she took her time, maybe no one would look to her for small talk. The moment was . . . less. Less exciting, less impressive, less big than she'd dreamt of all through her career. They'd accepted the photos, but no one was thrilled with her.

When the double doors of the conference room swung open, the last person she thought to see was Tanner. He still wore the slacks and green button-down he'd had on earlier. "How's it going?"

She licked her dry lips. She couldn't believe he was going to do this to her. There had never been anything in their relationship that had hinted at him being petty. She forced her mouth into a smile, but she thought she heard her muscles practically creak. "Fine. It's going fine. Tanner, what are you doing here?"

His blue eyes flashed, and she absolutely knew he was remembering how much she'd hated that he called her portfolio *fine*.

Tanner pinned Mr. Wakowski with an intense gaze. "Did she show you the rest?"

Mr. Wakowski shook his head, confusion darkening his eyes. "I'm sorry?"

"There's at least a hundred shots. Me on my deck with a cup of coffee? Or one where I'm just standing in waist-deep water?" Tanner's gaze burned into her from across the table.

Her stomach dropped to wiggle and flop around her toes. The thick, hard thump of her heartbeat washed in her ears. She realized she was slowly shaking her head. Could he possibly have misunderstood her that badly? To think she'd expose the heart of *them* for profit?

Mr. Palmer's head swiveled, as did the head of everyone else in the room. Including the advertising director, who was already halfway out the door. "Those don't sound at all familiar."

"They weren't . . ." She shut her mouth. Swallowed. "They weren't my best work."

"Bullshit," Tanner said. He fished around inside his pocket and held out the jump drive. An assistant took it. "They're art."

"Oh." Her heart fluttered again, this time in a way that made her head spin. She dropped into her seat when her knees wouldn't hold her up anymore.

The photos went up on the big screen and even under those less than perfect display options, they did look amazing. Emotional and realistic and everything she'd ever wanted to capture.

But they were also so raw it scraped her nerves. Such was the life of an artist, but if they'd rubbed her raw, she'd known they'd do the same to Tanner, who loved his privacy. She hadn't wanted to put either of them through this.

There was an entire roomful of people staring at her heart. And Tanner was one of them. The tips of her fingers tingled and short washes of anxiety went up and down her spine in rapid succession.

It only felt like half a second, but almost forty-five minutes passed before she could even unlock her throat.

Mr. Wakowski flattened his hands over his leather-bound notepad and sternly looked at Avalon over the tops of his wire-rimmed glasses. "I'm disappointed you didn't show these to us initially."

She shifted. It hadn't seemed right to share them. She'd taken the photos and she could barely stand to look at them sometimes. But across the table, Tanner smiled at her. His fingers stretched across the black marble, as if he'd reached for her.

Maybe the distance wasn't so great after all.

She swallowed down her fear. Though she addressed her words to Mr. Wakowski, she meant them for Tanner as well. "Do you like them?"

"Like?" He stood on a soft laugh. "They're some of the best work we've seen in years."

Johnny Carter, advertising guru, stood at his end of the table. "They're going to give us the spin we've been looking for. A taste of the end of an era, the passing of a star." He flushed slightly pink and bobbed his head toward Tanner. "No offense meant."

"None taken." His blue eyes were still boring into her. And she honestly didn't really want to escape. "But if you all don't mind, I've got something I want to discuss with Avalon."

Then he did the most remarkable thing. He held his hand out.

Steady, calm . . . and waiting.

She put out her hand. For him. In front of an entire roomful of people. Her heart was tumbling around her throat, but that was good. More than that, it felt amazing.

They met at the head of the table, and her fingers slipped into his. The warmth of his hand folded around hers, shot up her arm in a reassuring zing.

They were silent as they walked out of the building and across the parking lot. As if by unspoken agreement, neither said a word even when they were at the edge of the sand.

Avalon held on to Tanner's thick arm as she balanced on first one foot, then the other, to take her heels off. Then the sand's warmth took the soles of her feet. This was home. This was reassurance.

She could have almost any conversation on the sand. Even one that made her think she might pop right out of her skin. She tried to take deep, steady breaths to calm herself. The far line of the horizon glittered with afternoon sunlight. Nothing but heartache ever came when she got so overwrought.

Then Tanner touched her.

He curved one hand around the back of her neck, tugging her near. With his other fingers, he made her look. The expression on his face threatened to rip her to shreds from the inside. His eyes tilted down at the corners with deep emotion.

The thumb he rubbed over her cheek was wet. She hadn't even realized she was crying. But that was how deeply he affected her. "God, I'm so sorry," he finally said. The words were harsh with more emotion than she'd ever thought to hear.

"I am, too, but . . ." her voice trailed off. She ducked his gaze. The open collar of his shirt displayed his thick neck. Burying her face in that strength would be so incredibly comforting. And she even had a feeling he'd let her. They could quietly declare everything done, then carry on to take what they could from life.

Avalon pulled her head back to look at him in the eyes. A faint, glassy sheen hovered behind his lashes. She bit her bottom lip on the hard thud that echoed through her chest. Her heart, absolutely lost without him. "I should have told you, though. Anything worth doing is worth admitting to."

He shook his head. "I didn't give you a chance to explain after the fact, either."

"I could have made an opportunity. Except," she said on a quiet whisper. "Except I still don't think I was wrong to do it."

He sighed. The grip he folded around her upper arms was like coming home. "You weren't. God, you definitely weren't." He pulled her close, wrapping his arms around her. "I've been an ass."

With her face pressed against his chest, there was no missing his clean, soap scent. Not that she would want to. "You have been," she agreed. "Feel free to talk at length about that."

"I was an idiot, a jackass. It's gone really far back too." His hands roamed over her shoulders, mostly giving comfort. "I was playing God, like Dad did. But in an entirely different way. Thinking I had all the right answers. I'm so sorry, Avalon. I know you were only doing what you thought best. Hell, what you did ended up *being* what was best. Mom needed to prove it to herself that Mako couldn't touch us."

He bent his face to the top of her head, nuzzling his lips across her temple. But the hand he curved around the back of her head trembled the slightest bit.

There was one thing that had become clear to her over the past couple days. "I didn't tell because I was afraid of making you upset. Because making you upset could mean losing you."

"Never." He held her firmly. His hands were unmovable. Steady and real. "You're not losing me. Avalon, without you I'm lost. I need you. You're my girl. Everything to me."

She slicked her tongue over her bottom lip, wondering how to say what she needed to. "I . . . I don't know if I believe that. I want to. So badly, it makes me ache inside. But really I'm not sure I understand how you can need someone who hasn't made herself heard?"

"I don't know what you mean."

She nibbled on the inside of her cheek. The slight bite of pain centered her whirling thoughts. "It really, really bothered me that you didn't tell me about your idea to turn your mom's store into a surf school." When it looked like he was about to protest, she held up a hand. "Not that I expected you to consult me. I just wanted you to . . . think of me, I guess."

"I always think of you," he said solemnly. "You color the way I think, the way I see the world, my every move. Avalon, I love you."

The air in her throat thickened. Her lips parted on a silent gasp and her heart was beating so hard it felt like it was trying to slam out of her chest. "You love me?"

His big, strong hand was heavy against her jaw, his fingers on her neck. "I do."

"I love you, too, Tanner." The breaths that had been silent a second ago flipped into a tiny sob. She pulled back far enough that a wisp of breeze could move between them and flirt with the bottom hem of her blouse.

Her skin was sticky hot, but that was most likely the emotion of the moment. "Not just because I love Sage and your mom, but because you make me happier than I ever thought I could be."

She nibbled the inside of her lip hard enough to make it tingle with a hint of pain as one last worry nagged her. "The bigger problem is that I didn't speak up. I didn't tell you once I had a problem, like I was some second-class citizen who doesn't get to voice her problems. That's not happening again."

His grin did wicked things to her insides. "Sweetheart, that's absolutely fine." He ducked his head to skate his lips over her neck. Shivers washed out over her skin. "In case you haven't noticed, I love it when you're mouthy."

"Those photos . . ."

His mouth stilled against her flesh for half a second; then he pulled back. "Those photos were everything you were talking about the other day."

"You were listening to me."

"Of course I was. I listen to everything you say. It's a matter of me learning to unpop my head from my ass." He waved that off. "But those photos are amazing. Emotional and real. Everyone in that room stopped what they were doing. You deserve that."

"They're so intimate."

"I don't care. Not if it means you get the recognition you deserve. Making you happy means more to me than you realize. I'd do anything for you." He smoothed her hair. The emotion and power in his eyes was almost intimidating. Almost. It was also heartwarming and what she'd been looking for all her life.

Her fingers found purchase in the sides of his shirt. Through the fine material, the heat of his skin worked through her. The stinging pressure behind her eyes finally eased. "How about we make a deal?" Her smile worked all the way up from the tips of her toes to her head, easing the tension she hadn't even realized she'd had.

"Anything," he agreed automatically. "Anything so long as I get to keep you."

But she put the tips of her fingers over his mouth. "I'll promise to talk even when I think I'll upset you, if you'll promise to talk calmly with me before you run off at the mouth."

"Deal. I'm still so sorry, Avalon. Hurting you was the last thing I wanted." His fingertips trailed up the insides of her forearms. The rush of power she got off his earnest expression made her feel like she was in charge of the world. "Does this mean I get to kiss you now?"

She laughed and hooked her arms around his neck. With shoulders that wide, he'd never let her down. Not if she made sure of it. "Yes, you may."

But he took her mouth before the words had even hit the sand. A long, slow kiss that wound all the way down her body—and swept her away. She let her eyes drift shut, let herself go. Tanner was the man she'd never realized she was looking for. And they'd rescue each other, if they needed to.

But as she locked her wrists behind his neck and gave a little hop, Tanner grabbed her hips. He was her rock and her reassurance and her excitement, all in one. Her skirt rose scandalously high as he hitched her legs around his waist, as if he'd automatically known what she'd wanted. To be close to him. To be with him. To be *his*.

Like she would make him hers.

Epilogue

A sign installation should have been a no-big-deal kind of thing.

After all, Tanner had traveled the globe. He'd surfed fifty-foot waves in Punta de Lobos, Chile. Once he'd found himself less than fifteen feet from a great white shark. He'd had a huge career that meant people from all over the world admired him.

It's not like there hadn't been the Wright name on the building before. This was only a modification, not something brand-spanking-new.

And yet there he was, standing across the street, watching as the workmen adjusted the framework for the sign. He kept his thumbs looped through the back of his belt because that way no one would see them shake.

Christ, he was a big pansy.

But when Avalon ducked out of the storefront, then glanced up and down the street briefly before weaving behind the lone car, Tanner knew what was really going on.

He'd needed his girl at his side.

She looked absolutely amazing. Her hair had grown out a little bit, long enough that her ponytail trailed over her shoulder and the ends coiled on the topmost curve of her breast. The white shorts she wore showed off legs tanned by her most recent outing to the South Maldives, where she'd been on a shoot for *SURFING*. As their newest stringer, she didn't always get the choice gigs, but that one had been pretty good. Tanner would have gone with her, since he still grabbed the opportunity to make a few shots now and then, except he'd had too much to arrange for the school.

After all, it'd be opening in a matter of weeks.

He held out an arm to her and she tucked herself in along his hip. She fit perfectly with the soft sweep of her thigh along his. "I'm so glad I didn't miss it."

This day had been more than six months in the making, but kind of dreamlike at the same time. Tanner hadn't been ready to put up the sign yet, though he'd bought his mom out months ago. There'd been too much else to get going. Admissions and standards and the fine-tuning of what exactly he wanted out of the experience.

He'd have the chance to still surf and shape the future at the same time. Not that that didn't make him sound a bit egotistical. But whatever, it was the truth. The truth that Avalon had helped him find. He had a bit of an ego problem sometimes, yeah. Wouldn't have had the balls to go after a World Championship without one.

But the trick would be guiding the kids under him. Not turning them into miniature Tanners. He didn't get to dictate terms to the people around him anymore. And that was a damned good thing.

He rubbed up and down Avalon's slender arm, but he wasn't sure whom he was comforting.

Of course she caught on to his nerves. She spread her

hand over his stomach, giving him a pat. "Breathe. It'll be okay."

Even her presence was enough to make him feel like he could rule the world. Tucking a couple fingers under her chin, he turned her face up to him. The kiss he skated over her lips was more promise than anything else. The rest could wait 'til they were alone.

Except his feelings. Those didn't seem to want to wait anymore. "I love you, Avalon."

The green of her eyes flashed brighter. She gave a cheeky grin. "You mean it?"

"I do," he answered, just like he did every time they played this game. He kissed her again, this time because he couldn't help himself. "You're everything to me. I'll never let you down. Because you're my heart."

Her smile could lead him around by the soul. He'd have to make sure she realized that. If ever there was a woman who ought to know her own power, it was his Avalon.

She combed her fingers through his hair, pushing it back. Her touch worked through him in happy waves. "I love you too."

"Good." He grinned at her and took another kiss because she was his girl and that made everything right in the world.

"Oh!" she gasped as she pulled her mouth away from his. "You're going to miss it."

Tanner was of the opinion that everything worth having was in his arms at that very moment, but he looked anyway. Just in time to see the sign snapped into place. Sage had designed the simple black and white with a clean blue graphic of a single wave as a favor to her brother. Even the name was simple. Wright School.

Wrapping his arms around Avalon, he tucked her head under his chin. "Thank you," he said.

She startled a little bit. "But . . . why? This is all your thing."

He shook his head. Explaining himself was still difficult sometimes. But Avalon was worth trying for. "I know none of this would be the same without you."

She smiled and turned back toward the storefront. "Good. I'm glad you know that."

He laughed. The part of his woman that gave herself up to smooth things over seemed to be long gone.

And he was damned glad of it.

Read on for a sneak peek
of Lorelie Brown's next sexy
Pacific Blue Novel,

AHEAD IN THE HEAT

Available from Signet Eclipse
in February 2015.

Sean Westin had been to physical therapists before. Once, he'd sprained his knee on the North Shore of Hawaii and had to check in with a therapist near his home turf in San Sebastian for three months. That guy had worked out of a standard stucco-walled complex across the street from the hospital. The building Sean pulled up in front of was about as far from a doctor's office as humanly possible.

Sean double-checked his in-dash GPS. Right address. The California bungalow was where he was supposed to show up. The place looked more like a cottage than an office. There was a shallow porch decorated with white wicker chairs and a multitude of potted plants, which bloomed green or sprouted pink and blue flowers. Cupolas peeked out of the shingle roof, hinting at a second story. Lining the front of the porch were bushes with purplish pink blossoms the size of Sean's fist.

Getting out of the car wasn't pleasant. He moved slowly, bracing himself as he reached to unbuckle the seat belt. Didn't matter. A dull ache of pain spiked from his collarbone and radiated down his shoulder. The black sling he wore inhibited movement. The doctors said he'd need to work on mobility if he wanted to be able to regain his spot on the surfing World Championship Tour in time to keep his ranking in the top half of competitors.

He wanted to regain his spot.

He wanted to like hell. His entire career had been about consistency and determination. He had the skills, and he also had the means to move up.

This should have been Sean's year. The reigning champion, Tanner Wright, had retired to open a surf school and boink his supersweet girlfriend, so the rankings had all been given an exciting shake-up. If Sean didn't move into the top ten this year, he'd have to take a good, long, hard look at what he was doing. Maybe he wasn't meant to be the 'CT winner.

Sean wouldn't allow that. It didn't fit his plans.

A six-inch plaque by the doorbell confirmed yet again that he was in the right place. SANTA BARBARA REHAB on the first line. ANNIE BAXTER, DPT, was inscribed below. He rang the doorbell, but there was no response. He rang it again, hearing peals echo through the small house.

He wasn't completely surprised, since he didn't have an appointment. But he did have information that said Annie Baxter could always be found at her offices on Saturday mornings because she ran an unofficial drop-in program for disadvantaged teenagers.

He sighed, but damn if that didn't send another spike of pain through him as his shoulders shifted. He ground his back teeth together. He needed to talk to Baxter. It wasn't too much to expect the doctor to be where she was supposed to be.

A hollow wooden sound caught his attention. Even though he hadn't heard the noise in person for at least

five or six years, he'd have known it anywhere. Skate-
board wheels rolling over wood. More particularly, over
a wooden ramp.

It was coming from the back of the house. He followed the echo down the porch stairs, then down a path
lined with foxtail grasses, which were lush and verdant
despite the barely waking spring.

The backyard was skater heaven. The Japanese wave
painting Sean could never remember the name of decorated the sloping sides of an empty old-school-style pool.
At the far end, a ten-foot-tall half-pipe filled the only bit
of spare flat land.

A kid dropped his board from the table into the vert,
knees bending into the dip. He slipped effortlessly back
and forth, getting higher and higher until he finally
launched into the air at the other end. He kept it easy,
barely touching his board as he flew. He wore a helmet
and a dark blue hoodie, which swallowed his small frame
and contrasted with his slim-cut jeans.

Sean waited as patiently as he could until the skateboarder came to earth and drew to a stop. "Hey, bro,
have you seen Dr. Baxter?" The skateboarder paused for
a second before pulling off the black helmet and turning
around. Stubby dark-haired ponytail. Delicate features
with wide-set eyes.

Sean immediately rearranged his assumptions. "Sorry.
I mean—may I have a moment of your time, Dr. Baxter?"

One finely arched eyebrow lifted even higher. "I don't
deal with pros."

Being recognized wasn't anything new for Sean. The
first time, he had been at the mall in Brea, eating tacos at
the food court, when a couple dudes fell all over them-

selves talking about his first Prime tour win. And that had been before his pro career really took off, when he'd still been biking himself to the beach on the weekends and returning home to his mother's filthy house.

He hoped he never really got used to being famous. Because, damn, did it still feel good. His chin lifted and he probably smiled some. The hot satisfaction lifted his mood so high that he almost forgot about the constant throb that arced through his shoulder.

"So, you know who I am?"

She made a soft little *psh* sound and tucked her helmet under her arm as she started toward the back door of the house. "Everyone in California knows who you are. And everyone who knows surfing knows you were drunk and shouldn't have been on the water. Not to mention what the fallout could do to your career."

That was the downside. Everyone *did* know what a douche he'd been in Bali. He'd been drinking mai tais with a pretty waitress, and he had taken a rollicking turn toward trouble from that moment. He knew he should have never surfed, but he had done it anyway because he was such a fucking sucker for a pretty face.

His fists curled, but he immediately drew a deep breath as he tried to loosen up. Tight meant pain lately. He'd learned his lesson.

"Then you know how desperate I am for help."

She slanted a gaze at him out of the corner of her eyes, dropping her board to the ground and her helmet on a folding chair. "I've heard hints."

"I have a tweaked collarbone. It's causing some shoulder impingement. There's more technical stuff, but I'd have to have the files sent over to you. I have six weeks. I can't let recovery take any longer than that."

The laugh she dropped into the air between them sounded almost bitter and completely disbelieving. Her mouth was small but plump. She was kind of small all over. If she stood next to him, she'd only come to his sternum. "Recovery for a collarbone injury could take up to sixteen weeks. Maybe longer if you're foolish and push yourself harder than you need to."

"I can't allow that." He moved toward her, but not too close. Women were delicately balanced creatures, and there was a fine line between charming and an icky kind of invasive. "Six weeks keeps me out of competition at Bells Beach and in Rio. I'm missing the Margaret River Pro this very minute. Six weeks means I'm in the water in time for Fiji. I have no choice with Margaret River and Bells Beach, and I'm going to have to choke that up. I can probably even afford zeroing August's event. Probably. But I have to get back on the 'CT by Fiji. I can't afford to drop out of the top twenty-two. Considering that I'll still be in recovery, I'll have a hard enough time requalifying for next year."

"I can give you references to three very good physical therapists. They have a practice on the other side of San Sebastian."

"I don't want very good. I want *the best*." And according to every bit of research he'd culled in the week since his injury, that was Annie Baxter.

But she didn't give a crap. She wasn't even bothering to look at him, which was like nails on a chalkboard to Sean. He thrived on attention, and he usually got it. He wasn't above admitting that.

She pulled the blue sweatshirt off, revealing a cream button-down shirt with minuscule puff sleeves. Even though the blouse was completely feminine, the way it was paired with slim, low-slung jeans emphasized her distinct lack of curves. She had little breasts and boyish hips. Exactly the opposite of Sean's type, but that didn't seem to matter when he looked at that mouth of hers. Adorably filthy. "Then you're screwed."

But Sean knew there was one thing Dr. Annie Baxter cared a whole hell of a lot about. Finding info on that had been dead easy. He tipped his head down, looking at the petite pixie, and he found himself using his silkiest tone of voice when he said, "Do you want your drop-in center funded?"

Her eyebrows flew up toward her hairline as she whipped back to face Sean. "You've got a spare three million sitting around?"

He smirked. Everyone had a price, even if they thought themselves the noble type. It was only a matter of finding it. "I do. Do you want it?"

She gave another of those laughs and stuck her hand out, palm up. "Sure. Right here. You can make the check out to the Clear Ride foundation."

"Nothing is free."

She dropped into one of the wicker seats, hands resting on the arms. Her legs stretched out in front of her, as short as they were. She crossed them at the ankles and laced her fingers in front of her stomach. Her buckle was round and yellow with a black X across it. "You mean to pay me three million for physical therapy for a collarbone injury?"

"Sure. Is that an X-Men belt buckle?"

Bright red washed across her cheeks, making her look both older and younger at the same time in a mix of innocence and chagrin. "I know, I know. I'm a total geek."

He shrugged but instantly regretted it when pain smacked him upside the shoulder again. When he pushed too far, the hurt washed all the way through his chest and upper back. He was gonna be schooled out of shrugging right quick. Fuck, he was tired. "I recognized it. That's gotta be equally geeky."

She didn't answer for a long moment, and at first Sean wondered if he'd gone too far. He'd never been a hundred percent sure which side of the social line he walked. It wasn't like he'd had a normal childhood, which was when most people learned normal human interactions. He'd come from shit. Literally.

"Do you know *why* I'm the best?" Her eyes narrowed and a line knit between her straight brows. "Because I'll own you. Your diet and your exercise. How many times a week you get to surf. Whether you'll go running or do a stair-stepper. How much you stretch and *precisely* when you do it. How often you see me or any other *anything*. Including massages."

"Deal."

"Including sex."

"Deal."

She scoffed. "You're fucking full of it. This is one of the reasons why I don't work with pros. You're too damn full of yourselves. You don't even stop to question whether you can handle it."

His impulse was to cross his arms over his chest, but of course that was out. He settled for widening his stance and tucked one hand in the pocket of his slacks. "There's one thing you don't understand. I *will* stay in the 'CT this year. The only question is whether I permanently fuck myself up in the process."

Her mouth set into a mulish knot, but she pushed up out of her chair and stepped toward him. "You're an arrogant, foolish asshole."

"I am." He grinned because he knew her body language: unwillingly intrigued. "But I'm an arrogant, foolish asshole who's your patient."

Can't wait for Lorelie Brown's next surfer novel? Check out

ONE LESSON,

her special e-book novella
on sale now from Signet Eclipse
wherever e-books are sold!

Macy Beckett

MAKE YOU MINE
The Dumont Bachelors

For ninety-nine years, every man in the Dumont family has remained a perpetual bachelor—supposedly cursed long ago by a voodoo witch. In truth, the Dumont men have their own player personalities to blame, and Marc is no exception. As captain of his family's riverboat, he's broken hearts up and down the Mississippi.

But when his high school crush, Allie Mauvais, fills in as the riverboat pastry chef, old feelings are rekindled. But to reach Marc's heart, she must show him that the hex is all in his head. Will Allie's love be enough to finally make Marc hers?

Available wherever books are sold or at
penguin.com

facebook.com/LoveAlwaysBooks